Praise for *Looking Glass Lies*

"With her signature style—straightforward, poignant, powerful—Denman's *Looking Glass Lies* reflects painful truths . . . and healing hope."

—CANDACE CALVERT, bestselling author of *Maybe It's You*

"Who knew fiction could soothe my soul the way this book does? Through her beautiful story of brokenness, Varina Denman poignantly unveils shame, fear, unforgiveness, and feelings of worthlessness—the telltale symptoms of a shattered self-esteem. And it's her well-crafted characters that bring healing to some deep places of wounding in my own life. Only an anointed writer can do that. If you are a woman, this is a must read that will leave you encouraged and challenged in equal measure."

—CAREY SCOTT, author of *Untangled: Let God Loosen the Knots of Insecurity in Your Life* and *Uncommon: Pursuing a Life of Passion and Purpose*

"Varina Denman has done an outstanding job of telling a captivating story that addresses one of the 'hidden sins' in our churches and culture today. *Looking Glass Lies* honestly portrays the reality that pornography addiction not only destroys marriages, but that trust, self-worth, and dreams are often among the collateral damage left in its wake. This hard-to-put-down book offers the possibility of finding hope, healing, and joy in the midst of pain."

—VICKI TIEDE, speaker and author of *When Your Husband is Addicted to Pornography: Healing Your Wounded Heart*

"*Looking Glass Lies* is the essence of a good book. Varina Denman creates an abundant depth of character, and I closed the pages feeling like I had a newfound set of friends and was better having known them."

—JAMI AMERINE, *Sacred Ground Sticky Floors* blog

"Varina Denman has crafted a poignant account of a wounded soul on a journey to self-acceptance after enduring the fallout of a destructive relationship. Along with a memorable cast of characters and a sweet romance, *Looking Glass Lies* delivers a hope-filled message of healing and a wonderful reminder that identity should only be found in the One who created us."

—CONNILYN COSSETTE, CBA Best Selling Author of *Counted with the Stars* and *Shadow of the Storm*

"A brave and heartrending portrait of a woman searching to find her worth in a culture built on lies. Honest, relatable, and deeply moving."

—NICOLE DEESE, author of *The Promise of Rayne* and the Love in Lenox series.

LOOKING GLASS LIES

ALSO BY VARINA DENMAN

The Mended Hearts Series

Jaded (Book 1)

Justified (Book 2)

Jilted (Book 3)

LOOKING GLASS LIES

Varina Denman

Waterfall
PRESS

Text copyright © 2017 by Varina Denman
All rights reserved.

Published by Waterfall Press, Grand Haven, MI

www.brilliancepublishing.com

Amazon, the Amazon logo, and Waterfall Press are trademarks of Amazon.com, Inc., or its affiliates.

Scripture quotations are taken from the Holy Bible, New International Version®. Copyright © 1973, 1978, 1984 by International Bible Society. Used by permission of Zondervan Publishing House.

ISBN-13: 9781503942707
ISBN-10: 1503942708

Cover design by PEPE *nymi*

Printed in the United States of America

When a woman peers at her reflection,
she blindly believes the glass when it whispers, and is convinced
that others must feel the same about her skin, her face, her body,
her soul.

But sometimes . . . the mirror lies.

For those who hear the lies

Chapter One

I woke up in the middle of the night in our cavernous walk-in closet. Again. For a moment, I enjoyed the wispy memory of a not-yet-forgotten dream, but then I realized the plush carpet had become solid rock while I slept, its gritty fibers pressing against me as though I were wedged into a sandstone crevice instead of willingly tucked against the back wall beneath my hanging clothes.

Good grief. You have to stop this, Cecily. I told myself the same thing every blasted time, but so far I hadn't been able to do it. Even now, I didn't move so much as a pinkie finger, didn't open my eyes against the harsh fluorescent light, didn't crawl past Brett's shoe rack where I could see myself in the floor-length mirror. Not a chance. Because that would have broken the spell and sent me back to the real world, and—*no, thanks*—I preferred the fairy tale where high school sweethearts lived happily ever after.

My husband slept soundly in our pillow-top king, just on the other side of the closet door. The phrase *sleeping like a baby* crossed my mind, and I snickered softly because Brett's snoring was anything but child-like, and his seemingly undefiled slumber had been brought on by over-the-counter sleeping pills rather than the serenity of innocence.

Besides, Brett wasn't the one who was childish. He never scrutinized his reflection in the mirror late at night. He never beat his fists against his thighs until he had bruises, hoping a tantrum would somehow change things. He never bawled uncontrollably, wishing he could mold his body into what it ought to be—like Play-Doh—kneading and pressing until the flesh became aesthetically balanced.

He never once cried himself to sleep in the closet.

I uncurled my stiff legs, wiggling my toes and stretching while the shirts hanging above me caressed my skin like an old friend. The back of my hand bumped against solid wood: the leg of the chair where Brett sat every morning, tying his shoes like Mr. Rogers. Smiling.

For seven years it had been the same. On mornings when he found me asleep on the floor, he'd nudge me with his socked toe, wag his finger, and laugh. "Cecily, you silly girl. Get in bed where you'll be comfortable." Then he'd pat me on the butt as he slipped his cell phone in his pocket.

I hated that phone. Despised it. It was full of videos Brett didn't want me to see, websites he claimed he hadn't visited, pictures he made certain I never had access to. But his temptations didn't end there. When he left the house, there were billboards and magazine covers and posters in shop windows. There were advertisements and mannequins and sultry radio voices, and there were women, everywhere, in low-cut blouses, short skirts, and thick makeup.

I couldn't compete with all that. Evidently.

My hair itched my cheek, and I shoved it away from my face. Six months ago, Brett had showed me a picture of a style that he described as spunky and sexy—one side swinging alluringly over an eye, the other in a cute pixie—and he insisted the red tint would accentuate my green eyes more than my natural color had ever done.

Yeah, right.

I fingered a lock on the long side, pulling it past my chin and yanking it hard. Then I touched the tip of my finger to the short side. So very, very short. Brett had told me he would like it, but it hadn't been enough.

Of course it hadn't.

I realized his snoring had stopped, and my eyes popped open, then I held my breath, pushing the hanging clothes away from my ear to listen for bedsprings or squeaky floorboards, daring to hope that the closet door might open. That he might get on his knees, tell me he hadn't meant it.

His breathing faltered for three seconds, then the rhythmic snoring continued, and he went back to sleep. *Like a baby.*

Pressing my palm against the ivory carpet, I dragged myself out of the corner, sat in front of the mirror, and squared my shoulders as though I no longer needed to hide from reality. As though I'd be all right without Brett. As though his divorce papers fit neatly into my fairy tale.

"You can handle this," I said to my reflection. In a few short hours, I could start a new day, build a new life, create a new me.

I could go back home and start over. People in my hometown wouldn't be surprised things hadn't worked out between Brett and me— they had said as much when we'd started dating in high school. After a while I could settle into the complacent solace of small-town life, lick my wounds, and become invisible among the laid-back community that Brett had always deemed *unsophisticated.*

"You go, girl." I lifted my chin, but the girl in the mirror didn't seem convincing.

No matter. That's what I would do tomorrow . . . or next week . . . or maybe next month. Okay, so it might take a while, but at least it was a plan. And it was a heck of a lot better than crying in a closet. *Like a baby.*

Chapter Two

Eleven months, two weeks, and four days later

My life was a thousand-piece puzzle I couldn't seem to fit together. Or maybe it wasn't my life that was the problem; maybe it was my emotions or my circumstances or my sanity. Maybe I had multiple puzzles all dumped together on a tabletop, and I was trying to figure out what went where.

That's why I finally came home—the place where it all started—to try to figure out what to make of the chaos, or possibly to find a new puzzle with fewer pieces.

Home seemed like a safe place to work on things.

I used to compare my hometown to the quaint setting of *Gilmore Girls*, but ten years in Los Angeles had given me a more cynical and realistic perspective. My dad always said the university kept the town thriving, and so did the tourist trade. Families in minivans trekked across the country to gape at Palo Duro Canyon, hike its trails, and camp in its depths. But for me, Canyon, Texas, represented a million childhood memories, all of which melded together into a comforting poultice, and made me feel as though an enormous Band-Aid had been wrapped around me like a shawl.

"Cecily, you job hunting today?" My dad stood in the kitchen of our family cabin in his park ranger uniform, holding a coffee pot a foot above the table and peering at me with a perplexed expression, as though he couldn't believe I was truly sitting in his cabin, eating bacon and eggs.

"Sure am." I held my mug out toward him. "You know if anybody's hiring?"

Dad was only forty-nine, but since my departure after high school graduation, smile lines had appeared around his mouth. It was like his face kept grinning even when he told it to relax.

He lowered the coffee pot to the table. "Seems like I saw a sign in the window at the pool hall, but I reckon that wouldn't suit." He chuckled. "Olivia might have a position down at the visitor's center, though. I'll ask her about it."

Minimum wage at the state park would barely cover my car payment, much less rent for my own place, but with no experience and no degree, I couldn't be picky. "Thanks, Daddy."

The silence that followed wasn't awkward, and never had been. My dad and I had only seen each other a handful of times in the last ten years, but he still seemed as familiar to me as the day I left. I unscrewed the cap on a bottle of hazelnut coffee flavoring, poured a hefty dose in my cup, and then reached for a second bottle—French vanilla—and dumped in a little of it as well. My mom had taught me that.

I looked around the room, experiencing a sense of déjà vu that took me back to my childhood. When Mom died, Daddy had removed her personal things from the bedroom, but the open area that served as our kitchen and living room hadn't changed much over the years. It almost seemed as if Mom might walk in and sit between us like old times, passing dishes back and forth and chattering up a storm, laughing, and always, always telling me I was pretty.

"So." Daddy dipped his knife into the butter and scratched the stainless steel across a piece of toast. "You know you could have come home as soon as he divorced you, Cecily. Why wait a year?" He stabbed a slice of bacon.

His mention of my divorce didn't bother me, and neither did his aggression toward his breakfast meat. The question itself didn't even faze me because it was valid.

"Oh, you know . . . tying up loose ends." I supposed a stint in a psychiatric hospital could be termed a *loose end*, but I didn't mention it. Most likely, he wasn't upset that I waited a year to come home after Brett served me divorce papers, but because there were divorce papers at all. If I knew my dad, he was thinking that if I had come home earlier, he might have been able to help me. He might have saved his little girl some pain. He might have talked Brett out of it.

That was the real reason I'd waited.

I smiled weakly, then shoved a bite of scrambled eggs into my mouth with a chunk of bacon.

"Cess?" His chin jutted forward. "He didn't . . . hurt you . . . did he?"

"No, Daddy."

"Then . . ." The tines of his fork made two small circles above his coffee cup. "He was unfaithful?"

So many questions. "Brett just said he didn't love me anymore, and he wanted out."

The word *love* seemed to make my dad flinch. "And what Brett wants, Brett gets."

It went without saying that I was no longer what Brett wanted. I cut a bite of eggs with the side of my fork, picked at it, then mashed it flat. After a few more jabs, it resembled yellow sand. My self-esteem wouldn't allow me to explain my jigsaw puzzle past, or my sinking fear that the lid of the puzzle box, with the picture on top, had been tossed in the garbage. There was no way to convey the depth of my loneliness over the past year, or how crazy I'd felt while I was in recovery, or the emptiness that still consumed me.

He cleared his throat. "I bumped into Dr. Harper out at the state park yesterday, and I sort of suggested he call you."

"Dr. Harper? I don't remember him. And . . . I'm not sick."

His shoulders fell half an inch. "He's a counselor." His eyes met mine, and suddenly he was a bumbling giant in a glass cage, unable to move to the right or left for fear of breaking whatever strange new relationship we were forging. "He could help you, Cess." His gaze settled on my hair for a few seconds before he frowned thoughtfully at the wood floor.

My hair. I should have gotten it fixed before I came home. I should have tried to look like my old self. I should have pretended to be healthier than I was. My emotions were still a wreck, and my hair was proof.

The wonky red style had grown into a two-tone mop of fluff, and apparently Daddy couldn't make sense of it.

"I appreciate you asking him to call me." No, I didn't. "But doesn't it usually work the other way around?" That's all I needed. One more counselor telling me to *just let it go.*

He pulled his truck keys from his pocket. "That's what Dr. Harper said, but he doesn't mind making one call, seeing how it's you."

I squinted. "I remember Dr. Cushing, down at the Monday clinic . . . and Dr. Mendez, the veterinarian, but who is Dr. Harper? Where did he come from?"

"Aw, you know him, Cess, you went to school together." Daddy glanced at the time on the microwave oven. "And actually the Monday clinic shut down."

"Harper? Wait a minute. *Graham* Harper?"

He pushed his chair away from the table.

"Are you serious?" I followed him to the front door and onto the porch. "Graham Harper can't possibly be a therapist. Does he even have credentials? Daddy, they called him *Graham Cracker.*"

He adjusted his cap as he stomped down the steps. "Of course he has credentials."

"Daddy . . ." I could hear the whine in my voice as I called across the yard. "Did you really give Graham Cracker my phone number?"

As he opened the door of his truck, his neck disappeared between his shoulder blades as though he were being pelted with rocks. "No need to overreact. I'll tell him to forget it." He cranked the ignition and pulled away slowly, gravel popping beneath his tires like the last few kernels in a bag of Redenbacher's, but as he looped around the circle drive, his smiling eyes met mine one last time.

"Yes, Daddy," I whispered. "Tell Graham Cracker to forget it."

Chapter Three

A Dumas teenager was injured Thursday morning at Palo Duro Canyon State Park, said Randall County Sheriff's Office spokesman Sonny McNeill. The sixteen-year-old girl ventured too close to a sheer drop-off while hiking the CCC Trail with her family. She was airlifted to Northwest Texas Hospital, where she remains in critical condition.

The grandmother reciting the local news at the beauty shop didn't bother me nearly as much as the stylist cutting my hair. When I finally left the place, the hairdresser was grinning like she had salvaged a flea-market dresser and turned it into a trendy mini bar. My hair had returned to its natural dark-brown shade, and now fell in soft waves around my face. The full side of the asymmetrical cut hung only an inch or so longer than the short side, and the overall appearance was *delicate and girly*, as the beautician claimed.

"I don't know anything about you, hon," she had drawled, loud enough for everyone in the shop to hear. "But I bet you have a good excuse for letting yourself go. Probably taking care of a sick relative or something like that." She had eyed my reflection in the mirror, waiting for an explanation that never came. "But now you look right delicate and girly, and you'll feel all pretty on the inside too. That's how things work." She brushed tiny hairs from my neck and shoulders. "You'll feel like a new woman."

Since then I'd been to four businesses to fill out job applications, and so far, the *new woman* inside me hadn't had an ounce of luck in spite of the delicate, girly feels. Next on my list of employment possibilities was the Midnight Oil Coffee Shop, so I figured while I was applying for a job, I'd grab a cup of java. Caffeine would make me feel more like a new woman than any sort of haircut could.

Midnight Oil had been in the same place for years, on the corner of the square near the old courthouse, and even though it lay nestled among the nostalgic businesses in the old-town district, the shop looked a little worn. The sign—a huge cup with squiggly lines representing steam—needed painting, and a haze of dust streaked the plate-glass windows, almost obscuring the "Help Wanted" sign. Evidently, none of that deterred customers, because the shop was packed—mostly with college kids. Strange. I didn't remember it being a popular hangout back in my day.

The scent of coffee greeted me before I stepped onto the curb, and when I opened the glass door, the warm roasted aroma pulled me in. I noted the hanging plants, the squishy-soft couches along the exposed brick walls, and the small tables with mismatched wooden chairs, and I gave a silent nod of approval. A flat-screen television hung on a side wall, but the morning talk show was muted, and Ingrid Michaelson could be heard crooning from tiny speakers in the four corners of the room. I found myself at the end of a long line of customers and considered coming back later in the day, but immediately discarded the notion. I wanted a job, and the sooner, the better.

A blond girl behind the counter called over the hum of voices, "Welcome to Midnight Oil!" Then she continued with her work, holding a cup beneath a spigot and punching a button. *Barista Barbie.*

She reminded me of the dolls I played with in childhood. The slender Barbies had hobbled across my hearth on their rubbery legs, competing for best gown, best swimsuit, best hair. I only had two of them, Barbie and Skipper, and even though Skipper's freckles and flat chest were adorable, they didn't hold much weight in a competitive pageant. Hence her curvy older sister always won the glittering crown.

Fingertips touched my elbow. "Welcome to Midnight Oil, ma'am. This your first time in my shop?" A tanned man wearing a khaki apron smiled down at me, and apprehension slithered in my ribcage. If the blonde was a Barbie doll, then this was Ken. He certainly had the hair for it.

"Oh . . . sort of." He must've been the owner, and suddenly I couldn't think how to explain my ten-year hiatus.

"What's your drink of choice, ma'am?"

I faltered. My drink of choice was back home in Daddy's coffee maker. Morning roast with a medley of International Flavors poured in. To know what to order at Midnight Oil, I'd have to study the menu for a while. To even determine the size I wanted, I'd likely need to fall back on college algebra, if not my foreign language studies. "Just black coffee, I guess."

He raised his index finger and then walked away, smiling back at me over his shoulder.

I couldn't remember the last time a man with teeth that white and skin that tan had smiled at me. Maybe never. I took a step to follow, but . . . did he really mean to get my coffee? I wasn't next in line. Not even close. If I followed him, I risked losing my place, and how was I supposed to pay? I'd have to scan my debit card at the register on the other side of a small bundle of people who would all assume I was cutting in line. I should've just asked him for a job application and passed on the coffee.

But that smile.

"Here we go!" He approached again, holding a disposable cup stamped with the Midnight Oil logo. "On the house, in celebration of your *sort of* first visit to the shop." He ducked his head like a Japanese honor guard.

When he looked up again, the girl behind the counter caught his eye and tilted her head to the side. I thought he winked at her.

"Thank you." I took the cup from his hand and glanced back at the girl.

She looked like—

I squinted.

It couldn't be.

"You live around here?" Malibu Ken asked.

"Outside of town, on the canyon." Why did I tell him that? I crossed an arm over my stomach.

"No kidding. Did you hear about that girl falling yesterday?"

"Crazy, right?"

Ken kept smiling, but his gaze wandered to an adjacent table. "Have you lived in Canyon all your life?" he asked.

"Until I went to UCLA"—no need to mention a failed marriage—"but I'm back now, probably to stay a while." Why was he asking so many questions? Why was he talking to me at all?

"UCLA? We played them in the Cotton Bowl."

"Um . . . football?"

He grinned like a ten-year-old boy looking at a brand-new, just-released video game. "You're not a football fan?" He seemed unusually thrilled by the news.

"Can't say I am. Sorry. Did you play in college?"

His eyebrows quivered once. "I had a pretty good stint at UT."

"Hmm. The Longhorns, right?"

"That's the ones." He grinned. "So enough about me. What did you study at UCLA?"

"Music."

A UPS truck stopped on the street, and Ken glanced at it through the window. "Nice tattoo, by the way." His fingertips grazed my arm again as he walked away, calling over his shoulder, "I'm Michael Divins. Hope Midnight Oil becomes part of your daily routine."

Michael Divins? I stood still in the middle of the shop, staring after him. I was so stupid. Michael Divins was an NFL football star, a local icon (though I'd never met him), whose name had been splashed all over social media in the last year because of his unexpected and controversial retirement. I should have recognized him. I should've watched more sports so I'd have an inkling of what he looked like. I should have guessed he had a legitimate reason to talk to me.

After all, it was good business. Greet the new customers, make them feel welcome, invite them back again. Maybe even give them free product.

And to think, for a few minutes, I had thought my delicate and girly hairstyle had made a difference. Now I reassured myself, as I always did, that men were all the same.

Holding my coffee near my chest like a shield, I settled on a barstool at a tall table in the corner and took a sip of the hot liquid. I hated black coffee. Only someone like me could end up in a situation like this. Free coffee that I didn't even like, and no job application in sight.

I set the cup on the table and pulled out my cell phone. In a few minutes, I would get up the nerve to ask Michael Divins for a job, but in the meantime, I would pretend to check email and look busy.

"Thought you might want this."

I blinked. The Barbie doll was standing in front of me, holding a tiny plastic cup. Now that she was closer, I knew exactly who she was.

"I'm sorry?" There was a slim chance she wouldn't recognize me.

"It's caramel honey flavoring, and I've got milk if you want to make it a latte."

I removed the lid from my abandoned cup and held it out to her so she could pour in the additives. "How'd you know?" I asked.

"Nobody takes their coffee black except old men and college kids cramming for exams. And maybe the occasional forty-something woman, bent on making a statement to the world." She shifted her hips to the left, and the man sitting on the couch behind her seemed to appreciate the stance. "So . . . are you?"

"Am I . . . ?"

"Are you making a statement to the world?" When her chin jutted forward in a challenge, I knew she recognized me too.

I wanted to lift my chin right back at her, but I couldn't seem to muster it. "Been a while, huh?" *But not long enough.*

Mirinda Ross, Brett's annoying little sister, had flattened all four tires on my old Jeep when Brett asked me to the prom. She had been a kid at the time, and we had hardly seen each other since then. Of course, that had a lot more to do with her refusal to attend family gatherings than my determination to hold a grudge. But she had certainly changed physically. From a stringy-haired brat into a beautiful woman, gorgeous enough to turn the head of Michael Divins, who was possibly the most eligible bachelor in America.

He appeared at my table. "Where were we? Oh, yes. I'm Michael." He shook my hand, and I felt that warm touch again. "What's your name?"

"Cecily." I couldn't stop myself from smiling. "Cecily Ross."

He looked at Mirinda and then back at me. "Any relation?"

"No." Mirinda rested her elbows on the counter-height table and leaned over, her breasts nestling between her arms. "None at all."

Michael stood a little taller and smiled, first at Mirinda, then at me, then back again, as though he were watching a surprisingly happy game of table tennis. In the end, his gaze settled on me. "Cecily, would you like to catch a movie together?"

Was he asking me out? It certainly sounded that way, but . . . *why*? Suddenly I was pushed into the deep end of a swimming pool without the necessary intake of breath. No one had asked me on a date since the divorce. Even before that, really. Not since Brett and I dated.

"You just met her," Mirinda snapped.

"It's only a movie." His eyes met hers, and I wondered if he was trying to tell her something without saying it out loud.

Mirinda's mouth smashed into a less than doll-like line, and I figured she didn't know what she looked like when she did that. I bet every time she peered in the mirror, she smiled and spruced and primped her hair. Not many people happen to be looking at themselves when their attitudes and feelings and hurts—their personalities—leak out around the edges.

I hoped I wasn't making the same face. Because I wasn't entirely sure I wanted to go out on a date—even with Michael Divins—but the possibility had revived feelings I'd thought were long since dead, and for the first time in over a year, I didn't feel ugly.

I fumbled with the lid on my cup and decided a job application was out of the question.

Mirinda put a fist on one hip as her eyes scanned my face and body, lingering on my sleeve tattoo. Then her shoulders lifted and fell in a minuscule shrug, and with the gesture I heard her unspoken words: *No wonder my brother left you.*

To get back at her, I smiled at Michael. "I've been wanting to see that new action movie."

"How about Monday night?" He glanced at Mirinda and then back at me, and my heart gradually increased its beating, like a bass drum coming closer in a parade.

This could be okay. "Monday it is."

My former sister-in-law crushed the tiny cup in her fist and stomped to the counter, and I'm sorry to say I enjoyed it a little.

Michael and I exchanged numbers. Then I was left alone at my table, sipping coffee.

If Brett knew I had a date, he would be surprised. If he knew it was with his favorite quarterback, he would be shocked. *Yes, this could be okay.*

I lowered my gaze to my cell, and my thumb swiped across the screen. After a few taps I was sent to an old friend's Facebook page where I opened a folder of pictures, tapping my way through graduations and weddings and birthday parties. When my phone rang, I inadvertently hit the answer button as it popped up where the photo album had been a split second before. I hadn't had time to see who was calling, but I knew it would be Daddy, wondering about my job hunt.

I put the phone to my ear. "I'm at Midnight Oil Coffee Shop."

An unfamiliar male voice chuckled. "Well, I can already see that you have more sense than ninety percent of my clients."

Chapter Four

"Who is this?"

"Sorry." He laughed, maybe nervously. "This is Graham Harper. From back in school?"

I gripped my coffee cup until I thought my fingers might crack the brittle sides. The man on the other end of the line wasn't my interfering yet well-meaning father calling to check on my employment progress. It was my old friend from high school—if he had even been that much—cold calling because he couldn't scrape up business any other way.

And I had accidentally taken his call.

My next two questions should have been *How did he get my number?* and *What did he want?* but I knew the answers, and he probably knew I knew. Ridiculous.

"I heard you were back in town," he said. "Thought I'd give you a call and welcome you home."

That was a fib. "Did you?" I asked.

He laughed outright then, and the honest sound of it made me sit up straight. "Okay, no," he said. "Actually, I bumped into your dad the other day, and he asked if I could call you."

My fingertip dabbed at a drop of coffee on the lid of my cup. "I appreciate you taking the time, but I really don't need counseling." Internally, I gave myself a high five for sounding so calm and rational, but then I blubbered, "Just this morning I got my hair done for the first time in eighteen months."

When he didn't answer right away, I realized how much I had revealed in that single statement. Crap.

"It's not like that," he said. "Sure, your dad asked me to set up an appointment, but that's not really how I roll." That chuckle again. "I couldn't seem to make him understand, but since I promised I'd call, here I am."

"Dad doesn't generally take *no* for an answer, but he has no reason to be worried . . . about me." My voice evaporated.

There were a few seconds of silence, and then Graham asked brightly, "So what are you up to these days? Do you work in the music industry?"

"No," I answered quickly. Music wasn't even a part of me anymore. "I lost interest years ago."

"I always thought you'd be a concert pianist. Van Cliburn. Yiruma. Somebody like that." His voice sounded different than it had in high school, more mature, like one of those deep baritones on radio commercials—the ones that make you want to buy a luxury car simply because the guy sounds so authentic and real. Maybe Graham wasn't hiding as much as other men, or . . . maybe he was just an extravagant used car salesman with a nice voice.

"I studied music at UCLA." I squirmed on the barstool. "But I dropped out before I graduated."

The crowd in the coffee shop was thinning, and Mirinda was now moving from table to table, wiping coffee rings and muffin crumbs. As she drew near, I noticed her doll-like persona extended all the way to her fingernails, which were long and brightly painted, and I wondered how she managed to keep them so nice even though she worked in food service. I slipped my left hand under my thigh as she passed.

Graham cleared his throat.

"What about you?" I asked. "How did you become *Dr. Harper?* Last I remember, people were calling you *Graham Cracker.*"

He hummed good-naturedly, as though my words had scratched the surface of his pride, but a dollop of ointment would make everything better. "The nickname was unjustified," he said. "I never did crack cocaine. That was a nasty rumor."

"But you admit you did other drugs?"

"Just marijuana, but I did enough of it that it's a wonder my brain isn't fried."

And this was the man my dad wanted me to confide in.

"In the end," Graham said, "I learned I wasn't the only one with issues, and when I discovered I had a knack for helping people face theirs, I enrolled in college and never looked back."

"So you have a degree?"

"Three."

"From where?"

"Bachelor's from West Texas A&M here in town, master's and doctorate from Texas Tech."

A mother and three small children moved into the table next to mine as though they were setting up at a campground for the weekend. A little girl, probably four or five years old, rested her elbows on the table as she held an iPad in front of her face. Even though I couldn't see the screen, I recognized the Disney music. The girl swayed dreamily, and I knew she was there, in the castle, dancing with the prince. I smiled along with her before tightening my grip on my cell.

"So, what exactly did my dad tell you?"

Michael hovered one table over, asking the mother the names of her children. The woman seemed smitten with Michael and flattered by the attention, so I gathered she didn't notice Mirinda brushing against him as she delivered their breakfast.

When Mirinda's eyes met mine, I tugged down the sleeve of my shirt in a futile attempt to cover the tattoo that ran from my shoulder to my wrist. I needed to wear long sleeves.

"Did you hear me?"

Graham was talking, and, no, I hadn't heard him. For crying out loud, I had just asked him what my dad told him, and then I didn't listen to his response.

Irritation punched through my curt answer. "What did you say?"

I thought he laughed again, but it was so soft, I couldn't be sure. "Your dad only said that you and Brett recently split, and that you're wallowing." He held the word *and* longer as though he didn't want to get to the *wallowing* part. "He just wants the best for you, Cecily."

Dad claimed he wanted the best for me, but his real problem was that he was still grieving Mom. He had no right to project his problem onto me and insist I was grieving my husband. "I don't even miss Brett."

"That's good to hear."

I sat up straight again, having gradually melted into a slump. "When he divorced me, I was sad, but after a few months, I knew a huge burden had lifted. Brett had been suffocating me for years, and when he left, it was like I could finally breathe again. Since then I've hardly thought about him, and all my other problems seem insignificant in comparison. I've done my grieving, and I've moved on." My fingertips tapped against my lips. I hadn't meant to say all that.

"As long as you're facing your problems squarely, your dad should be at peace."

"That's the second time you've mentioned *facing problems*, and I just want you to know that I am. Facing my problems."

"Good for you. It's an important step in recovery, Cecily."

"I know all about recovery." I stood, walked toward the trash, and tossed my half-empty cup. "Dad doesn't really understand the situation, because if he did, he wouldn't accuse me of wallowing in grief. Brett left me over a year ago, and I'm fine now. I went through months of counseling after the divorce, and I'm taking steps to get on with my life. Like moving back to Canyon, getting a job, spending time with my dad." I realized that I'd frozen in place by the trash can, one arm tightened across my waist while Mirinda watched me from the back of the shop, her head cocked to one side in curiosity. I shoved through the door and out onto the sidewalk. "So you see, I don't need your services, Graham, but thank you for following through on your promise to my dad."

"I'm glad to hear you're doing well," he said softly. "But I think I may have led you astray. So, before you go, can I set the record straight?"

I paused on the sidewalk, and my reflection in the shop windows smirked back at me. "Okay."

"It's just that your dad didn't tell me you were wallowing in grief. I never said that."

Was he lying again? Or was I remembering things wrong? Sometimes my brain was so foggy. "You used the word *wallowing*. I remember that."

"But I didn't say you were wallowing in *grief*." I could hear him take a breath, and his next words came cautiously. "Your dad said you were wallowing in *self-pity*."

The breeze caught my hair, whipping the long side in spirals that landed across my cheek, and as I reached up to hold it away from my face, my tattooed arm formed a right angle—a sarcastic salute to my haphazard confidence. And on the other side of the window, Mirinda, in all her perfection, let her gaze sweep over me one last time. I turned away from the glass and both images vanished from my sight.

"Graham?" My knees shook, and I couldn't seem to get away fast enough. From the Barbie. From Michael Divins. From Graham Cracker, who had sounded authentic at first but was now gently picking away at my sanity. "Please don't call me again."

Chapter Five

Cecily, it's Brett. Listen, your dad called me this afternoon, and the more I think about it, the more it rubs me wrong. He was asking questions he could've just asked you, so I figure you're not talking, but good God, it's been a year, right? I know you've still got hang-ups, but it's not my problem anymore. You know? So . . . could you please ask him to stop calling?

Brett wanted my dad to leave him alone. And he had said *please.* Probably he thought one word of politeness softened the entire voice mail, and maybe it did in a way. At least he hadn't been as demanding as in the past. I listened to the message one more time, then dropped the phone to the carpet in front of the mirror that hung on the closet door.

I stood in my pink-and-white teen girl's bedroom and examined my body. My nightgown fell loosely around my breasts but puckered near my waist and tightened at my thighs. Brett had never liked this gown, and there was no question as to why. Gripping the satin, I jerked the garment over my head and wadded it into a tight ball. I hurled it toward the mirror, but the silky fabric merely brushed against the glass and fell to the floor, an insignificant demonstration of emotion. To make up for it, I balled my hands into fists and pounded my thighs as hard as I could, but just like all the other tantrums I had pitched over the years, nothing made the injustice go away.

My inpatient therapist had told me I placed waaaay too much emphasis on body image. Well, *duh*, anyone who had known me more than a week could've figured that out and for a fraction of the cost. What I needed to know was *why*. Apparently emotional abuse from my narcissistic husband wasn't enough to send me to the loony bin, and there must've been a deeper, more fundamental reason. *Whatever.*

I reached for a pair of athletic shorts and stepped into them, then pulled on an old T-shirt, being careful not to look in the mirror again.

My bulletin board, covered with teenage keepsakes, caught my eye. Tonight was just as good a night as any to purge all those childish mementos and begin the process of turning my room into an adult woman's sleeping space. I reached for my pink mesh wastebasket and started decluttering.

The first pushpin came out with a squeaky pop, a satisfying sound, and the movie stubs it had been securing fell neatly into the can. Next came a newspaper article, an empty wrapper from a Snickers candy bar, and the paper insert from an *NSYNC CD. I held it up and studied the boy band I had idolized in junior high. I ran a fingertip across their faces, remembering myself at twelve years old as I morphed from a laughing child into a timid adolescent startled by the fact that people noticed what I looked like. At first, that knowledge had made me feel important—mature—and I paid close attention to clothes and speech patterns and status symbols, but by the time I was grown, I had become frustrated by the impossibility of it all and told myself I didn't care. But I lied.

I tossed the paper insert into the trash can and returned to my task.

A spirit ribbon from a regional basketball game went into the bin as well. Then a love note from Brett that I didn't bother to read. I paused when I uncovered a birthday card from my mother. She hadn't written anything other than *Love you, Mom*. I clicked my thumbnail against the edge of the cardstock, then tucked it into the top drawer of the dresser next to a pair of scissors.

Those were Mom's old sewing scissors, and as I let my thumb and fingers slide into the orange handles, I imagined her working with fabric and yarn and paper. She had loved to make crafts. I carefully set the scissors on the floor by the mirror, making a mental note to give the horrible nightgown what it deserved when I'd finished with the bulletin board.

The next pushpin released a piece of sheet music, something I had written for one of my teachers. I hummed a few bars of the melody, which only made me want to hear every note of every chord, but I decided against playing the piece on the piano in the living room.

I popped out two more pins, releasing a small advertisement for a sample of Shalimar perfume, a dried and withered corsage from a piano recital, and a flattened, rainbow-striped snow cone cup. But then I stopped.

Nestled behind a college brochure was a picture of Brett and me, taken just before we left for college. I brought it close to my face and scrutinized my eighteen-year-old self. I had thought myself pretty then. The girl in the photo had long—almost waist-length—hair, thinner hips, no tattoos, but she was definitely me. Same flat chest, same pug nose, nothing special. And there was Brett, as handsome as ever, his arm hanging limply over my shoulders.

Even then Brett hadn't been completely satisfied. Even with my long hair and thin hips and flat, smooth stomach, he had wanted something—*someone*—a little better.

I yanked everything else off the bulletin board in five groping handfuls. Brett Ross could take a flying leap right into the pink mesh trash can. Just like he'd said on the phone, I was no longer his problem.

Peeking into the mirror, I ran my hands through my hair, wishing for the length I had back then and remembering the day I got it cut. I had obediently followed Brett to the salon, and the hairdresser had obediently followed Brett's instructions, and when we left the shop, I felt confident and attractive.

The girl had gone on and on about my thick hair and smooth complexion, but now I figured she had simply been trying to sell more products. She knew as well as I did that Brett's bank account ran deep when he wanted something. Turns out they were both liars, and I was a fool to believe them.

I wrapped my fingers around the long side of my hair and yanked, *hard*, as though I was pulling a rope in a tall bell tower, while Brett's words from that day echoed in my mind.

It's not quite what I had envisioned.

Somehow I thought it would be different.

You're still beautiful, though. Of course.

My teeth ground against each other as I stared at the limp hair in my fist, and I growled. Then in one sudden movement, I fell to my knees and snatched the scissors from the floor. My hands trembled as I stuck my fingers through the handles, and the blades slid against each other noisily as I drew them to my forehead.

But then I stopped and stared at myself in the mirror, startled.

And I laughed bitterly.

No wonder Daddy was worried about me.

I dropped the scissors and retrieved my phone from the floor, intending to slip it into the pocket of my shorts, but there was no pocket. Instead, I found myself listening, just one more time, to my ex-husband's voice mail.

Chapter Six

It wasn't everyone who could rappel fifty yards from their back deck, but our property sat right on the edge of the canyon, and hurling myself off cliffs was something I had learned when I was tiny. The canyon itself had been the source of so many family outings that it overlapped my childhood memories like an intricately woven bedspread.

The cozy size of our cabin stood in sharp contrast to the broad expanse of the canyon, but our home had always been big enough for the three of us. As my dad and I stood on the rim, buckling harnesses around our waists, I realized the house felt too spacious now that Mom was gone, as though her personality had taken up more space than her five-foot-six-inch frame should have.

"How long's it been since you rappelled?" Dad tightened a strap on his thigh.

"A while, but it's like riding a bike, right?"

"I reckon it is." His mouth lifted on one side to reveal a crooked incisor in the line of otherwise straight teeth. Mom had always called his smile distinguishing, and I couldn't argue. At the moment, his simple grin told me several things. Like how much he enjoyed rappelling, and how he was glad our time apart had finally come to an end—even under the circumstances—and how, as always, his heart contained an overpowering void in the shape of my mother.

"Things going all right out at the state park?" I asked.

"They're making changes again, new rules and regulations, more inspections." I noticed a tinge of gray hair at his temples as he busied himself, flaking the rope by coiling it into a neat figure eight so it wouldn't get tangled when we tossed it down the cliff. "It's always something," he said, "but what about you? You see any old friends in town?"

Dad was undoubtedly referring to Graham Harper, but I didn't take the bait. In the past twenty-four hours, I had done a fairly thorough job of ignoring any mention of the good doctor.

"Only Mirinda Ross." I rolled my eyes. "She's a little fancy, but we could probably hang out."

My dad laughed loudly, and I liked the sound of it. "She dates Michael Divins. Did you know?"

I froze. "No kidding?"

"Well, they've been on-again, off-again for a while now. One or both of them can't make up their minds, I reckon."

I breathed in. I breathed out. No wonder Mirinda had stomped away when Michael asked me to the movie. No wonder Michael had seemed tense. But why had he asked me out in the first place? "Holy crap," I muttered.

Dad frowned for a split second before asking, "Where did you run into her?"

"At Midnight Oil. I ran into both of them." I yanked the straps of my harness, making sure everything was tight, and decidedly not telling him about my pending date. If Michael was trying to make Mirinda jealous, he was stirring up a hornet's nest.

"So how's the job hunt going?"

"Crappy."

He picked up the rope. "You never used to talk like that."

"Like what?"

"Crappy." He pointed his voice into the canyon, making the adjective seem shallow and weak.

Good grief. I was a grown woman, and if I wanted to use hard language, I would. I scrunched my nose. "I never used to be job hunting in Canyon, Texas, either. It requires a whole new set of vocabulary words."

He worked in silence then, attaching one of the red straps of the belay anchor to a strong cedar and the other to a thick metal rod that he had driven deep into the ground years ago. As he worked, I watched an eagle soaring in the distance, occasionally dipping down to the treetops before sailing skyward. Probably the bird was hunting for a mouse or a rabbit or some other small animal to eat. Hopefully she would have better luck with her hunt for lunch than I was having with my hunt for a job.

"You know?" Dad uncoiled a few feet of rope. "Now that I think about it, there was a "Help Wanted" sign in the window of Dr. Harper's office. He's in that strip shopping center on Twenty-Third Street, where the Monday clinic used to be."

I refused to look at him.

"It wouldn't be the worst job in town," he continued. "I bet he pays better than minimum wage, and he'd be reasonable if you needed a day off." Dad seemed to have forgotten the task at hand, and he now stood holding the ends of the anchor straps in one hand and the rope in the other. "Come on, Cess. I know Dr. Harper called you, and I know you're ticked with me, but could you at least give it a try?"

If Dad knew Graham had called me, then he must've talked to him again. I sighed and I could feel my pride seeping out with the oxygen. "Wallowing in self-pity?" My voice broke on the last two words, so I tightened my diaphragm before adding, "Why did you tell him that? I'm not wallowing in self-pity."

"Maybe not." His eyes softened and he gazed far across the canyon. When he spoke again, his voice was so low, I barely heard him over the swish of the wind through the cedars. "It's just that I see you're hurting, Cess. I can't help you, but I know Graham could."

How did he know that? I squinted at his profile, closing one of my eyes against the morning sun, then closing them both against his sadness. Poor Daddy, missing his wife, remembering her long battle with disease, wishing year after year that he could have helped her. A thought crossed my mind, and I dug my thumbnail into the nylon fibers of the rope I was holding. "Have you ever gone to Graham for counseling?"

The question prompted him to resume his work with the belay. He took the middle of the rope and attached it to the anchor, then he attached a personal anchor to the harness on my waist. I didn't push him, knowing if he never answered, it would be all right.

He tightened the carabiners, then double-checked that they were locked. "I'm still paying off your mother's medical bills." He looked away from me, away from the house, probably away from his own memories. "Sometimes I get real stressed, and I just need someone to talk to." When he looked back at me, I noticed that his eyes—which only moments before had been filled with concern—now appeared hollow.

"But you're all right?"

"Aw, sure." He shook his head slightly, as though he were clearing his mind of cobwebs. "I shouldn't have said 'self-pity,'" he said. "Maybe I shouldn't have talked to Dr. Harper at all."

A hundred questions flooded my mind, but Dad tossed the rope over the side, indicating he had done all the sharing he could stand. I stepped to the edge of the cliff, and he checked my gear one last time.

"I'm just worried about you, Cess," he said.

Suddenly I was his little girl again, rappelling down the canyon for the first time, and as I stood on the edge of the abyss with my dad in front of me, anchoring me to safety, I was incredibly glad to have him in my life. He wouldn't ask me how I had been broken, but I heard the implication, and I knew he wanted to fix me. He'd always been the fixer, and here he was, talking to the local therapist, helping me find a job, offering his bumbled words of encouragement—all in hopes that I would change back into the person I had been ten years ago.

I stood on tiptoe and kissed his cheek. "I'm alright, Daddy. Truly." Then I leaned back over the rim of the canyon and let myself fall away from him.

Chapter Seven

Dr. Graham Harper's note-to-self (as scribbled on a yellow Post-it):

1. Buy extra tubes for bike tires.
2. Check on details for new support group.
3. Call Mom back.

Graham Harper's thoughts were focused on Cecily Ross as he swiveled in his office chair, tapping a ballpoint pen against his leg. He was hardly ever still. His father chalked it up to the *H* in *ADHD*, but Graham knew it wasn't anything so clinical. Motion simply helped him focus, always had, and right now he was focusing on a gray SUV in the parking lot. He wasn't positive it was Cecily, but he had a strong suspicion.

Dub Witherspoon had called him again, asking if Graham knew of any place in town looking to hire an inexperienced, untrained, slightly depressed young woman. Graham imagined Cecily's dad was only doing what any good father would do: overreacting. But that didn't keep Graham from wanting to help—more out of compassion for Dub than for Cecily. Graham remembered Cecily as an ambitious yet humble girl who knew what she wanted in life and quietly worked to make it happen. He had never been able to figure why she'd hooked up with Brett Ross—other than the fact they looked good together.

The end of the ballpoint pen found its way into Graham's mouth, and he chewed on it gently as he glanced at his wall clock. His next client was due in thirty minutes. Tossing the pen on his desk, he stood and rotated his arms like a wind-blown whirligig, trying to loosen tense muscles in his neck and back. He stepped into his break room, following the worn path in the thin carpet, and poured himself a cup of coffee.

He supposed he should hire Cecily. He actually needed a receptionist because Veda Lopez's maternity leave had morphed into stay-at-home mom status. Besides, if Cecily ever found the nerve to get out of her car, the least he could do was be brave enough to give her the job. He sipped his coffee, enjoying the triple-digit temperature of the liquid as it slid across his tongue, but he almost spit it out when the bell above the front door jangled.

Hurriedly, he set his cup on the counter, then strode down the narrow hallway. "Can I help you?"

Cecily stood at the corner of the small receptionist's desk, peering at the posters stapled to the wood-paneled wall, but Graham got the feeling she wasn't reading them. When her eyes met his, he understood Dub's concern. Where there once had been purpose and hope, there was now timidity and emptiness. Then she blinked and those things were tucked away.

"Hello, Graham." Her forearms rested against her abdomen, and she gripped one elbow, worrying the skin with her thumb. "I bet you never thought you'd see me in this office." She smiled, but her gaze swept to the air vent on the ceiling, then the two vinyl chairs across from the desk, then the outdated magazines on the corner table.

"You were fairly clear about that." He pulled on his earlobe, trying not to stare at her but failing miserably.

Two of her fingers jerked away from her elbow and toward the front window. "My dad told me about your 'Help Wanted' sign. If you're still hiring, I'd like to fill out an application."

"No application necessary." He nodded, then nodded again. "Let's just take a seat in my office and talk." He pivoted and started down the hallway, uncertain if she would follow.

She didn't.

"I don't actually want the job," she called after him with a small laugh.

Graham stopped, turned, shrugged. "Okay . . ."

"I just need to apply."

"To get your dad off your back?"

She visibly relaxed, and her smiling eyes seemed to plead with him. "Something like that."

He considered offering her a chair in the waiting room, but she probably wouldn't want to get that comfortable. He moved to stand behind the receptionist's desk.

"Sorry about the other day," she said. "I practically hung up on you." She pushed one side of her hair behind her ear with a manicured fingertip. He had forgotten her willowy piano-player hands. So delicate.

"No worries," he said. "I shouldn't have called you in the first place."

As she peered around the room, Graham took the opportunity to study her. She was neatly dressed, so apparently she was taking better care of herself than when Dub had first called him. She wore dark jeans and high-heeled sandals, with a long sleeved shirt. He took a few moments to peruse the open appointment book in front of him, giving Cecily the opportunity to study him too, if she needed to.

"My dad is something else," she said.

"He's just worried about you." Graham rested his knee on the chair, itching to ask her a few leading questions but remembering her insistence that she didn't need counseling. "So about the job," he said. "It's just a basic receptionist position, answering the phone, scheduling clients, brewing the occasional pot of coffee. A full forty hours, but the schedule varies. I work from eight to five three days a week, but on Tuesdays and Thursdays, I come in late so I can see clients into the evening." He realized he had shoved his hand in his pocket and was fiddling with his keys and loose change, filling the office with a loud tinkling sound. He pulled his hand out and crossed his arms. "It pays ten an hour, but I'd do my best to give you an increase as soon as possible."

"You look different." Her fingers interlocked loosely in front of her body. "I guess it's the beard."

Did that mean the beard was good? Or bad? He smiled. "So you're still not interested. In the job?"

"Sorry. No." Her thumbs traded places, then returned to their original position, dancing a stilted, round-and-round waltz. She had said she didn't play the piano anymore, and he wondered why. Music had practically been her life before she left. It had been her oxygen.

"But there are some pretty sweet job perks," he said. "Every Wednesday, I take the staff to Soccer Mom's for lunch."

"The staff?" She glanced toward the hallway.

"That would be you. Assuming you decide to take the job."

"Hmm. Who's Soccer Mom?"

"Oh." He'd forgotten how long she'd been gone. "Sayakomarn's. It's a Thai restaurant down on the square. Everybody calls it Soccer Mom's."

Her eyebrows rose, and she chuckled. "That's Canyon for you." Her laughter bounced around the room like a balloon she had swatted with the palm of her hand.

When the sound floated to the floor in the corner, Graham shook his head. "Any chance you might want a temporary position for a few hours a week? Until I find a permanent receptionist?"

She squinted. "Probably not." When she ducked her head, her gaze fell on the appointment book.

"What's this X?"

She was asking a lot of questions for someone who didn't want the job. Maybe she didn't know what she wanted.

"That's a regular client who comes in every Thursday evening. She's a little . . . shy."

"Her name is X?"

"No . . . She just doesn't want other clients to see her name and discover she comes in."

"Why couldn't you simply keep the book closed?" Her sassiness made Graham smile.

"This client doesn't want any person, including my not-yet-hired, temporary, part-time receptionist, to know she comes here. But once she heals a little, I think she'll be more confident and less sensitive."

"If she doesn't want anyone to see her, then clearly I shouldn't take the job and be sitting here when she walks in."

He smiled. "I appreciate your compassion, but I need you here." That sounded too pushy. He didn't need *her*; he needed *someone*. "If you were to take the job, you'd have to wait in the break room on Thursday nights while she was here. But you'd still be in the office, and that's what counts."

"What do you mean?"

"I don't like to counsel women when I'm here alone. That's the reason I have a receptionist in the first place, but since I'm in a bind, I've relaxed my policy so that I'm not counseling women alone *after dark*. Which is just Tuesday and Thursday nights."

She stared at him, clearly trying to work it out in her head, then she chuckled. "You're worried there might be gossip."

She hadn't asked for more information, but he couldn't seem to hush himself. "Yes, but believe me, most of my clients aren't my type." His hand went back into his pocket. *Clink clink.* "But even if they were, it's against the code of ethics for me to date clients because it infringes on their vulnerabilities." He cleared his throat.

"Code of ethics?"

"In other words, it's against the law."

"So . . . you've never dated a client?"

"Definitely not. My lawyer would go crazy."

"You have a lawyer?"

"Everyone has a lawyer."

She eyed him skeptically, and Graham's knee pushed against the swiveling office chair in front of him. A little to the left, a little to the right. Cecily had somehow managed to swing the conversation away from herself, and now Graham felt as though a bright spotlight was focused on him. She didn't seem to have done it on purpose, or even to know she had done it. Most likely it was a defense mechanism to protect herself, but on the other hand, she was still standing there, chitchatting, no longer in a hurry to leave. Graham made an educated assessment.

Cecily needed someone to talk to.

"No wonder you're not married," she said. "You've probably counseled every woman in Canyon at one time or another."

"That may be more true than you know."

"Are you interested in Madam X?" Her eyebrows inched upward accusingly.

"No, no, no. Like I said, she's not my type." Good grief, why did he keep saying that? Graham prayed she wouldn't ask what his type was.

"Why does type matter anyway?" She took a step away from the desk to investigate the magazine rack. "I'm going out on a date, and I'm pretty sure he's not my type."

"You're dating?"

"I'm not *dating*," she insisted. "I have a *date*. There's a big difference. I barely even know the man." Her head jerked as though she realized, a little too late, how that sounded.

Graham paused before asking his next question. "Are you positive you're ready to date?"

"Oh . . . sure." Her expression clouded. "All the books say wait a year, and it's been a year. Since my divorce."

"The books also say to wait until you're emotionally ready."

She lowered her chin, leveling her gaze at him, but she didn't reply.

He raised his hands as if she had pulled a gun. "Line crossed. My bad."

Her shoulders rose and fell dismissively. "I'll consider the temporary position and let you know in a few days." She walked to the door, then turned and smiled. "But don't hold your breath."

"Couldn't ask for more. I'm just glad you'll think about it."

She lifted one eyebrow as she pushed through the door, and Graham knew one thing hadn't changed about Cecily Witherspoon Ross. She was still sharp as a whip. If he wanted to insert bits of therapy whenever he bumped into her, he would have to be subtle. And sneaky.

But he could certainly do that.

Chapter Eight

Text from Graham to Cecily: *Thanks for almost applying for the receptionist position. The rest of the staff is looking forward to your decision.*
Cecily: *So is my dad.*
Cecily (three hours and four minutes later): *If I take it at all it will only be temporarily.*
Cecily: *In the evenings.*

I considered breaking my date with Michael Divins, but in the end I kept it, mostly because Graham had told me not to, but also out of curiosity—*Why had Michael asked me out?*—and because I knew it would rankle Mirinda.

Now Michael's elbow rested next to mine on the arm of the theater seat, and I was questioning all three motives.

"Why'd you cover up your tattoo?" He asked.

"I don't exactly love it." I tugged my sleeve over my wrist. "I never thought I'd have a tattoo, much less one that covers my entire arm."

"That must've been one heck of a party."

"It wasn't like that."

He nodded. "I'd love to have a good look at it."

He wanted to see my tattoo. Most people glanced at my arm, then looked away. Some would peek at it again, trying to see the design in the ink, but few people ever really inspected it. What could it hurt? I pulled my sleeve up to my elbow.

Michael's touch trailed across my forearm. "It's sort of sexy." He laughed nervously. "Though I probably shouldn't have mentioned that."

I tried not to make eye contact. Not because he had mentioned the sexiness of my tattoo, but because I had heard those words before. From Brett.

Three teenage girls giggled from down the aisle, drawing Michael's attention. They wore short skirts and tank tops, clearly having dressed to match each other. Since there was security in numbers, I didn't blame them, but I envied their confidence. Following behind them, fully clothed, were three lanky boys. They seemed to be a few years younger, though I doubted that was the case.

I studied Michael discreetly, wondering if I hadn't seen him on a Gatorade commercial. He could just as easily have been in an ad for designer jeans. Or expensive red wine. Or *shampoo*.

"So, how do you know Mirinda?" he asked.

Irritation pricked at me. He had mentioned Mirinda while we were eating dinner at Soccer Mom's. Apparently he had gotten a text from her, and I figured she had planned the timing. "Actually, she's my sister-in-law." When his eyes widened, I clarified, in a softer tone. "*Ex*-sister-in-law."

He seemed to hold his breath in a mild, what-have-I-gotten-myself-into panic. "You were married to her brother . . . Brett?" His eyes squinted. "I've never met him."

Had he met the rest of her family? "In a town as small as Canyon, everyone has a connection somehow." I tried to make light of the situation, relieved that the movie previews were starting. "Where did you grow up?"

"Amarillo." He settled back into his seat. "Not much bigger, but decidedly different," he whispered.

Decidedly different. Like this date.

The movie opened with an action scene, but ten minutes in, the male characters predictably followed the bad guys into a night club where a beautiful girl danced provocatively on stage. I sighed. My first counselor, years before the divorce, had warned me not to watch movies. *Hollywood is not a healthy standard of measurement, Ms. Ross. You'll always find yourself lacking if you hold yourself to standards set by models and actresses.*

But that had been a long time ago.

Two hours later, the heroes were in one helicopter fighting the bad guys who were in another. All of them had powerful guns and bulging muscles, and each of them wanted more money and the beautiful girl.

"Want to get an ice cream when this is over?" Michael leaned toward me, and I wondered if he was less than impressed with the movie too. "There's a new place. You'll love it."

"What makes you think so?"

His shoulders bounced, one after the other with a split second between, like a bowl of Jell-O. "Because I said so?" he teased.

His innocent words triggered an emotional reaction, reminding me of Brett and transporting me back in time. *Because I said so* had been Brett's answer to so many questions.

Why should we paint the kitchen gray?

Why should I drop out of school?

Why should we stop trying for another baby?

"Actually, I need to get home," I said.

In the light of the screen, I could see a hint of relief in his eyes, and I knew he had come to a decision. He had worked through his what-have-I-gotten-myself-into panic and determined that dating me was too great a risk. Mirinda—his on-again, off-again girl—was worth more.

On the screen, the hero reveled in the glory of his accomplishments with a long-legged beauty standing next to him, and I thought, *How appropriate.*

Mirinda couldn't have planned it better herself.

Chapter Nine

By the time Michael dropped me off at the cabin, we had toiled through a stilted conversation about my history with Mirinda, which led to an even worse discussion about Michael's relationship with her. Apparently he worried that she was only interested in him for his status and for the money that was still rolling in from his guaranteed contract.

His lengthy explanation came across as an apology for asking me out in the first place.

"I couldn't believe you didn't know who I was," he said. "You seemed like a breath of fresh air." He couldn't seem to look me in the eye. "I didn't realize you were related to her, but regardless, I was a louse for asking you out right in front of her. I apologize for that."

He should apologize to her, not me, I thought. But I didn't say so.

Just as I got out of his fancy car—he had informed me it was a 1979 Corvette—he offered me a part-time position playing piano in his coffee shop.

"You're looking for work, right? Mirinda says you play, and I've always thought it would be cool to have live piano for the evening crowd. Mood music, you know?"

Music had always calmed my spirit, but I wasn't convinced it would compel customers to buy more caffeinated drinks or sugary pastries. I gripped the edge of the car door and bent down to peer in at him. "I already have a job. Thanks, though." And, instantly, working a temp position for Graham Cracker seemed so much better than it had earlier in the day.

"You sure? It would be the perfect job for a girl like you."

A girl like me. Yet another of Brett's phrases.

"Pretty sure."

"Okay, then. See you around. And, Cecily? I'm sorry again."

I didn't watch him drive away.

The glass storm door bumped my backside as I let myself in. Dad always left the cabin unlocked, and why not? There was no one around for over a mile. Unless you counted the Smithsons' hunting lodge, but the canyon jutted between us and them, and the only way to get there was the long way.

A note from Dad lay on the kitchen counter next to a box of Cheerios. *Have a meeting tonight. Be home late.*

I tossed the note in the trash, tucked the box of cereal under my arm, and trudged to my room. Ten minutes later I had changed into my nightshirt and was leaning against my pillows, eating Cheerios by the handful. I figured it didn't count as gorging because they were made from oat bran—and it was heart healthy and all that. I frowned. What had Dad called it? *Wallowing?* I still didn't think my behavior fell under that definition because . . . surely wallowing involved chocolate. Or at least Cheetos.

Sometimes Brett used to bring me chocolate, and I always felt it was his way of trying to get me to stop whining. I didn't want to be that way, but once our problems had started, I so desperately needed reassurance from him—in the form of compliments, hugs, even eye contact—that I hung on every word he uttered, every facial expression he cast my way, every sigh of frustration. But it didn't matter. Even if he had done all those things perfectly, he never could have convinced me that I was what he wanted.

Because I wasn't. And we both knew it.

I reached for my phone, tapped my way to the saved messages, and listened to his voice again. Then I tossed the phone on the bed. A moment later, I found myself standing in front of the narrow closet door, scrunching my nose at my reflection. I missed the big walk-in closet I'd had in California—a safe cocoon where I had spent many sleepless nights curled on the floor and sheltered from the world, from my problems, from my husband.

I sighed, longing to hide away in the depths of that closet once again. My childhood room barely had a closet at all, much less a walk-in. When the door was shut, it pressed against the clothes hanging from the short rod, and the lone shelf above them was crammed with boxes of cosmetics and old dolls. The floor was packed wall-to-wall with bags of unwanted clothes.

As I stood there, I peered into the skinny mirror my dad had bolted to the door long ago. It had been an eight-dollar purchase from Walmart the year Mom and I reworked my bedroom. In one quick weekend, we had transformed the room from a hodgepodge of Hello Kitty into a teenager's paradise. We'd put away my toys and covered the walls with posters. The mirror, twelve inches wide and four feet tall, had been perfect for applying makeup and checking my ever-changing outfits, and I had stood before it every day for years, always ducking to see my hair. I didn't duck now, because I didn't want to see the new haircut.

My nightshirt hung from my shoulders, a far cry from the silk gown I had tried to wear three days before. This garment was soft cotton—affordable, practical, comfortable—just right for a divorced woman on her own. Just right for *a girl like me*.

What kind of girl was I?

Damaged? Like an appliance sold at a discount in the scratch-and-dent department?

Brett had said as much, though not with words. When my body changed and my clothes started to fit differently, he'd stopped looking at me from across the room. He stopped grabbing me from behind when

I was pouring his orange juice. We no longer made love spontaneously. We still did it, but it seemed more like a chore on his part, and we always did it with the lights off. He only touched the parts of my body he still liked.

My right palm traveled up and down my left arm, and I wished I could wipe away the permanent ink of my tattoo. Really, it was Brett's tattoo. He was the one who wanted it on me. He was the one who said barbed wire was sexy. He was the one who said it would make a difference.

I scratched at one of the pointed barbs and smirked. What a perfect illustration of my relationship with him. The barbed wire, coiling and circling my arm, was just like his vibrant personality that had tightened around my heart until it drew blood.

I lifted my nightshirt to inspect the stretch marks covering my abdomen like ripples on the surface of a lake. A wrinkle of skin pillowed below my belly button, and I gripped it. I didn't understand how I could have that much extra skin, when I still had pounds I could lose. I lifted my shirt farther, and scowled at the pear shape of my body, so disproportionate, so undesirable, so deformed. *No longer attractive*, as Brett had said.

And tonight it had become clear to me that I was just as insignificant to other men. Michael Divins had chosen Mirinda over me, and even though I didn't care a lick about the man, his actions had convinced me, once and for all, that all men were alike.

Stifled sobs wrenched from my throat, and I replayed my memories of Brett frowning at me, turning away, shaking his head. And then I replayed my evening with Michael, who seemed so relieved that I didn't want to go out for ice cream. I didn't try to hold my tears back. Instead, I used them as a weapon, stoking the flames of injustice until I burned with rage.

I dropped to my knees and pounded my fists against my thighs like I always did, trying to hurt myself or hurt Brett, hoping I'd leave bruises, evidence of the disgust I felt toward myself for becoming so pitiful. Good girls are supposed to be above that. According to my therapist, I wasn't supposed to put emphasis on my appearance because, after all, beauty is only skin deep. Healthy women are supposed to be happy with themselves, drawing strength from their accomplishments and their dreams and their God. *We're all fearfully and wonderfully made*, he had said, and when I could believe that, I wouldn't have these problems.

When I looked once more in the mirror, I saw a weak woman pitching a tantrum with tears streaking down her face and her fists clenched. She was lost. She was nothing. And I hated her.

Shifting my hips to the carpet, I sat on my bottom, bent my knees, and slammed my heels against the closet door, cracking the mirror. My fury felt a smidgen less powerful, but then the size of the crack—so small and ineffectual—angered me again. I pounded my feet against the crack over and over, venting my hatred until the glass shattered into a hundred lines. I only paused for a split second—to appreciate its beauty—before I kicked one more time, sending warped triangles of glittering light to the floor as smaller fragments sprinkled onto my hair and shoulders.

An animal scream erupted from my throat, and I reached for one of the knives I had just created. Holding it shakily between my finger and thumb, I ran it softly along my leg, leaving a thin red line from which blood seeped in droplets. I deserved to hurt. I longed for it.

The glass grew slippery from sweat or blood, and I gripped it tighter between my fingers, not quite able to bring myself to clench it in my fist. That inability made me even more furious, and I dragged the shard firmly across my right thigh, crying out from the pain. I felt a release of tension, and I knew it was what I deserved. I scraped it across my left thigh, faster and deeper, back and forth from one leg to the other, two then three times, four, five, six, until I dropped it.

Exhausted.

Satisfied.

Empty.

My muscles turned to pudding, and I leaned sideways against my suitcases, blood trickling down my legs until it dripped to the carpet and was hungrily absorbed.

Holding my hands in front of me, I inspected my palms. What had I done? Brett would be so put out with me. No, Brett didn't care anymore. Daddy would be upset, though. And sad. So sad. I pulled my nightshirt over my head and pressed it against my legs, staunching the flow of blood as I came to my senses. I had gone too far this time. This was more than crying and venting and leaving bruises.

Maybe I really was wallowing.

Well, of course I was.

Wallowing had nothing to do with Cheerios or any other food I might use to drown my sorrows. It involved mirrors and shards of glass and lies that I couldn't stop believing. Accusations screeched through my mind like an eagle's cry deep in the canyon, bouncing off the jagged walls of my mind and reaching into every crook and cranny, until it gradually diminished and became so faint, so distant, that I couldn't be sure I had heard anything at all.

And even though I had thought the lies were a distant echo, I was wrong. Even though I had tried to replace that jumbled thousand-piece puzzle with something new and fresh, my life, my emotions, and my sanity were still an impossible mess. Lies were still a part of this new person I had become, because playing the part of a well-adjusted woman hadn't changed me on the inside at all. Not only did I still believe the lies . . . they consumed me, heart and soul.

Chapter Ten

Text from Graham to Cecily: *Still considering my job offer?*
Cecily: *I can come Thursday night. Just this once. To help out.*

As I stood at the pharmacy counter, my legs vibrated with pain. The skirt I had slipped on that morning rubbed against the cuts, which still oozed watery blood, and I was desperate to bandage them before my dad noticed. Even though the wounds were on my thighs, my legs ached all the way down to my calves and ankles. Thank goodness the pharmacist didn't ask what the bandages were for.

"You new around here?" He smiled.

"Sure am." I lied to keep things simple, wishing he would hurry.

He placed the items in a white paper sack, then narrowed his eyes. "You feeling all right? You don't look so good."

"Haven't had my coffee yet."

"Ah." He grinned. "My wife has to have coffee to wake up too. She's a cappuccino girl. Used to buy coffee every morning on the way to take the kids to school, but I bought her a cappuccino maker for her birthday. Now I get up a few minutes early, make her a cup, and take it to her before she gets out of bed. My brothers tell me I'm whupped, but I don't care if I am."

The guy was a middle-aged Hispanic man with shiny smooth skin and black hair that wanted to curl. "Sounds . . . blissful."

"She makes it easy for me." He smiled. "Not only is she good to me, she's gorgeous. Not that looks matter," he said quickly, "but she's a knockout, and I'm lucky to have her."

Another Barbie doll. Or maybe a runway model, leggy and slim, with waist-length hair and tons of eyeliner. Yes, that would make marriage easier, wouldn't it? I handed him a twenty-dollar bill even though he hadn't told me the total.

The skin above my knees quivered like the aftershock of an earthquake. The cuts would take a while to heal, but not as long as my mental health would take to recover. *And I had thought I was doing so well.* Maybe the date with Michael Divins had put me over the edge—if it could even be called a date—but more likely the straw that broke the loony's back was running into my sister-in-law. Miranda's mere presence had triggered an onslaught of dangerous memories, and I had tortured myself with them long into the night.

"That'll be eight forty-seven," said the pharmacist. "So, your change is . . . eleven fifty-three." He counted the money into my palm. "You sure you're okay, hon? You look a little pale."

If he told me I looked bad one more time, I would scream. Or claw his eyes out. Then again, if he was used to looking at his tanned runway model wife, I probably did appear washed out. I smiled before I told him one last white lie. "I couldn't be better. Thanks."

Picking up the paper sack, I walked stiffly to the car, holding my skirt away from my legs and not caring if I had to lie a million more times. Dishonesty seemed trivial compared to the rest of my struggles.

I had almost killed myself last year, and the fact that I didn't want to kill myself now gave me a haunting sense of confidence. Even as I processed the thought, I recognized it as distorted thinking, and I chastised myself. Who was I kidding?

I needed help.

Chapter Eleven

Dr. Graham Harper's favorite motivational poster (stapled above the sink in the break room where he could see it every day):

It's a good thing to have all the props pulled out
from under us occasionally.
It gives us some sense of what is rock under our feet,
and what is sand.

- Madeleine L'Engle

Graham had gotten the impression something was bothering Cecily when she arrived at his office, but he knew better than to ask. He knew that whatever she shared about herself would have to be offered freely, and that she would talk when she was ready. After his last appointment of the evening, he ushered the client—Madam X, as Cecily had called her—to the back exit of the office and locked the door behind her. Then he turned toward the break room where Cecily was waiting discreetly.

And his pulse quickened.

Cecily Ross was swiftly getting under his skin, and because of her, his world had lightened ever so slightly. She was a stinker, for sure, but she made him smile, and smiling was good therapy. But there was something he couldn't quite put his finger on. He had watched her on and off during the evening, as she sat at the receptionist desk and interacted with clients, and he'd gotten the impression that some of her smiles were only a surface mask. Every now and then the mask would slip, and Graham saw darkness in her eyes, as though she were a lost child with no hope of finding her way home.

"All safe and clear?" She opened the break-room door two inches, but she didn't look into the hallway.

"Mission accomplished. Thanks."

"So, that was the famous Madam X?"

He pulled on his earlobe. "You saw her?"

"No." She stretched the word out. "Relax. I don't know who she is, but honestly, I've been away from Canyon so long, I probably wouldn't recognize her anyway."

Graham didn't reply, just nodded.

"It's not the old drama teacher, is it? That woman was a basket case for sure."

"Mrs. Kilpatrick?" He smiled, and then laughed as he realized that the retired teacher probably could have benefited from a few sessions.

"Remember the time she went into hysterics when those three boys refused to accept tardy slips?"

"You took drama?" Graham asked.

"No, I just heard about it." She wiped crumbs from the table and sprinkled them in the trash can, and suddenly Graham speculated that she might have agreed to work tonight merely to appease her dad.

He put his coffee mug in the cabinet, forcing himself not to stare. Every time he looked at her, he relived that night years ago and wondered what she remembered. Had those few minutes made as huge an impression on her as they had on him?

Somehow he doubted it.

He dried his hands on a dish towel and turned to find her standing by the trash can. She had removed the liner, tied the bag, and was now holding the white plastic bundle in her arms like a baby. When Graham looked into her eyes, a heavy weight of concern pressed on his shoulders. A moment ago, she had been chattering about nothing in particular, but now, surprisingly, she was no longer hiding her feelings behind that mask of hers, and she peered at him with wide eyes. The pressure on Graham's shoulders slid down to his chest.

"I went out on that date I was telling you about." A smallish sort of laugh crossed her lips, but then she sucked it back in before another could follow.

"Did you?" He rested his hand on the counter, trying to still his jitters. If this were a counseling session, he would ask Cecily to sit down and relax—but he didn't dare suggest it.

"You were right that I'm not ready yet." Her head bobbed to the side. "Turns out I have a little problem with self-esteem. I should've known you were right, and my dad too, but I've just been telling myself I'd be fine." Her eyes didn't meet his.

Graham spoke cautiously, so as not to prompt a fight or flight response. "Did something happen?"

"Not on the date . . . no." Her fingertips swept her throat. "That's probably not what you meant, but the man is harmless. Quite the all-American good guy. Every girl's dream."

Was she talking about Michael Divins? Graham's palm pressed against the Formica. The crowd at Midnight Oil had quadrupled since it changed ownership, mostly because of college-aged girls. Rumor had it the football star was looking for a bride, but Graham had also heard that Michael had found one: Mirinda Ross. Whether that rumor was true or not, Graham didn't know, but he did know Michael well enough to be confident that he wouldn't knowingly hurt Cecily. "You're all right?" Graham asked.

"Just a slight meltdown. Nothing like Mrs. Kilpatrick or anything." Her voice trailed off.

"Self-esteem can be a monster." He shoved his hands in his pockets in an attempt to appear laid-back, as though he wasn't hanging on every word of the conversation. "But it sounds like you recognize it for what it is."

"Oh, I've known all along." She settled the trash bag in the seat of a chair. "Believe me, my low self-esteem and I go way back."

"So . . . you know you need to accept your responsibility in the matter? And not lean on others to make you feel better?"

"Knowing it in my mind and being able to do it in my heart are two entirely different things. The emotions rule the kingdom, so to speak."

She really had been through a lot of counseling. "But you're on the right track."

"I guess a little more therapy might not be such a bad idea after all." She fumbled with the tie on the trash bag, curling it around her index finger, then unrolling it, then twisting it again. Her next words spilled over each other in a rush. "I penciled myself in for Tuesday night . . . in the next available time slot."

For the first time since Cecily had come back to town, Graham stopped fidgeting.

"My dad will be thrilled." She noticed she was still touching the trash bag and pulled her hand away.

This was monumental, a huge step for Cecily, but Graham found himself at a loss for words. He hadn't expected her to consent so readily, or so soon. "Okay."

She exhaled slowly, thoroughly.

"When was your date?" he asked.

"Monday night."

Three days. Had she spoken on impulse after Madam X's appointment? Knowing someone else suffered from insecurity might have given her a boost of courage. Either way, Graham was glad, but the thought of Cecily's name in his appointment book made him want to crumple to the floor in self-defeat. His heel began to bounce.

"I'm not sure you need more counseling." His fingers went to his mouth involuntarily, but he pulled them away, frowning down at his palm as he recognized that his own subliminal action signaled he was lying. *Of course she needed counseling.*

"Are you serious?" She seemed simultaneously relieved and leery.

"Like you say, you've been through months of it already. Maybe it's time for a different approach." He picked up the dish towel and busied himself with folding it, not looking at her.

"You're not going to tell me I need shock treatment, are you?"

He chuckled. "Not just yet. No."

"Then what did you have in mind?"

"A friend of mine is starting a support group—just two or three women—battling the same type of struggles. It might be good for you."

Cecily's face was controlled, a vacuum, void of any telltale emotions that could hint at her thoughts. "Where?"

"I think they're planning to meet at Midnight Oil." He cringed inwardly, wishing the leader had chosen somewhere else. The location alone could be Cecily's undoing.

"Do I know these women?"

He bit his lip, wondering how he could make all of this sound better . . . but the fact that Cecily knew Shanty wasn't necessarily a bad thing. "Actually . . . yes. I don't typically give out names, but Shanty gave me permission to let people know she'd be leading the group."

Cecily's eyebrows flickered with skepticism. "Shanty Washington? Who graduated a few years ahead of us?"

Actually, Graham thought, she never graduated. "That's the one, but she's Shanty Espinosa now. Married. And she's surprisingly good at these things. She led her first group a couple of years ago, and since then, she's helped a lot of women."

"Espinosa?" Cecily narrowed her eyes. "Tell me she didn't marry one of those Espinosas who lived out on Hereford Highway, twenty-five of them in a single-wide mobile home."

"A cousin of theirs from New Mexico."

Cecily was silent as they made their way down the hall, and Graham clicked off lights as they went. She would be weighing her options now, trying to decide which was the lesser of two evils—counseling with him or a support group with Shanty.

"She's actually quite good," he repeated, trying to convince himself, as well as her, that it was a great idea to meet with a support group led by a woman she didn't respect, at a coffee shop owned by the man she went out with three days ago. Graham ran a hand through his hair, his own self-esteem dragging along behind him and leaving a greasy trail of guilt on the worn carpet. "And you and I could still discuss things on the side."

"Like unofficial counseling?"

"Exactly."

"Okay . . . I'll do it." Her haunting eyes held his for five long seconds, then she nodded and pushed through the door.

Graham watched her walk to her car. He told himself he was watching her for her own safety because it was late at night and she was in a dark parking lot, but truthfully, nothing very worrisome ever happened in Canyon. The real reason he watched her was because he liked what he saw. He liked the way she pushed her hair behind her ears. He liked the way her shirt swung back and forth as she walked. He liked the shiny little slippers on her feet.

But remorse washed over him as he headed out the back entrance . . . to his car waiting in the alley, to the dumpster where a few rats scurried, to the darkness where he could hide his shame. Certainly, he liked what he saw in Cecily Ross, but if he was honest with himself, he would admit that those shiny little slippers were black, just like all her other shoes. And her clothes were either black, gray, or brown. Even her SUV was dark gray. And her hair? It was styled in such a way that she could easily let it fall across one eye, partially hiding her expressions, her emotions, her pain.

Graham distinctly remembered the hardtop Jeep Wrangler that Cecily had driven in high school. It had been refurbished, probably by Dub, and spray-painted bright yellow, with a smiley face sticker on the back bumper. And he remembered her wardrobe—after all, he had looked at her enough—as nothing fancy, just jeans and shirts, but she was obsessed with matching her shoes to her blouses. Red shirt . . . red sandals. Green shirt . . . green Converse sneakers. Pink shirt . . . pink heels, pink earrings, pink scarf, pink purse.

Graham remembered Cecily very, very well.

And he knew she needed his professional help. He knew she did, and he wanted to help her. He wanted to give her advice, listen to her problems, steer her away from the self-inflicted darkness she was hiding so well from the world. But more than all that, he wanted to get to know the twenty-eight-year-old Cecily, to hear her laugh, to find out what could make her happy. He wanted to date her.

And he wouldn't be able to do that if she became one of his clients.

Chapter Twelve

Text from Graham to Cecily: *To be yourself in a world that is constantly trying to make you something else is the greatest accomplishment.*
Cecily: *Is that just off the top of your head or what?*
Graham: *Actually, it's Ralph Waldo Emerson.*
Cecily: *Of course it is.*
Graham: *Have fun at group.*
Cecily: *Right. Fun.*

"Sess-uh-lee With-uh-spoon!"

Shanty's cry met me as I opened the door of Midnight Oil on Saturday afternoon, and I almost shuddered. She had always been a loud one, and the gaze of every coffee shop patron swung from her waving palm straight to my face. And to think, I had sat in my car for ten minutes, fretting over whether I would recognize her.

I waved tentatively, then walked past the counter, greeting Michael with a cheery *hello*, as I'd planned. To his credit, he did the same. Mirinda, on the other hand, looked back and forth between him and me with a smirk on her face.

Shanty sat at a booth deep in the shop, and a young girl sat across from her. Shanty looked the same, but different. Her creamy brown skin—a mixture she got from her African American father and Asian American mother—was set off by frosted makeup. I had forgotten how pretty she was, but surprisingly, I didn't find her intimidating.

As I came closer, I could see that the young girl sitting across from her was actually a young woman, college aged, who leaned in the corner of the booth as though trying to disappear into the vinyl. Her arms were crossed tightly, and a student backpack sat on the bench beside her, discouraging anyone from getting too close. She fingered the leather cover on what I assumed was a Kindle e-reader sitting on the table in front of her.

I pulled a stray chair to the end of the booth. "Hi," I said simply, glad Shanty didn't seem compelled to stand up and hug me.

"Been a long time, girl, but you look good," Shanty said. "Love the wonky hairstyle." She tilted her head from side to side, indicating my bi-level cut, and as she did so, her own beaded braids bounced around her shoulders.

I had never seen Shanty with long hair. Before I moved away, her curls had been kept short in a halo of black fluff. Maybe the braids were extensions.

"Cecily, this here is Nina Guiterrez," said Shanty. "She's a sopho-more at the college. I was just telling her how you and I go way back even though we never ran in the same crowd or nothing. You were probably still in school when I married Al and settled down."

I nodded toward the girl but didn't speak to her directly, fearing she might have an anxiety attack if I did. "Do you guys know each other?"

"We've known each other all of"—Shanty made a production of looking at her cell phone—"seven minutes, but we've hit it off really well so far. Don't you think, Nina?"

The girl had been sipping her iced coffee, and when Shanty addressed her, all at once she set her cup down, swallowed her coffee, and nodded. The hurried combination of actions left her with coffee dripping from one hand, and she patted her wrist with the tiny napkin her drink had been sitting on.

I pushed my chair back. "If you need to wash up, I can let you out."

"I'm good. Thanks." Her cheeks warmed from a shade of soft honey into dusty peach. She was pretty in a natural way with long straight hair that was so black it almost looked blue. I remembered seeing her in the shop before.

"Anyway," said Shanty, "looks like this is us. There was another woman thinking on coming, but her husband was against it, don't that beat all? Seems like he'd want his woman to feel good about herself, but whatever." She leaned her elbows on the table where a bagel, smeared with strawberry cream cheese, sat next to a large coffee. "I don't know what Dr. H told y'all, but this group is all about self-image, self-esteem, even self-love if the term makes you happy, and my goal is to help you girls get out of your funk. Personally, I have a constant battle with self-esteem, but when I help other women fight their own, it helps me fight mine." Her smile slipped, but just barely. "Have any questions?"

Could you please speak quieter? "Um . . . what do we actually do here?" I asked.

"Just talk. And maybe whine a little. Lean on each other for encouragement."

She grinned, and I felt the urge to smile back.

"But I don't want y'all to feel apprehensive about sharing your stuff." Shanty held up her index finger, and its glittery nail wagged back and forth. "What's said in this group, stays in this group. None of us will go blabbing things around town—that's not productive—but there is one thing I won't hesitate to act on, and that's anything that hints that one of you might be a danger to yourself or others." She placed a palm on each of our hands. "And in that case, I'd only be doing it to get you the help you need."

I slipped my hand from beneath hers, pretending I had an itch on my shin. Would the cuts on my thighs classify me as a danger to myself?

Probably, but I was over that now, getting help, moving on. But still . . . I made a mental note to myself: *be careful what you say.*

"What do we talk about?" Nina could barely be heard over the general noise of the shop, but I was glad to discover she could speak up when she wanted to know something.

"Our problems mostly." Shanty's expression grew grim. "Our fears. Whatever makes us feel insecure that day. And we'll chat about the forces that are working against us."

"What forces?" Nina asked.

"The media, mainly, not to mention all those thoughts that churn through our minds and cause us to beat ourselves up." She batted her palm through the air. "Anyhoo, we need to be aware of what we're up against. I trust you wouldn't be here unless you were down on yourselves a little bit, so we'll root out your particular brand of hang-ups, but we won't harp on them. We'll just put them all out there and talk about your options."

Poke them with a stick.

Shanty leaned toward me. "Nina was just telling me she paints with watercolors. Ain't that something?"

"Oh?" I settled back in my chair, trying to recapture my personal space while marveling that Shanty had been able to glean even that much information from the timid girl.

She continued to study me, then bounced gently, squeaking the springs in the padded bench. "What hobbies do you have?"

My mind went blank. "I guess I read sometimes."

"What was the last book you read?"

"I . . . I can't really remember."

"Then you need a new hobby. Something you enjoy doing just for yourself. Something that makes you happy. Think you can find something before we meet again?"

"Is it really that important?"

"I'm just telling it like I see it. Honestly, Nina couldn't admit to painting much either, and I put it to her the same way. You girls need hobbies." Her lips puckered like a duck, and she looked back and forth between us. "Something you *like* to do, so that you will *like* yourself while you're doing it. Make sense?"

No wonder Nina seemed to be pushed into the corner. After seven minutes of interrogation by Shanty, she could have looked a lot worse.

But finding a hobby was the least of my worries. "Sure," I said.

"Excellent."

Shanty seemed to have an agenda, but what did I expect? It was a support group, for crying out loud, but still, I felt as though she was pressing me like an overexuberant spin class instructor when all I needed was light yoga.

"Let's get to know each other a little," she said, "by sharing our stories." She shoved the table half an inch toward Nina to give herself more room, and I looked away. Shanty could stand to lose a few pounds.

"Our stories?" I asked.

"You know . . . how you ended up needing this group. What happened in your life, recently or even in childhood, that caused you to have low self-esteem."

Again, I wished she would talk quieter, but nobody around us seemed to be paying any attention. "I think I'm going to get a coffee first. Since we're here and all."

"Oh, right. I'm jumping ahead of myself as usual."

I escaped to the counter, taking my place behind three other customers and wishing the line were longer. Shanty Washington—no, she was Shanty Espinosa now—was a steamroller, full speed ahead, and Nina and I were going to have to hold on tight or get slung off at the next curve. Could I do this? Did I even want to?

Shanty was so . . . *open* about her self-esteem, whereas I didn't even like to say the word aloud. I glanced back at the booth where Nina was rotating her cup in front of her. She had stopped drinking from it, as though her throat was too tight to swallow. Shanty, on the other hand, was still talking faster than a time-lapse video.

When I turned back to the counter, the line had disappeared, and Mirinda was tapping a fingernail against the cash register.

"Caramel honey latte, please," I said. "Grande."

Mirinda busied herself with making the drink. "So I guess things didn't work out between you two." My mind was so far away from Michael Divins that it took me a minute to register what she was saying.

I peeked around the restaurant and located him. He was standing at our table, greeting Shanty.

"No, things didn't work out," I said, wondering what Michael had told her.

"Can't say I'm surprised. I never figured you for his type."

Well, he hadn't turned out to be my type either, but I had actually known that going into it, hadn't I? And I had been desperate and needy. I handed her my money, then stalled at the napkin dispenser and waited until Michael left our table.

Shanty started talking before I sat down. "That Michael Divins was asking how I know you and all that. Are you friends?" Her left eyebrow inched up until it was hidden by beaded braids.

"Sort of. I went to a movie with him last week, but we didn't really hit it off."

"You went out with him?" Nina sat up straight, bolstering her courage in order to solicit the information, and I suddenly had an overwhelming thought. *You're Madam X!* It seemed obvious, and I wondered why Graham had even sent me to the group if her identity was supposed to be such a secret. Did he think I wouldn't figure it out?

"We only went out once and probably won't again," I said softly.

Shanty placed her palms on the table. "I'll share my story first 'cause I'm not nervous about it."

Her transparency made me uncomfortable.

"My issues go way back to when I was a little girl." Her voice finally lowered. "My parents were both workaholics, never home, and they didn't have much time for my sisters and me. Turns out I didn't suffer too much from Mama's absence, seeing as how I had older sisters to baby me, but it would've done me good to have Daddy in my life." Her face lost its animation. "He's gone now, but still, I wish I could just hear him one time, saying, *Shanty, you're beautiful, just as you are.*" Then, suddenly, she snickered. "Course, I don't know he wasn't thinking that every day of my life, but that's just it . . . I don't know. I don't know that he ever even noticed I was around, one way or the other."

Nina patted her forearm.

"Thanks, darlin'." Shanty fanned her face with her palm, drying her eyes. "I'm married to a loving man who tells me I'm a pretty little girl. That makes me laugh cause there's not nothing *little* about me, but we have a good thing going." She dabbed at a tear. "Anyhoo, now I write a blog about body shaming called *Shame on Shanty*. You girls should check it out if you haven't already. There's lots of good info on there, and a guest blogger every week—stories from all sorts of women. I try to keep it encouraging."

My mouth must have fallen open, because Shanty looked at me and guffawed.

"I know it!" Her smile was back full force, and her bronze skin glowed. She really was pretty. "I know what you're thinking, Cecily. Who would've thought little ole Shanty would end up a big-time blogger, but there you go. I'm not able to do as much online as I'd like, seeing as how I've got four kids underfoot, but I do what I can. And it's rewarding for me. Makes me feel like I'm helping this crazy world a little. One woman at a time."

My lips curved upward. I knew they did because I told them to, but I wasn't sure it was a believable smile. Not because I wasn't happy for Shanty, but because I knew I was expected to tell my own *story* now.

"I'll go next." Hopefully my nervousness wouldn't be obvious. "I don't remember being unhappy with my looks when I was young." I shrugged. "I don't remember thinking about myself one way or another, but when I was a teenager, suddenly everything mattered. I looked at the other girls with their silky hair and designer clothes, and I didn't match up. Or I didn't think I did—who knows the truth, right? But I started trying very hard to fit in, to be what I thought I was supposed to be, and to get praise from other people, especially boys."

Nina nodded, but she didn't seem like she was going to comment, so I continued.

"Brett and I dated in high school, and everyone said we looked great together. We kept dating in college, and then we got married after my sophomore year." I paused while I decided there was no need to mention the secret I had discovered about Brett after the wedding. "We had a few rough years, and eventually he told me he didn't love me anymore and he wanted out. But I don't think it was about love at that point." I swallowed what felt like a cotton ball lodged in my throat.

Nina's fingertips brushed the back of my hand, startling me with their reassurance.

"Pretty boy Brett Ross didn't love you anymore? That fool." Shanty's lips pursed like she'd tasted a sour lemon. "Girl, you're better off without that one."

"I agree, actually, but I can't seem to pull myself out of the mud he tossed me in."

Shanty hummed softly. "Thank you for sharing your story, honey bunch. I know it ain't easy. Let me tell you, we're gonna get you outta that mud puddle, you just wait, but we'll work on you, not Brett. He's got to take care of his own problems now." She looked at Nina and tucked her chin. "Okay, girlie, you're gonna have to speak, but I promise we won't bite."

Nina smiled, nodded, smiled again. "I know you won't. I've just always had a difficult time speaking up . . . When I was a child, they worried about me."

Shanty spoke gently. "Does your shyness lend itself toward insecurity?"

Lend itself? Every so often, I got a glimpse of the writer Shanty claimed to be.

"Yes . . . ," Nina said slowly, "and vice versa. If I was more confident, I wouldn't be as shy. And if I wasn't as shy, I would be more confident."

She took a sip of coffee, then settled her shoulders as though she was finished speaking for the day.

Shanty kept nodding at her and didn't look away.

"And"—Nina's eyes stayed focused on her drink—"over the years, I've had trouble standing up for myself, you know?"

Shanty's head bobbed, and after another long pause, she must have decided that was enough torture. "Thank you for sharing your story." She looked back at me. "Both of you. I know it's not easy telling others your problems, especially when they're things like we're talking about. It's so much easier to let them lie in the dark closets of our minds. Problem with that is those silly little memories turn into monsters if they're left unattended. So . . ." She intertwined her fingers on the tabletop. "I've got some homework for you."

"Besides finding a hobby?" I asked.

"That was a freebie." She grinned. "For homework, I want you to smile at yourself in the mirror."

Nina and I looked at each other, both frowning.

"That's it?"

"Yep, easy smeasy, girls. Just smile at yourself in the mirror. You in?"

"Sure." I shrugged. "I'm in."

"Okay," said Nina.

Shanty pulled her phone toward her. "Let's exchange cell numbers so I can send you reminders and such. And do you girls wanna set up a regular time to meet each week? Maybe Monday or Tuesday night?"

"Tuesdays I have night class," Nina said.

"Monday then?"

Nina nodded, and they both looked at me.

This was all weird and unusual, and I didn't want to be a part of it, not really. But when I thought of the shards of glass still lying in the bottom of my pink mesh trash can, I nodded. "Yes, Monday's good." But like Shanty said, I would work on myself and not Brett, so come Monday—or any of the following Mondays—I would still have no reason to mention Brett's addiction. This group was about self-esteem, not pain or humiliation or fear, and no amount of *sharing* would change that.

Besides, I had no real reason to be afraid. Not really. And I had no reason to explain the question that raced through my mind every time I talked to a man, whether it was my dad, or Michael Divins, or Graham. Or even that pesky pharmacist with the runway-model wife. It didn't matter who the man was, I always wondered the same thing: *Do you have a secret too?*

Chapter Thirteen

Line C—Auto registration and renewal
Please have paperwork filled out before getting in line.

The man was caught by surprise the first time it happened.

He had been standing in a long line at the county tax office, waiting to renew his auto registration with a dozen others, all of whom undoubtedly wanted to be somewhere else just like he did. One minute he was scrolling through sports statistics on his cell phone, and the next minute he was looking into the eyes of a beautiful woman, there on the phone's small screen, wearing nothing but lace and eyeliner. She sat on an antique settee like the one his grandmother had in her apartment at the retirement villa. Actually, the woman wasn't sitting on it. She was lying on it, which seemed out of place because the piece of furniture wasn't meant to be lain on. He envisioned his grandmother perched on the edge of its satin cushion with her cup and saucer balanced on her knees.

But this woman was not his grandmother.

He glanced around to see if anyone was watching him, but the teenager behind him didn't look up from the textbook she was reading, so he nonchalantly dropped his gaze back to the screen. He studied the way the woman leaned back on one elbow with her legs crossed neatly at the ankles. She had silver high heels on. She looked about twenty-five, but she could've been older. Her blond hair had been swept around the back of her neck, and it fell down her front, covering half her chest. He had the urge to reach into the picture and gently push it back over her shoulder . . . because he wanted to see more.

The line shifted, and he let the phone fall into his front pocket before he took a step forward. He crossed his arms, feeling the tension in his shoulders from too little sleep and too much stress. The lawyers were still after him. Would be until he got the ordeal settled once and for all, but in the meantime, he'd be wise to find a way to vent his frustrations. Usually exercise was his go-to, but even that hadn't been helping lately.

His phone vibrated in his pocket, and he pulled it out, holding it at arm's length as though distance might lesson the sting of whatever message was coming through this time. But, no . . . it didn't. His thumb made a single tap, and the words disappeared from his sight—but not from his mind. He supposed the lawyers were only doing their jobs.

He inched forward in line again, then closed his eyes momentarily, wishing his problems away. When he opened them again, he glanced down at the screen. He had forgotten the woman on the settee, but she was still there, smiling. As though she wanted him. As though he hadn't made a mess of things. As though the two of them shared a secret.

Chapter Fourteen

Group text from Shanty to Cecily and Nina: *I really enjoyed meeting with you two!! Thanks for trusting and sharing. Looking forward to Monday night, but between now and then . . . think happy thoughts!!!*
Cecily: *See you then.*
Nina: *:)*

Sunday afternoon, I sat in the stone gatehouse at the entrance to Palo Duro Canyon State Park, watching my dad work. As a maintenance ranger, he typically spent his time building, repairing, or cleaning the park's facilities, and he didn't often find himself checking in visitors behind the front desk. "They're short-staffed today," he had said. "Come and keep me company."

And the idea had sounded perfect.

The gatehouse had been built eighty years earlier out of local stone and rock, and I'd always felt the building, though outdated, fit the canyon perfectly. It was rugged and earthy, so it blended with its surroundings, and it was appropriately small in comparison to the immensity of the canyon that lay just out of eyesight. I had grown up in and around the park's rock buildings, and they seemed as much a part of Dad as our own cabin.

"How's the new job?" He didn't look at me when he asked—an indication of how badly he wanted to know the answer.

"I'm just helping until Graham finds someone permanent, but it's going all right, I suppose. Sometimes it's pretty boring, just sitting in the office. I'm thinking I might"—why was I telling him this?—"take up a hobby. Something to do while I'm waiting."

He didn't say anything for several seconds, and when he did, I heard laughter behind his words. "Knitting might be just the thing. Not too loud or distracting."

"I'm not knitting." I plopped into a chair near the window and rested my foot on the sill. "And no embroidery or cross-stitch either." My mother had tried to teach me all three with little success. Not that she had been interested. She'd just gotten it in her mind that a mother and daughter ought to experience that sort of thing together, but my best memories were those times she didn't try to *be with* me. We just were. Painting our nails, making cookies, buying groceries.

Dad's elbows rested on the counter, his fingertips touching to form a tent near his chin. He gazed, unseeing, at a display on the wall, and I knew he was thinking of Mom too.

"We should get out more," I said.

He hummed. "You mean you should."

"No, I mean we both should. I'm not the only one who gets lonely."

"I don't get lonely." He frowned as though I had said a string of curse words.

"Do too."

"Don't."

"How often do you get out of the house? And work doesn't count. I mean out of the house just for fun."

"Aw, now. I have a pretty good time at work, Cess. You know that."

"Yeah." I stared out the window, wrinkling my nose at the scraggly brush that dotted the pasture. "She'd want you to get out more. She'd want both of us to."

He didn't answer, and a few minutes later, he seemed glad when a car approached the gate. "What do you know, there's Michael Divins. And I bet Mirinda's with him." The Corvette, still fifty yards away, approached slowly as though its occupants were looking at the scenery.

I still hadn't admitted to Dad that I'd gone out with Michael, and I didn't plan to admit it now. Seeing him with Mirinda was awkward enough, even though I had assumed they'd get back together. Barbie and Ken.

Dad stepped onto the porch as the driver's door opened.

My foot slid off the windowsill and hit the floor, and I leaned forward to watch through the dusty window. When Michael climbed out of the car, he had an amused look on his face, as though he were the only one who knew the answer to a riddle. He took a step toward Dad and gave him a casual fist bump.

And then there was Mirinda. The two of them could have made their own commercial. Two larger-than-life models in a sleek car. *If you spend eighty thousand dollars on a vehicle, you can look like this too! You'll be beautiful and sexy, and the envy of all your friends!*

I only got a glimpse of my ex-sister-in-law, but it looked like she had her hair in a ponytail. Michael and my dad talked for a few minutes, but it didn't seem like the detached conversation of a park ranger and a random guest. They were chatting like they might have been continuing a conversation they'd started earlier.

When Dad came back in the gatehouse, I didn't even wait until he had closed the door. "You know Michael Divins?"

Daddy straightened two brochures in the rack by the counter. "We've met."

"Where?"

"Aw . . . here and there, I guess." He rubbed his jaw with his thumb. "Canyon's a small town. By the way, did you hear that he's hosting next week's fundraiser, that big bingo night to raise money for the tornado victims? I heard he's the emcee."

"That'll be good publicity for Midnight Oil."

"I don't think it's just that, though . . . I get the impression Mirinda asked him to help out."

So Mirinda had a soft spot for disaster relief. Who knew? "It's sort of weird that Mirinda's at the park," I said. "I never figured her to be the kind to enjoy the outdoors."

"Rumor has it Michael has fallen in love with the canyon—hiking especially—and Mirinda has fallen in love with Michael."

So now it was love. "Wait. Mirinda *hikes*?"

"Apparently."

I got the feeling there was something he wasn't telling me, but I didn't push. If he wanted to talk about something else, I had something in mind.

"So, tell me about those medical bills." I cocked my head to the side and waited.

Daddy tucked his chin. "You're so much like your mother."

"So they tell me."

A puff of air slipped between his teeth. "Well, there are a lot of bills, Cess. Hundreds of thousands of dollars of debt."

Suddenly the room felt like a suffocating sauna. "Good Lord, Daddy," I whispered. "Have you been paying on it since she died?"

"I'll be paying it the rest of my life." He frowned. "But there's no chance of you inheriting the mess. Or so says my lawyer."

I was stunned. Daddy had been carrying this burden all alone, and now that I had finally come home, I had nothing but a measly income. I was no help at all. "It's impossible," I said.

He sat in the only other chair, halfway across the room. "There's a way out."

That sounded so dramatic. *A way out.* Like a movie where the hero single-handedly digs himself out from under the thousand-pound wreckage of a collapsed building. "What do you mean?"

His gaze fell to his hands, which were sitting limply in his lap. "I could sell the cabin."

Those five words sent a wave of desperation through me, like a violent wind blowing through the canyon's depths. How could he even think such a thing? Our family had been canyon dwellers for generations.

"Selling the cabin would be like selling your soul," I said.

He nodded slowly, not taking his eyes from mine, and we stared at each other without speaking. We didn't need words to understand what the other wasn't saying. We were mourning. First for my mother and all the memories that went along with her, then the possibility of losing ourselves. Of becoming ordinary people living in an ordinary house on an ordinary lot on a street in town.

"So, your job's all right then?" Daddy rubbed his palm against the arm of the chair, seeming to study the grain.

"Yes. The job's all right."

He wasn't asking about my job. He was asking about me, about my emotional health, about Dr. Harper and whether or not he was counseling me. About whether I would be able to handle it—mentally and emotionally—if he had to give up the spot of land that acted as our family's anchor and tied us both to my mother.

I shook the negative thoughts from my mind. "Graham sent me to a women's support group that meets at Midnight Oil."

His shoulders relaxed, so I kept talking.

"Turns out there are only two other women besides me, and one girl won't hardly talk, so I'm not sure she counts. And you'll never believe who leads it." I laughed. "Shanty Washington. Remember her?"

"Espinosa. She's married to Al."

"How do you know Shanty's husband? I thought he was from New Mexico."

"He was, I reckon, but he's been in Canyon for years now. He's a regular guy."

This surprised me. I hadn't figured Shanty to have a regular guy for a husband.

"So . . . ," he said. "Shanty leads this group you're in. What do y'all do?"

"Just talk, but she wants me to get a hobby."

"Hence the knitting."

"I'm not knitting."

Daddy glanced out the window and then stood as another car approached the gate. "So what else does the fearless leader want you to do?"

"Smile at myself in the mirror."

Daddy paused with his hand on the doorknob. "That one might be harder, I reckon." His face grew so solemn it seemed his skin might crack. "Yep. That one might be harder."

Chapter Fifteen

Dad and I ended up playing gin rummy for an hour, and as I unlocked my car to head home, Michael and Mirinda drove by the gatehouse on their way out of the park. Michael didn't seem to notice me, but Mirinda's pouty gaze held mine until they passed, like a three-year-old with a new toy. *Mine!*

Whatever.

I settled into the driver's seat and frowned at the sports car, then opted against following along behind them all the way back to town. Instead, I turned the other way and headed deeper into the park, content to wind back and forth through the canyon while I nursed my mellow mood.

Lowering my window to enjoy the fresh air, I marveled that the canyon floor was so different from the hazy view I saw daily from the back deck of our cabin. Down here in the depths, the view was near-sighted and tall, and I inhaled the earthy scent of juniper along with another smell that I could only describe as *rock*. It didn't seem like stone should have a scent, yet the smell of the canyon had always been the same.

Two miles into the park, I pulled into a lot near the Capitol Peak trail to enjoy the scenery, but the last rays of the sun reflected in my rearview mirror, causing me to squint. A quick shove to the glass put it at a safe slant, and I nestled a hand behind my head as I watched tourists snap pictures of the sunset. I heard myself sigh, but when my eyes passed the skewed mirror, my smile startled me.

I grinned often enough, but I didn't usually see myself doing it. Now that it had happened, Shanty's challenge rang in my ears. My smile had been a result of the beauty and peacefulness of the canyon, and I couldn't fool myself into believing I had smiled at myself in the mirror.

My eyes narrowed as I watched the girl in the glass with her head lying at an angle against the headrest. She looked calm, unperturbed, somewhat confident. Her lips twitched as though a gnat were buzzing around them, and then the corners lifted, resulting in a smirk instead of a smile. I sat up straight, gripped the mirror in one hand, and swiveled it so I could study my reflection. I was frowning now, put out with myself.

Blinking to erase my scowl, I lifted my eyebrows. My teeth showed a little, and smile lines appeared on my cheeks, but something about the entire thing seemed artificial, like a store mannequin with a molded expression and hollow circles for eyes. I shoved the mirror away and let my hand fall to my lap, sending a slash of pain across my thighs.

The cuts hadn't yet healed, but I had downgraded from gauze bandages to oversized Band-Aids. Just that morning I'd stopped at the store for more ointment, and the obnoxious pharmacist had once again rattled on and on about his wife's beauty. It was enough to make me cut myself again.

Not really.

I started my car, then paused, with one hand on the steering wheel and another on the gear shift, as something—someone—caught my eye from the road.

A man was on the shoulder, pushing a mountain bike, and from the looks of things, he was having trouble. He was too far away to have seen my debacle with the rearview mirror but not so far away that he wouldn't notice my car. I instantly recognized his scruffy beard and stocky build. Graham Cracker.

I rubbed my palms across my cheekbones and, without thinking, pinched my lips between my fingers, smashing any remaining trace of my ridiculous smile. Graham was the last person I wanted to see immediately after failing at something so trivial, but I could hardly turn around and drive away.

When I pulled my car onto the road and climbed out, I got a better look at him. Judging from his cycling shorts and matching shirt, he was an avid cyclist. He was even wearing the funny shoes. "I didn't know you were a biker," I called.

"Exercise helps me relieve stress." His helmet hung from the handle bars.

I looked at his bike, not expecting to know what was wrong, but it was obvious. "How'd your wheel get bent?"

"Came down hard off a steep jump and had the front end turned too far to the right." He thumped the wayward wheel with his finger. "What are you doing out here?"

"Just driving. I hung out with my dad at the gatehouse for a while."

"I didn't see you when I came in, but I've been here since early afternoon."

He looked tired, and dust had dried on his arms and neck along with sweat, leaving brown paths up and down his skin. The area around his eyes was a little cleaner, and I noticed sunglasses dangling from a cord around his neck.

"Do you need a ride somewhere?"

He wiped his forehead with the back of his arm. "My car's down at the Givens, Spicer, Lowry trailhead, but I'm doing all right."

"That's over a mile." I glanced at his footwear. "And those shoes aren't made for walking."

"No, I suppose not." He lifted one foot.

"What do they do?"

"They're designed so I can clip in. They attach to the pedals."

"Ah."

He grinned as though his pride had been knocked down a few notches. "And you're right. I feel like I'm walking on marbles."

The good doctor seemed different today, more relaxed, but maybe it was just the bandanna around his forehead. Or the tight shorts. It seemed cool for shorts, but I supposed he warmed up when he was cycling.

I opened the hatch of the SUV, and Graham maneuvered the bike into the back end. As I settled into the driver's seat, I adjusted the mirror.

"I started with Shanty's group yesterday," I said as I pulled away.

"Yeah?"

"She's quite a character."

"Sure is. Did you ever hear about her chaining herself to the flag pole?"

"That was her?" Graham and I had been in junior high at the time. "Why did she do that?"

"Some kind of protest, but I don't remember what. She's always had strong opinions."

"I get the impression she's out to change the world." And change Nina and me right along with it.

"Does that make you uncomfortable?"

I pretended I didn't hear him. "Do you ever do any hiking, or are you strictly a biker dude?"

"I hike every now and then, but I'm addicted to the speed that comes with biking."

The wind whipped through my open window, and I tugged on my rolled-up sleeve, suddenly aware of my tattoo. But maybe Graham wouldn't notice. I cut my gaze toward him. "I heard a hiker fell the other day."

He didn't say anything.

"Oh, my goodness. You didn't know her, did you?"

"No, I was just thinking about the man who died from a fall a few years back. At that same spot on the trail." He held his water bottle in his hand, opening and closing the pop-up lid.

Was he nervous? Were we both nervous?

"I always wondered if that guy jumped off," I said. "That would be a horrible way to go."

"I heard he fell," said Graham softly.

"You said your car's at Givens, Spicer, Lowry?"

"Yep."

I maneuvered into the parking lot and stopped next to his Toyota pickup.

"So . . ." He turned toward me with his eyebrows raised.

"What?"

"You avoided my question back there." He shrugged. "Does the support group make you uncomfortable?"

What a persistent little bulldog. "Only a little." I glanced at the mirror. "Shanty seems to know what she's doing."

"She's been around the block a time or two."

"The other girl barely said a word. Nina? You know her, I guess."

"I do." He nodded. "But I can't discuss her situation."

"Of course not, but if I wait for her to talk, I may never find out her story."

"Her story?"

"That's what Shanty calls it. You know, what each of us has been through."

"I call it a journey."

"I call it a nightmare."

In the glow of the dashboard lights, I could see his eyes soften. He had nice eyes. He started to say something but stopped himself.

We sat quietly then, neither of us reaching for the door handles, neither of us continuing the conversation, and I wasn't sure why we weren't. It just seemed right to sit there. With Graham Cracker, for goodness' sake. I remembered sitting quietly with him in a car years ago. We had talked a while. Then sat a while. Then . . . he had held my hand.

I looked toward him, wondering if he remembered that day, but he was only watching a cloud of flies swarming in the beam of the headlight. Then he blinked. He wasn't watching the insects. He was staring into space. And thinking.

He turned and caught me watching him.

"Cecily?" he said softly.

I lifted my eyebrows as though whatever he was about to say would be light and casual.

"A lot of people live through nightmares." His smile was genuine. "You will too."

Suddenly we were in high school again, and Graham was holding my hand and listening to my problems. Only we weren't in high school, and he wasn't holding my hand, and I didn't want to tell him my problems. The feeling in my stomach was the same, though, and so was the pull I felt. As though he were magnetized and I were a paper-thin sheet of metal. "Thanks," I said. "I know you're right."

He popped his door open and the spell was broken.

But that was silly because it wasn't a spell. It was nothing more than a veiled memory from a time when I was young and naive. The only reason I was even thinking about it was because that night, long ago, Graham's friendship had seemed so uncomplicated. He still seemed that way, but I couldn't let myself make more of it than was real.

Graham was just an old friend. My boss. A recovering drug user.

But more than all of those, he was a therapist.

Chapter Sixteen

Text from Graham to Cecily: *Even if you're not a biker, you should exercise. It's excellent therapy.*
Cecily: *Thanks for the tip.*
Cecily (Two hours and thirty-nine minutes later): *BTW, I've decided to take the job on a permanent basis. I'll be there at 10 a.m. tomorrow.*
Graham: *Excellent!*

The volume on the television in Midnight Oil was turned up, and a male character and female character, on a beautifully staged daytime drama, were in the throes of a bedroom romance. Shanty stomped behind the counter, snatched the remote control from a lower shelf, and pointed it toward the love affair. She flipped through channels, landing on a game show, then tossed the remote to Michael as she returned to our table.

"Okay, ladies, come clean," she said. "Did you smile at yourself in the mirror?" She wasn't wasting any time.

"Not me." Nina turned off the Kindle she had been reading, but her eyes didn't leave the device. "I don't see the point."

"That's all right, hon," said Shanty. "You can do it later if you want."

I looked between them, expecting a discussion, if not a debate, but Shanty only smiled at the top of Nina's head—as close to eye contact as she could get—then turned her gaze to me.

"How did you make out, Cecily?"

A part of me wanted to stare at the tabletop, just like Nina was doing, but what good would that do? If I was going to get over my stinking problems, I was going to have to go along with Shanty's assignments, whether I liked them or not. "I did it." Or did I? "Sort of. It felt weird."

Shanty nodded in empathetic agreement. "Like you were faking it?"

"Yes! And like . . . like it was vain for me to be doing it."

"As though you're not supposed to like yourself?"

"As though I don't deserve it." I slumped back in my chair. "But that's ridiculous, isn't it?"

"It's not ridiculous," said Nina. "Your feelings are real, and you shouldn't ignore them."

I let her words roll around in my head for a second, then answered her cautiously. "Feeling as though I don't deserve happiness is one thing, but telling myself—rationally—that it's true? That's counterproductive. Logically, I know better, but emotionally, I believe the lie."

"Yes," Nina said slowly, "we need to pay attention to our emotions— respect them—but not let them take over our minds."

"I'm pretty sure my emotions have been in the driver's seat for a while now," I said, "taking me on one heck of a wild ride." I sipped my coffee, hiding my face behind the cup.

"My emotions have been all over the place this week." Shanty rolled her eyes dramatically. "My husband's family has been bickering over his uncle's inheritance, and he's been on the phone with lawyers and cousins and whatnot." She sighed. "But enough about me." She rubbed her palms together, then rested her hands, one on top of the other, on the tabletop. With her long, brightly painted nails, she looked as though she were doing a commercial for nail polish. "It's only been a few days since we met, but I'm wondering how you've been doing, what's been going on in your lives, how you've changed your thinking so far." She looked back and forth between the two of us, but didn't give us time to answer. "While you're thinking on that, I'll fill you in on what's been happening in my world. I think I told you guys the other day that I write a blog." She paused until we nodded. "Well, I heard about a blogger up north somewhere holding a demonstration to raise awareness of body shaming, and now I've got a bee in my bonnet to do the same thing."

"What kind of demonstration?" I asked.

"This is what I'm thinking." Shanty grinned. "I'll do it at the mall in Amarillo. My goal is to get people to see their own prejudices, and the judgmental attitudes of others. So my plan is to stand in the middle of the mall in my bikini, holding a sign that says something about body shaming and how I've struggled with self-esteem my entire life." Her lips pursed as she thought. "And as shoppers walk past, I want to get their feedback in some way, but I'm not sure how. Maybe have them sign their names on the poster or write their own struggles. What do y'all think?"

I thought she was absolutely insane. "That's an interesting idea."

"What good will that do?" Nina asked. "People will just make fun of you."

"Well, there's always that possibility," said Shanty, "but I like to think the human race isn't as foul as it seems. And even if people laugh at me . . . I'll still make an impression on them, because later, when they think about what they saw and the reactions of others, they'll have to figure out what they think about it, what they've been told, and what they believe. Maybe even ponder the lies that the world tells us." She shrugged and her voice lost its intensity. "It's not like this one demonstration is going to change the world, but it could change the hearts of a few people in our area. It could start a domino effect of awareness. Just enough that people will start thinking for themselves instead of latching on to whatever notion they're spoon-fed."

"Wow." I honestly didn't know what to say. "I would rather die."

Shanty's laughter seemed to echo in the small shop. "Bless your heart, Cecily, I had a feeling you'd say that. But, hon, rest assured you don't ever have to do any kind of demonstration. That's my calling; not yours." She leaned her elbows on the table. "But what has your life looked like the past two days? Better? Worse? The same?"

I picked up my coffee cup and swirled its contents, feeling the pressure of the mini waterspout inside that mimicked the pressure in the pit of my stomach.

Shanty said nothing, just waited.

"Okay." I set the cup down and slid my hands into my lap where I pinched them between my knees. "I spent some time with my dad at work."

Nina's eyes met mine.

"It was nothing monumental," I continued. "Just sitting with him at the ranger headquarters, but I had a good time, and it made me think how I ought to be enjoying myself more often." Daddy had been right after all, and as I said the next words, the pressure inside me eased. "I need to stop wallowing in self-pity and try to be happy."

"Well, praise the Lord and pass the ammunition!" Shanty's smile was contagious, and I softened in spite of myself.

"I'm beginning to believe I can get over the problems Brett caused me."

Shanty's grin froze. "You saying Brett caused your problems?"

"Well, he sure didn't help." A spark of indignation singed my pride.

"Ain't that the truth, though?" she said. "Making the decision to be happy, regardless, is probably the greatest secret to beating anything life throws at you." Instead of looking at me, she leaned toward Nina. "Don't you think?"

The girl nodded, but she did so hesitantly, as though the concept of happiness were a little far-fetched.

"But . . . ?" Shanty prodded.

"It's just not as easy as it sounds," Nina said. "A person can't simply decide to be happy and be done with it. Not always, anyway."

"You are so right, girl," Shanty said. "Sometimes it's the hardest thing in the world, but it's not impossible." Her eyebrows lifted. "What have the last two days looked like for you, Nina?"

"Well . . . I know it doesn't sound like much . . . but this morning, I walked through the JBK during the busiest time of day."

"What's the JBK?" I asked.

"The student center on campus. It's named for some man, but everybody calls it the JBK. I usually avoid it because so many students hang out there, and it always seems like they're making fun of people. My friends don't go there either."

Shanty lifted an eyebrow. "How'd that work out for ya?"

"It was all right, I guess. I walked really fast, and sort of ignored anyone who might have said anything to me, but"—she shook her head a smidgen—"I made it through. That's what counts, right?"

Shanty's nod was slow, and I got the feeling she didn't completely agree. "You were brave and you didn't allow your emotions to dictate your actions. That's good." She squinted. "But some people are just mean, you know? You don't necessarily have to expose yourself to them, especially now—you can keep yourself in safe places until you're ready for the tough spots."

Nina lifted her hands helplessly. "Now's as good a time as any."

"How you ladies doing?" Michael appeared at our table, his hand on the back of Nina's chair. "Your coffee all right?"

Nina smiled for the first time all evening, and Shanty answered enthusiastically, "Fabulous as always, Michael. How do you do it?"

"Oh, it's not me. The girls make all the drinks." He tilted his head toward Mirinda and another girl, who were working behind the counter, then his hand eased from the chair onto Nina's shoulder. "Nina, isn't it? You've been in a few times before, I think."

She tucked her chin and smiled, and I watched as she became a different person.

"Yes, I'm not usually here this late, but I've started meeting my friends here." She seemed to think Shanty and I were something to be proud of. And maybe we were.

"I've been trying to talk Cecily into playing the piano here," Michael said, "but I may need you two to convince her."

"You play the piano?" Nina asked me.

"Now there's a hobby for you," Shanty pointed at me, then Nina. "And you're going to start painting more, right?"

I wasn't sure if Shanty knew I didn't want attention drawn to my piano-playing abilities, or if I just got lucky, but either way, I was grateful.

"You paint?" Michael asked Nina.

Even though I barely knew her, I felt a protective urge to slap him away. Not because Michael was necessarily a bad guy, but because Nina didn't need him around, confusing her.

Mirinda interrupted. "Michael?" She inserted herself between Michael and Nina, pressing her breasts against his arm.

The way she used her body parts as props made me sick to my stomach.

"There's a delivery truck out back," she said. When she walked back to the counter, her eyes caught mine for a split second, just long enough to give me the impression that she wanted Michael away from me as much as I wanted him away from Nina.

"I'll have to check on that," said Michael, and then he disappeared behind a door labeled *office*.

Shanty clucked her tongue. "That one's causing fruit basket turn-over around here," she mumbled.

Nina nodded absentmindedly as she watched the office door. "I got his autograph when he held his book signing. Stood in line all day."

"You were a part of that hullabaloo?" Shanty shook her head. "Girl, we've got a long way to go with you. Anyhoo, I've got two things I want y'all to do this time."

"More homework?" I teased Shanty, but honestly, I was a little worried about what she would dish out.

"A little homework and a little fun." She held up a printed list for each of us. "This is my *Be You Challenge*. I post this stuff on my blog all the time, and my readers love it. It's just a list of ten challenges that I'd like you girls to try. See here, the first one is just to make a list of things you like about yourself. Easy smeasy, no problem."

Easy smeasy? That's what she had said about smiling in the mirror. I took the list and skimmed the first few items, feeling doubtful but willing to give it a try.

Make a list of things you like about yourself. Name at least five.

Write and tell yourself you are beautiful and amazing. Then tell yourself why.

Write about a mistake you made and how it impacted your life in a positive way.

"Do we have to do all ten before we meet again?" I asked.

"Oh, honey! You don't *have* to do any of them, and certainly not in a week. This is just a tool for you to use when and if you're up to it." She tapped her nails on the table in front of Nina. "What do you think?"

Nina shrugged. "I like writing."

Shanty looked at us as if we were her pets and had just learned a new trick.

"You said there were two things you wanted us to do," I said.

She nodded her head like a show horse. "The other one's not work, though, it's just a lot of fun. Al and I are having friends over for a barbecue on Saturday afternoon, and we'd like you girls to come. Don't need to bring anything except your appetites."

"Dinner at your house?" Nina fingered a lock of hair near her shoulder.

"And bring a friend if you want," Shanty said. "Or come together, there's an option. I know it's hard to walk into a party alone, so whatever works for you girls is good with me. Cecily, maybe your dad would like to come with you. Nina, do you have a roommate in the dorm? Anyhoo, y'all come on over Saturday. I'd love you to meet my Al. He's a riot."

She'd love us to meet her Al.

When I thought about going to a barbecue at Shanty's house, I felt a leather band tighten around my lungs. This sounded worse than the *Be You Challenge*. It was worse than smiling at myself in the mirror. It was worse than meeting with two strangers in a coffee shop. But I was determined to manage it. One way or another.

Chapter Seventeen

Text from Shanty to Graham: *FYI group is going GREAT. Thanks for hooking me up with those two sweetie pies!!*
Graham: *Appreciate all you do. Let me know if you need anything.*

Graham had to send the text discreetly, so Cecily wouldn't notice Shanty's name on his phone. Somehow he didn't feel right taking Cecily to Soccer Mom's for lunch, even though he had taken Veda there every Wednesday for months. Cecily wasn't Veda. Instead, they got Pizza Hut to go and took it to the park. They sat in empty bleachers next to a ball field, Graham turned halfway in his seat, and Cecily sitting backward on the bench so she could see the lake behind them. While they ate their thin-crust pepperoni, Graham noticed that the noon sun caused the natural highlights in Cecily's hair to glow. Or maybe they weren't natural, but they were pretty either way.

"This place is full of memories," Cecily said, "but then again, every place in Canyon reminds me of something. Is it that way for you too?"

"Not so much, because I never really left. Even when I was at Tech, I'd come home most weekends."

"Your parents still live here?"

"They're in Amarillo now."

"You see them much?"

The easy banter felt good to Graham. "A lot more than I want to, that's for sure."

She brushed an ant from the bench. "I've gotta ask what you mean by that."

"Oh, I don't know. Things are all right between us." He was leaning with an elbow on the bench behind him, trying to look laid-back, one ankle resting on the opposite knee, but his foot was jittering. He laid a palm on his ankle to still the nervous tic. "It's just that my dad called this morning to give me his biannual declaration of disappointment."

"What's he disappointed about?"

"Me."

Cecily had been sitting in such a way that her shoulders bunched around her ears, and when she heard his words, her neck straightened in surprise. "But . . . why?"

Graham wondered why he had started talking about his parents—a topic he never broached with anyone. "In a nutshell . . . I'm an only child. I was supposed to grow up and fulfill all of Dad's dreams, but frankly, I fell short."

"You're successful . . . you're independent . . . you're not on drugs . . ." Her eyes swept the sky. "What more could he want?"

"An accountant."

"Your dad needs an accountant?"

"No. My dad *is* an accountant. And he thinks like an accountant, analytical and logical, and he expects me to think the same way. And want the same things."

Her lips puckered in a tiny frown. "He doesn't understand your job."

"No, but Mom's all right with it."

"She's not an analytical type?"

"Not hardly." He reached for his drink. "She babysits in her home. Sort of like a home daycare, except she only works with three kids. And she dabbles with crafts on the side. Nothing professional, just a hobby, though she has sold a few things on Etsy."

"Now you're beginning to make sense to me." She started rolling up her sleeves, hesitated, then continued.

"You were going to say I'm a mama's boy, weren't you?" he asked.

"No, I was going to say you're a lot like your mother. There's a difference."

Graham wanted to ask which of her parents she favored most, but her phone rang. Besides, he thought he already knew.

She glanced at the screen and grimaced. "I should take this." She moved to climb out of the stands, then seemed to think better of it, and settled back, almost in defeat. "Hello, Brett."

Instantly, Graham found himself wishing Cecily's phone battery would die.

"No, I didn't know," she said.

Graham took the opportunity to look at the tattoo she kept so well hidden, a tangle of barbed wire covering her thin arm. Then he realized his knees were bouncing, and he pressed his palms on his thighs to stop the movement.

"I'll talk to him," she said, "but I can't make any promises. Daddy's his own man. You know that." She fidgeted with the seam of her jeans and slowly closed her eyes. When she opened them again, she was looking at Graham, and the eye contact sent a vibration through him. "Okay," she said into the phone, then tapped the screen to hang up.

Graham could feel her tension from three feet away. Her posture had changed during the call, and now her muscles looked as hard as the metal bench. She sat bolt upright, one hand gripping the bleacher, the other clenching the phone so tightly that her knuckles whitened. Her feet were flat on the board beneath her, as though she might scurry away at any minute—a flight response—to escape her problems.

Graham bit his lip to hush the invasive questions that were trying to slip out.

When she finally spoke, she covered it with laughter. "You're not the only one who has problems with their dad."

Graham felt the problem was with Brett, not Dub, but he continued to keep his mouth shut.

"And apparently your phone number is not the only one Dad has on speed dial," she said.

Graham hurt for her, and he found himself wanting to make her feel better and maybe make himself feel better too. He wanted to massage her tight shoulders until she relaxed, and kiss her forehead and tell her everything would be all right, that he would take care of things, and that she wasn't alone. He wanted to do a lot of things.

"Your dad hasn't called *me* this week," he said. "If that helps at all."

She didn't answer, just rocked back and forth, and Graham worried that she might snap. He hadn't seen her interact with Brett in years. As he watched her now, he realized Cecily was not only stressed from her ex-husband's call, she was holding back a tidal wave of emotion, pushing it down inside herself in an attempt to . . . what? Hide it?

Graham felt as though he were standing by, watching as she drowned herself.

"Can I hug you?" he asked. When her eyes doubled in size, he hurriedly explained himself, his words tripping over each other. "Hugs are good medicine, you know? In fact, sometimes physical touch can do more for the soul than just about anything."

Thoughtless, stupid words. What was he thinking? He never would have asked a client for a hug—not in a million years—but Cecily wasn't a client. She was a friend, if they were even that much. And he had just crossed the line.

"I'm sorry I said that." He tried to laugh away his idiocy. "That was inappropriate."

"It probably was." She spoke softly. "But still . . . a hug would be nice right now."

He froze. Had he heard her right? Had she meant she wanted him to hug her? His foot slid from his knee. "Wait," he muttered. *"What?"*

She laughed then, an airy release of some of her tension. Or possibly another cover-up to hide it. "It's just a hug, Graham, and I'm only your receptionist, not a client. I'm practically nobody."

"You're *not* nobody." He looked pointedly into her eyes and imagined a gentle flurry of hope there, but then it was gone. He closed the distance between them and slid his arms around her shoulders. She felt stiff and unyielding at first, but then she softened and rested her chin on his shoulder.

"I can see how this could be beneficial."

Her hair smelled like coconut, and Graham fought the urge to inhale deeply.

She gave his chest two short pats before she pulled away. "Dad's not a hugger." She giggled at the thought. "That was always Mom's department. In fact, now that I think about it, she used to tell me she needed my hugs."

"I call it *touch therapy*."

"Of course you do."

Her quick retort surprised him, and he chuckled. "Your mother was a smart woman, Cecily. Your dad means well too."

Her shoulders slumped. "But I'm an adult, you know?"

"I know exactly. Believe me."

"Does he not think I'm doing all right? I'm working, I'm going to a support group, I'm talking to the famous Dr. Harper at the park. It doesn't get better than this."

Graham knew Dub was transferring some of his own pain to his daughter. "I guess both our fathers are alike in that they want the best for us."

"I suppose." She said it grudgingly, then pulled a pizza crust out of the box. "Ducks?"

"Actually, they're geese." Graham grabbed two crusts and tossed the empty box in a trash barrel, then followed Cecily to the bank of the lake, where a group of geese paid close attention to them but kept their distance.

"At least Brett wasn't horrible this time," she said.

"Is he usually?"

"Only every now and then, but I never know which Brett I'll get." She glanced toward Graham, seeming to make a decision about what she would say next. How much she would say. "Sometimes I have weird, crazy dreams about him. Not quite nightmares, but strange." She tore off a small piece of bread and tossed it to the closest goose.

Since she was making light of it, Graham did too. "I love crazy dreams. Tell me."

"Well, there's not much to tell. Sometimes Brett will be stuck high in a tower. It might be the Empire State Building, or a ride at an amusement park, or just a really tall tree, and then the tower or tree explodes or disappears and he's standing in front of me with an ax. Or sometimes it's a rose or a box of tissues or a hamburger. Crazy stuff. And he always tries to give me whatever he's holding, but I never take it from him. And then he gives me a kiss on the cheek, and I wake up." She lowered her head. "See? Isn't that weird?"

She tossed a hunk of pizza crust into the lake where three geese began squawking and fighting over it.

"Oh, I don't know. I once had a dream I was a giant pigeon and I got stuck in my car." He took a quick look at her. "Okay, actually, I dream that one fairly often."

"Is it the car you drive now? The little truck?"

"It's never my own vehicle. Sometimes it's a sports car. Sometimes it's a bus. One time it was an orange-and-yellow plastic Little Tykes coupe."

"I have a visual image now that I'm never going to be able to get out of my head. Were you a gray pigeon or a white one, or what?"

"Enough already." *She was so easy to talk to.* "Don't forget, I can fire you at any time."

"Don't forget, I can quit." She smiled, but it faded as though the sun went behind the clouds. "So do your dreams mean anything? Do mine? And why do I keep having them?"

"Well . . . it's probably because Brett is on your mind—not that you're deliberately thinking about him—but your subconscious is working things out." The geese lagged behind them.

"You're saying I'm still hung up on him." Impatience nipped at the edge of her voice.

"Not at all. You don't seem hung up on him to me, but you've been through a lot, and your brain and your emotions are scrambling to catch up. And while you sleep, they're working on things so you don't have to figure it all out by yourself in the daytime."

She stopped walking. "That makes sense, but what does the tall tower mean?"

"Actually, I don't put much stock into dream interpretation. To me, it's just a jumble of things bouncing around in your head."

"Like a bunch of puzzle pieces dumped on a card table."

He smiled at her perfect analogy. "Just like that."

"So you don't think it means anything?"

"I think it could mean something, and because of that, dreams can be useful in helping you make sense of your problems, but I look at it from another perspective. Instead of trying to figure out what the dream means, I simply acknowledge it, store it in my memory, and let my subconscious work on it. Then later, when I'm actually thinking about my real life, a little piece of a dream may help me make sense of it all."

She frowned. "So instead of figuring out what the dream means, you use the dream to figure out what your life means."

"Yes. Because dreams are funny. The thing I dream about could be a mirror image of what needs to happen in my life, or it could be the opposite of what needs to happen, and if I go trying to analyze it, I'm likely to end up even more confused."

Cecily motioned toward the walking trail, then pulled her phone out of her pocket to check the time. "We're okay still."

"Sounds good." Graham threw the remainder of his crust into a trash barrel, and they settled into a slow pace, side by side, heading toward the playground. They wouldn't be working off any pizza calories at this pace, but he didn't care. Cecily seemed lost in her thoughts, and he was fine with that. He had his own thoughts that needed pondering. Like, *what on earth was he doing?* Cecily probably viewed their lunch date as nothing more than an impromptu counseling session, but his mind wasn't buying it, and he knew that in the future he'd have to keep his thoughts and actions in check.

"My dad wants to know what happened between Brett and me." She blurted out the words as though saying them faster would dull the sharp edges. "It's like he needs to know I'm justified in getting a divorce."

They walked twenty paces before Graham answered. "I suppose that's understandable. After all, you're his—"

"I'm his little girl, I know, and I'll tell him everything—when I'm ready—but until then I just wish he would leave me alone. And definitely leave Brett alone."

Graham knew her irritation wasn't meant for him, and he sort of felt sorry for Dub, should Cecily ever unleash it on him. "If you never feel like telling him, that's all right, you know."

"I owe him an explanation."

"No, you don't."

She nodded. "Okay, but I do want to explain eventually. Just so he'll know it wasn't—" Her hand went to her mouth, and she didn't finish the sentence.

"It wasn't your fault." He finished it for her, willing her to believe it, hoping it was true.

"Brett was . . . Brett hurt me."

"Physically?"

"No." She peered in the direction of his truck.

Graham didn't change the pace she had set, but he veered away from the path and started walking to the parking lot. She followed him. "You don't owe me an explanation either."

"I suppose I should pour out my heart to Shanty Espinosa, right? Have you ever been on her website?"

"I looked over it one day. She's got a lot going on, and big-name bloggers are over there too."

"Goes to show you never can tell."

"Speaking of Shanty," he said. "She invited me to a barbecue picnic out at her house on Saturday, and she mentioned that you were coming. I checked with Nina to make sure it wouldn't bother her for me to be there, but I wanted to ask you as well, even though you're not actually a client." He pulled at his earlobe. "Just seems appropriate somehow."

"Honestly, I had been a little worried about that party. Having you there might actually help settle my nerves. Do you think we could ride together?"

Graham tripped over a rock and caught himself. "Sure, if that will make it less awkward for you."

"It's the walking-into-a-room-full-of-strangers part."

"I hate that too." Okay, so he would take her to Shanty's barbecue, but after that, he would keep a safe distance.

They were standing in front of his truck now, and she turned toward him. "Thank you for letting me rattle on about my silly dreams and whatnot." She looked up at him, but the sun blinded her and made her squint.

Graham took a half step to the left so his shadow would shield her eyes, wishing he could shield her from all of life's troubles. Wishing she would trust him to do it. Wishing he could hug her again. "That's what I'm here for, Cecily," he said. "To help you."

He just hoped he could help instead of hurt her.

Chapter Eighteen

Group text from Shanty to Cecily and Nina: *What lies behind us and what lies before us are tiny matters compared to what lies within us. (Ralph Waldo Emerson said that)*
Nina: *thats cool thanks*
Cecily: *What is it with RWE?*

Shanty had suggested I bring Dad to her backyard barbecue, and while I knew she meant well, the thought of going with my dad reminded me of kindergarten when I refused to walk into class without him by my side. The party gave me the same nervous jitters, mainly because I had no idea who would be there, other than Shanty and Nina. *And Graham.* Maybe I shouldn't have asked to ride with him, but it seemed all right somehow. Neutral.

As I hiked from our back deck down into the canyon, I worried, not about the barbecue, but about Shanty's *Be You Challenge*. It had fallen onto the floor of my car with a jumble of Midnight Oil cups, and it had stayed there until I fished it out, deciding I'd ignored the assignment long enough. It had been four or five days—depending on how you counted it—but knowing I'd see Shanty the next day gave me an urgency to at least begin the task.

I sat on a natural ledge in the canyon wall, letting my feet dangle over the side. A spiral notebook lay open on my lap, and Shanty's list perched on the rocky ground next to me, the corner tucked beneath my thigh to keep it from drifting away. I frowned down at the first challenge.

Make a list of things you like about yourself. Name at least five.

I copied the task onto the top of my notebook page. This sounded easy enough. I only had to list five.

Chewing on the end of my pen, I considered my talk with Graham. He had said Dad was only worried about his little girl, and Graham should know, right? He'd seen people in crazier situations than I was in. He'd said people lived through nightmares all the time. Every day.

I smiled. Shanty's challenge didn't rank as much of a nightmare, with its curlicues and flowers around the edge of the page, but still my hand poised above the notebook, and then the tip of my pen made a tiny dot just above the first line. I neatly turned the dot into a number one, traced over it twice, then circled it. If Shanty had been around the block a few times, then she could be hiding as much as me. Clearly Nina was. I traced the circle, over and over, until it darkened around the number one. Then I filled it in completely, forming a black blob that dented the paper.

Shanty and Nina may have been harmless, but I was fairly certain they would never understand the crux of my problems. Shanty was happily married, and Nina was so idealistic she was probably still waiting for Prince Charming to whisk her away. I leaned back on one palm and rested my head on my shoulder, wondering if I shouldn't have told Nina I had gone out with Michael. The girl seemed to be a bit of a copycat.

Leaning over my notebook, I wrote three words:

My new hair.

I really did like my haircut. It was nice to have it brown again, as though I had renewed a friendship with someone I hadn't seen in a long time, and the style fit my personality. Not flashy. Not sexy. Not red. And for the first time in years, I didn't long for the waist-length locks I'd worn as a teenager. The new cut made me feel as though I had stepped into my role as an adult. A role as myself.

Combing my fingers through it, I pushed it behind my ear, then let my fingertips trail down my neck. The touch felt good. *Touch therapy.* Graham's hug had felt good too—maybe too good—but I shoved the thought out of my mind as I remembered Brett's hands on my body. When we were in college, I pushed him away as he groped for more contact. After marriage, we became comfortable with each other, and I lost some of my shyness, allowing him to look at my body and touch me.

I shivered. Even though the sun was warm on my bare shoulders, an icy current ran through my veins. But Brett was part of my past, not my present.

What else could I write on Shanty's list? My figure wasn't worth a mention. Sometimes other women told me I should be proud of my weight, but no. Not with these hips.

My gaze slid from my thighs to the ground next to me where a beetle trekked across the gravel. I touched my pen to the dirt right in front of him, compelling him to turn to the side, and then I blocked that way as well. After sending him in frantic circles, I allowed him to pass, and he went on his way. His journey. Graham had preferred the term *journey* instead of *nightmare*, but he didn't really understand what I had been through. How could he? Even if I told him—which I wouldn't—no man could ever understand.

I crossed my legs and rested my elbows on my knees. Maybe I should ask Shanty and Nina what they thought about Graham. I wondered if he had a girlfriend. If he had ever had one. I wrote a number two beneath the dark blob:

My job.

Shanty might not count that one since it wasn't truly something about myself, but I liked that I had taken the job, and I liked that Graham had offered it to me. I liked that I could earn money while reading books and playing Solitaire. If I stretched it, I could claim I liked my *decision* to take the job. I rolled my eyes and groaned. I didn't have to explain my reasoning to Shanty. "She probably won't even look at this," I said under my breath.

Quickly I wrote a number three, then:

Back home.

It was nice to be in Canyon, even if Dad was driving me a little crazy. I supposed he couldn't help it. Men had a way of trying to handle things. Dad. Brett. Maybe Graham too. Were they all alike?

No.

My dad really, really meant well.

Graham probably did too, but I didn't know him well enough to trust his motives.

I fanned myself with the notebook, surprised at how warm it was for March. My face was even a little damp from perspiration, and I lifted the bottom of my shirt to wipe it away. Graham had done the same thing on Sunday when I found him on the side of the road with his bike. He'd been hot and sweaty, his freckled face glowing pink from exertion. And then pink from embarrassment.

I chewed on the end of my pen again, thinking about him, wondering what his story was—his real story, the one he kept hidden—and I pictured him walking down the side of the road when he noticed me pulling up. He had been surprised to see me there, and he had smiled.

Graham had a nice smile, which I knew was the result of years of orthodontia. And his eyes were friendly, as though the grin came from deep inside, not just on the outside where his lips moved. When we had walked through the park, he had smiled at the ducks, or geese, or whatever they were, and he had smiled at a story he was telling me about his mother. And he had smiled at me.

When had Graham transformed from a skinny, braces-on-his-teeth drug user into an attractive man?

I tapped the pen against the notebook, then put two hard lines through the last two items on my list.

Coming back home and getting a new job were not things I liked about myself. They were decisions I had made, and even though I was glad I had made them, they hardly ranked as characteristics of Cecily Ross. I slapped the spiral notebook closed and stood, dusting my backside. Apparently my haircut was the sole thing I actually liked about myself.

But I'd also discovered I liked . . . Graham Harper's smile.

Chapter Nineteen

Group text from Shanty: *Come to my barbecue today! (Can't wait for you to meet my Al) please Please PLEASE come!!!*
Cecily: *Relax. I'm coming.*
Nina: *if cecily is i will 2*

Shanty's cookout was as uncomfortable as I'd thought it would be. At least forty people milled around her spacious, manicured, perfectly inviting backyard, all talking and laughing. Men played Frisbee in the grass, women fussed over a buffet table on the deck, and children swarmed the play fort like a bed of fire ants that had been stepped on. Graham and I had entered through a side gate, and when Shanty greeted us, he had given her the impression we just happened to arrive at the same time. I wasn't sure she bought it. Now she was watching us as if we were the stars of a reality television show.

I spied Nina on the far side of the yard, standing alone with her back to the fence. Bless her heart. I headed her way, taking the opportunity to distance myself from Graham.

"I'm glad you finally got here," Nina said. "I don't know anybody."

"I recognize a few, but they're Shanty's age, so they probably don't even remember me."

"At least they're familiar faces." She crossed her arms. "Oh, look. There's Dr. Harper."

I didn't look where she pointed.

Across the yard, Shanty clapped her hands loudly, and the adult chatter ceased. The children's laughter barely lightened, but Shanty seemed used to talking over it. She stood on the brick edging of a flower bed. "I think we've got enough people here now to play a little game."

A low groan sounded among the adults, but there was just as much laughter mixed in.

"Everyone needs a seat," Shanty said. "I've got camp chairs and folding chairs leaning against the back of the house, and you'll need to make a circle in the yard. We're gonna play a game called Take a Hike."

Most people had looks of skepticism as they moved to find seating, and I considered sneaking inside and hiding in the bathroom.

Evidently, Shanty's children and their friends knew they weren't expected to participate because they didn't even slow down their play. I watched them enviously as I pulled a chair across the yard, then struggled to unfold it and balance it on the grass. Nina sat next to me.

"Nice circle!" Shanty stood in the middle with a man I assumed was her husband. He looked familiar, but I couldn't remember where I knew him from. "For those of you who don't know my man . . ." She put her hand on his shoulder and shoved him. "This is Al. And of course . . ." She curtsied. "I'm Shanty."

"And she's one of a kind. Beautiful inside and out." Al grinned and kissed her on the lips, which prompted catcalls from the guests.

Suddenly I remembered where I knew him from. *Holy cow.* He was the pharmacist, and Shanty was the wife he praised constantly. The one whose description reminded me of a skinny runway model. I blinked slowly. I didn't know which was more bizarre: that Shanty was married to such an ordinary guy, or that her husband was blind to her weight problem.

A man on the other side of Nina called out, "Shame on you, Shanty!" He wore a bright-lime-green shirt with matching green Nikes.

Shanty grinned. "That's right, shame on Shanty."

I wasn't making sense of any of it until I remembered her blog was called *Shame on Shanty*, but even then, I didn't see as much humor as everyone else seemed to.

"This is how the game works," she said. "Whoever's in the middle of the circle makes a statement, then yells, *Take a hike*. And if you fit the description, then you have to get out of your chair and run to another chair. But of course, there aren't enough chairs." She cackled. "So if you don't make it into a seat, then you're the one in the middle, and you have to think up something for the next round."

"For instance," Al said. "On my turn, I might say, *If you've ever been to Disney World . . . take a hike*! Then all of you who have been to Mickey's paradise would run to a different chair. Everybody got it?"

My face warmed, and I pressed my palms against my thighs, hoping the scabbed-over cuts wouldn't hurt if I had to move quickly. Maybe Nina and I could work together and simply trade seats every round.

"But there's one thing we forgot to tell you," Shanty called. "We want to make this a little more difficult, so we're asking that you snag a partner. When a statement is called, you and your partner will run together, holding hands, if it applies to either one of you."

"But it'll be hard to run holding hands," the man in green whined, even though he clearly wasn't upset.

"That's the idea," Al said. "So y'all find a partner, then sit back down in your circle."

My nerves actually settled. Nina and I could be partners. Even if we got caught in the middle, at least we wouldn't be alone. I turned toward her with a sigh.

"It'll be fun!" The man in green was holding his palm toward Nina, and she looked over her shoulder at me as she slipped her hand into his.

She smiled slyly.

"I've played this game before," said the man with a wink, then he looked at me and lifted his chin. "Better find a partner, doll."

I turned away from him, surveying my options, but almost everyone had already paired up, and the pairs were starting to sit back down. The bathroom hideout was looking better all the time. Just then, a hand touched the small of my back. "Looks like I don't have a partner. Would you mind too much?"

Whether it was the touch of Graham's hand or the calming tone of his voice, my anxiety lightened, and I motioned to a pair of open chairs. There was only time for me to say a quick *Thanks*, and Graham squeezed my hand in a silent *You're welcome*.

Al bellowed the first statement. "If you've ever played this game before . . . take a hike!"

About half the chairs emptied, and a scramble commenced. Nina and the man in green leapt from their chairs and ran across the circle, slamming into another set of chairs just before another couple got there.

"Nina's played this before?" Graham asked.

"No, that guy has."

"His name's Jason."

The next couple whispered to each other for a few seconds before the woman called out, "If you've ever been to Al and Shanty's house before . . . take a hike!"

Graham and I settled back in our chairs, and I slid my hand from his. "Maybe we'll get lucky," I said.

That time Shanty and Al ended up in the middle again, and she had quite a bit to say about it not being their turn yet.

The man in green—Jason—called out, "Shame on you, Shanty. You should run faster."

She smiled, then conferred with Al, and they both nodded. "If you've ever been out of the continental United States . . . take a hike!"

Graham looked at me questioningly, but I shook my head. Apparently neither of us had done much traveling.

Jason was next, and he strutted around the circle, pulling Nina behind him. "It's about time we livened this game up, don't you think?" He looked around the circle with a challenging grin. "If you've ever done drugs . . . take a hike!"

Graham gave a tiny sigh before grabbing my hand and jerking me out of my chair. He lunged to the left, but when another couple dove into the chairs he was heading for, I yanked him a little farther around the circle, and we made it to the last two remaining spots.

Nina and Jason had gotten caught in the middle again, and I speculated about whether it was deliberate.

"I've got an interesting one." Jason grinned. "If you've ever had sex in the backseat of a car . . ." He laughed out loud. "Take a hike!"

I looked at Graham, but he only shrugged, and then I rolled my eyes. Brett and I had sex *everywhere*. I yanked Graham to a standing position, and I thought I heard him chuckle. Fortunately, the couple next to us ran across the circle, and we merely slid down into their seats.

The next pair in the middle smiled as though they had a great scheme planned, then they called out, "If you've ever been pregnant . . . take a hike!"

Panic radiated up my spine, and my brain fogged in the same way it did whenever I was unexpectedly called on to speak in public. *What answer did you get on number five, Miss Witherspoon?* But this time, instead of stuttering an answer about music history, I involuntarily stood up. I moved slowly, as though my brain couldn't make sense of the dilemma, and my body was stalling.

Almost all the other couples moved too, and the circle turned to chaos. Graham was watching them and laughing and didn't immediately notice I had stood, and when he did notice, my mind registered what I had done. I plopped back into my seat, focusing my gaze on the grass at my feet.

Everything happened fast after that, but I felt as though I were watching it in slow motion. Graham stood at the same time I sat down, but before I could tug on his hand, another couple slammed into his seat, laughing and nudging me out of their way. Graham looked at me in confusion, then his confusion changed to compassion, then his compassion changed to urgency as he lunged forward to find another chair. The two of us and another couple were left scrambling for two remaining chairs, but they weren't side by side.

"Scoot down!" Graham called to the couples who were already seated, but they all moved down in the other direction, leaving the two available seats out of our reach.

Then we were alone in the middle of the circle, all eyes on us, and I was glad he was still holding my hand.

If I had been standing there naked, I wouldn't have felt so conspicuous. Now everyone in the yard knew I had been pregnant. Even though most of them didn't know me. My pregnancy wasn't something I talked about, not even with the support group. But now, of course, Shanty and Nina knew as well.

Graham didn't even pause for breath. "If you've ever been to Canyon, Texas, take a hike!"

And instantly, we were no longer standing in front of all those people, being scrutinized and judged, and sweating under an imaginary spotlight. Instead, Graham was pulling me solidly to the closest chair. As we sat down, I gripped his hand too tightly, but I couldn't seem to ease up.

He didn't look at me, just kept smiling at all the commotion, but his eyes seemed to be seeing something other than Shanty's backyard. I wondered what he was thinking about me, but when his thumb rubbed gently across the back of my hand, I knew that whatever he was thinking, it wasn't negative. And I tightened my grip on his fingers.

Thirty minutes later, the chairs had been rearranged into small clusters, and we sat balancing paper plates of barbecue on our knees. Graham had stayed fairly close to my side as I filled my plate, and I didn't mind.

I nibbled my barbecue sandwich and listened, but in a lull, green-shirted Jason turned to me.

"So, you have kids?" he asked.

I swallowed. "Um . . . no. I don't."

"But you've been pregnant before." His eyebrows lifted. "I sense a story there."

"A lot of women have been pregnant before." Al settled into a chair next to us. "It doesn't mean there's a story in it." He reached out and shook my hand, then Nina's. "Good to meetcha. Thanks for coming."

He didn't mention me buying bandages, so I liked him immediately.

"You sure know how to grill," Graham said as he lifted his plate. "Best barbecue I've had in a while."

"Best barbecue around!" Shanty seated herself next to Al. "Thanks for cooking, babe."

The yard was quieter than it had been all afternoon, and as the guests' stomachs got full, their moods mellowed. Even Nina seemed more comfortable. "When are you planning your demonstration, Shanty?" she asked.

"Next Friday. You coming?"

Nina's eyes widened. "Can I?"

"Sure! I need somebody to videotape it." She chuckled. "And to lend some moral support."

"Would I have to—"

"Not a thing, hon. Just stand back real inconspicuous like, and record it with one of our phones. Easy smeasy." She glanced at me. "You wanna come too?"

"Maybe?"

"Fair enough."

Graham leaned forward to look at Shanty, his toe tapping the ground. "What's this demonstration?"

"It's to raise awareness for body shaming. It's basically me holding a sign in the middle of the Westgate Mall . . . in my bikini."

Jason grunted, and his gaze traveled down Shanty's full figure.

Her head snapped toward him. "What was that for? Don't look at me like you don't know what I'm talking about. I may be fat, but I'm not deaf. You just made a sound, and I wanna know what you meant by it."

Al shook his head. "Now you've done it, man."

Jason gave her a court jester grin. "It's just that women like you don't usually wear bikinis."

"Women like me? Don't wear bikinis? Maybe not this time of year, but I'll have you know I wear my bikini all the time in the summer. In the yard doing my grass, to the pool, sometimes we go up to Lake Meredith. I wear it quite often and don't think twice about it." Now her head jerked toward her husband. "Ain't that right, Al?"

"I'm staying out of this one, but she does enjoy wearing the thing." He took a large bite of barbecue, then talked around it. "Won't hear me complaining, though."

"Al, you're one of my favorite people in the whole entire world," said Jason. "But honestly, if women weren't so obsessed with their appearance, they wouldn't take things that personal."

Shanty gripped her plate so fiercely, I thought it might flip off her lap and onto the grass, but she seemed to calm herself when Al patted her back, and she spoke slowly. "It's a little more complicated than that. Women didn't just decide one day that they wanted to be beautiful. Aw, no. It's how God made us. We have a deep need to feel attractive and cherished, and that's natural. But then the fashion industry comes along and exploits the entire concept, telling us we need *these* clothes and *that* makeup and *those* hair products. And after a while, a girl starts to look around and compare herself to supermodels and actresses and airbrushed photographs. And the men . . . *like you* . . . go along with it, and treat us like we're inferior if we don't happen to look that way."

Jason leaned an elbow on one knee and frowned at her. "Well, Shanty, you've got to look at it from a man's perspective too then. *Sex sells.* And it's not just the fashion industry that knows it. Beautiful women are in front of us 24/7."

Al seemed all too ready to jump in and soothe the conversation. "That's true." He said the words with a calming rhythm. "It's all over sports channels. Men are constantly being brainwashed—not only into thinking their women should look a certain way, but also believing that we deserve a woman who looks like that."

"Well, don't we?" Jason's mouth was full.

"Dr. Harper?" Shanty pointed at Graham and shook her head. "I may need to move my appointment up. I have a *lot* of frustrations I'm trying to work through right this very minute."

Graham smiled. "It's a sticky subject for men and women both. Society has a lot of us confused about the natural order of things. But, Shanty?" He smiled at her. "You're doing a world of good with your blog."

"Thanks to you, I'm not going crazy while I do it."

Fortunately, the conversation shifted to something less controversial, but my mind stayed locked in place. A tightness had formed across the back of my shoulders, and I knew I'd need a hot bath later in order to relax. But something else was nagging at me, and it took a few minutes for me to realize what it was.

Shanty had mentioned in our group that she went to counseling occasionally for a tune-up, but today she'd made it sound as though she might be going in sooner than later. And Nina was almost definitely Madam X, so clearly she went to Graham for counseling too.

This puzzled me. Granted, Nina may have been a little further over the edge than I was, but Shanty certainly wasn't. If anything, she was healthier, and that's what didn't make sense. If Graham had no problem counseling Shanty every so often, why did he not want to counsel me?

Was he hiding something?

Chapter Twenty

WHO WORE IT BEST?

FIVE CELEBRITIES SPORT THE SAME DESIGNER SWIMSUIT!
CLICK HERE TO CAST YOUR VOTE!

The man felt as though he was hiding when he shut himself in his bathroom, but he'd had a long day, and it felt good to lock the door, figuratively leaving his problems out in the hall. It was a welcome break from the letters he'd just read, and the implications they held. He'd have to ask his lawyer if the accusations held any merit, but regardless, they were clearly designed to cause damage.

He peered at himself in the mirror and wondered when the dark circles had appeared beneath his eyes, causing him to look older. Tired. Defeated.

Like a loser.

Reaching for the cold water knob, he splashed his face. Then he leaned his elbows on either side of the sink and watched the water churning in the basin before it swirled down the drain. When had life gotten so hard? A few short months ago, he had thought himself quite successful, but now things were spiraling out of control, and no matter what he tried, he couldn't stop the frenzy.

He shoved the faucet off, but didn't stand up straight. Instead, he groped for a hand towel, dried his face, then lowered himself to his knees. He was on all fours for a moment before shifting to sit on the tile floor, leaning against the door. Habitually, he reached for his phone, not willing to go more than a few moments without checking his messages. Too many people were depending on him.

There were only two fires that needed putting out, and he addressed them with short explanations, then he opened the app for his favorite news website. Most of the articles didn't apply to him, and none of them related to his personal life or his career, but he found himself scrolling through them daily, reading the ones that caught his interest, learning tidbits of information that came in handy in conversation, getting a glimpse into lives that were different from his own. It was a calm distraction from his troubles.

His thumb swept the screen slowly from bottom to top, and then a woman appeared, scantily clad but not all that beautiful. He zoomed the picture and studied her. Stringy hair, girl-next-door face, incredible body. He hadn't taken the time to see what the article was about, but he didn't really care. The way she smiled set off a spark inside him, not of lust, but of confidence. It was stupid, really. He knew she wasn't smiling *at him*. She was looking into a camera lens, but his mind and body felt as though he had gotten his first drink of water after thirty days in the desert. And he was so thirsty to believe in himself that a picture of a random stranger boosted his self-confidence.

He enlarged the image a little more, then considered finding a better picture. Maybe of another woman, not quite as homely. Not a naked woman—that was wrong—just another image to give him another boost. He typed a few words in his search bar, and a grid of eight images filled the top of his screen. Eight women who didn't require anything from him—and they were all smiling as though his life were uncomplicated, as though he hadn't made a mess of things, as though he were competent.

A grid of eight women. And in tiny font were the words *see more images.*

Without hesitating, he tapped the link and began scrolling through the crowd of women, and as they swirled through the shadowy places of his mind, they filled him with boldness, self-assurance, and renewed purpose. It had been so long since he felt at ease with himself that the sensation surprised him. And it surprised him how good he felt. And it surprised him how easy it was.

Chapter
Twenty-One

Group text from Cecily: *I keep listening to Brett's voice on my phone. I'm a psycho.*
Nina: *prob not a good idea ouch*
Shanty: *Girl, don't do that to yourself. DELETE THAT THANG THIS INSTANT! I thought you said you were over him?!!*
Cecily: *I'm over him. Honestly. This is more like self-torture.*
Nina: *oh yea i do that 2*

"Cess, how many bingo cards do you want?"

"One'll do."

Bingo had never been my thing—it was all chance and no strategy—but I agreed to go along with Dad because the proceeds were going to a good cause: helping a town south of us that had been hit by a tornado the previous fall.

The gym at West Texas A&M hummed with voices as we made our way to seats at one of the long tables. I'd actually only been on campus a handful of times, and compared to UCLA, it seemed small and well worn, but the smell was the same and brought back memories of college. And Brett. When I thought of him, I glanced down, realizing I hadn't taken the time to change clothes after work, or to freshen my makeup, or even to comb my hair. I probably looked like a tornado victim myself.

Dad and I helped ourselves to hot dogs and cake while I deliberately shoved thoughts of Brett from my mind—per Shanty's instructions—but twenty minutes later, the shadow of his memory was still a cloud over my mood. We sat alone at a table, waiting for the game to start, and when Dad lifted his hand to wave at someone across the gym, I leaned forward to see who it was.

An electric charge went through my chest when I saw that it was Graham. He smiled at Dad, then looked at me and grinned, and I found myself wishing he would come toward us, wishing he would talk about his biking or his parents or his work, wishing he would sit down with us and play the game. Just wishing.

My gaze followed him to the edge of the makeshift stage, where he stopped next to Mirinda. I hadn't realized they knew each other, yet there they were, deep in conversation. Not small talk where you smile and look around the room at other people and take a step away before going to talk to someone else. It was the kind of conversation where both foreheads are strained and the people alternate between looking at each other and studying the ground, as though an answer to their dilemma might be found in the stain of the hardwood floors. Graham and Mirinda must have known each other fairly well.

Dad waved to someone else.

"Who are you waving at?" I asked.

"Only Olivia."

His coworker stood just inside the door with her daughter and grandson. She was holding the little boy, bouncing him on her hip, and I decided Olivia didn't look old enough to be a grandmother.

As they moved to find seats, Olivia's gaze flitted back to us. To Dad, really.

I bumped his shoulder with mine. "Should you go talk to her?"

He arranged our bingo cards on the table and positioned the paint marker between us. "Olivia? Why? I saw her a few hours ago."

And I had seen Graham a few hours ago, but clearly it didn't make a difference to me. Maybe it ought to. "I think she might be interested in you."

"Olivia?"

Sometimes Dad could be obtuse. "Yes, Olivia. She was looking at you just now."

"Probably because I waved at her. People tend to do that, you know."

"But she looked at you again. After that."

His gaze returned to the spot he had last seen her, and he chuckled. "Not Olivia. We just work together, Cess."

"Or . . . maybe you're stuck in the past."

He gave me his can-we-talk-about-something-else glare.

"Graham says to think positive thoughts and get on with living life." I smiled, realizing I had started feeling differently about Graham's advice. And it had happened at Shanty's cookout.

"I know what Dr. Harper says," Dad snapped, "but it's easier said than done."

His quick reply startled me, and proved that he knew just how hard it was to purge one's mind of negative thoughts. Even if they were the result of years of happy memories.

"That reminds me . . ." I turned in my seat to frown at him. "You've got to stop talking to Graham about me, and for goodness' sake, *stop calling Brett.*"

He rubbed a knuckle across his chin. "If I stop interfering in your business, will you stop interfering in mine?"

"You mean Olivia?" I noticed the wrinkles around his eyes. "Maybe."

"Okay, then *maybe* I'll stop talking to Graham and Brett."

"Give me a break. At least stop calling Brett. That's not helping anything."

His eyes became slits, but then a grin slid onto his face. "Agreed. He's a turd."

I looked past Dad to a group of college girls who could have stepped off the pages of an American Eagle brochure. Their shirts were flowy, and their jeans had holes in the knees in that perfect way that said *money*, not *poverty*, and they all had exactly the same hairstyle. Shoulder length, layered, and board straight.

No wonder Graham hadn't come over to talk to me. My look said, *I don't care what people think.*

Just then, the university president called the room to order, thanked everyone for coming, and introduced Michael Divins.

Dad leaned toward me. "Mirinda's supposed to help him."

Well, of course.

Michael stood on stage, holding a microphone in one of his over-sized hands, thanking us for coming. His untucked dress shirt gave him a refined, untouchable appearance as he explained that the proceeds were going toward tornado relief—as if nobody knew. Then Mirinda joined him, and the two of them began the process of calling out num-bers, Michael spinning the cage of balls, Mirinda pulling one out and handing it to him, then Michael announcing the number.

Mirinda wore a tight T-shirt with *Tornados Suck* printed across her chest, and once again I thought of her as a Barbie doll. Plastic, stiff, and—should any defect ever be found—fully refundable by Mattel.

Dad tapped the tabletop next to my bingo card. "Stop staring at Michael and mark B-8. You've got it top left."

Snatching the marker, I crossed out the square and felt my face warm. I wanted to explain that I hadn't been staring at Michael, but what could I say? That I'd actually been staring at Mirinda? I bit my lip, trying—and failing—to think good things about the woman. All for the simple reason that her look, her body, and her movements were exactly the standard I had always measured myself against.

The dark shadow hovering over my mood now tightened around me, pressing against my good intentions and threatening my ability to be part of this normal, insignificant social activity. My eyes stayed focused on my bingo card as I tried to make sense of the weight that seemed to be holding me down, dampening my spirits until the phrase *Think happy thoughts* was no more feasible than winning a blackout in the first round. In the past twenty minutes, my emotions had gradually transitioned into melancholy. But as much as I hated to admit it, I knew Mirinda Ross wasn't the cause.

It was Graham Harper, and yet again I was placing my happiness in the hands of a man.

When would I ever learn?

An hour later, I was making my way back from the ladies' room when I looked across the gym and saw Michael and Mirinda standing at our table. Dad caught my eye, and his gaze fell to the floor momentarily.

Bless his heart. I gave him too much grief about getting over Mom. He may not have been gallivanting around town every evening, but he had a good life, and somehow his friends included a former football star. I straightened my shoulders and marched toward them.

As I approached, they finished their conversation—something about Michael's NFL contract and his lawyers—and they turned toward me. Mirinda clung to Michael's hand with a fake smile Scotch-taped to her face, but Michael looked at me with genuine friendliness even though his gaze held a trace of hesitation.

I smiled warmly yet generically to let him know I had no hard feelings.

"Michael," said Dad, "this is my daughter, Cecily."

Michael's eyes widened, enough to let me know he hadn't put two and two together yet, but not enough for my dad to notice. "We've met," he said.

"Oh, right." Dad nodded. "At Midnight Oil. You've got a nice shop there, Michael."

"I'm having fun with it. You enjoying the bingo game, Cecily?"

"I am."

"I'm ready to win a prize," said my dad. "Seems like the fella calling out the numbers could do a better job."

"It's all her." Michael poked his thumb toward Mirinda. "She's the one choosing the white balls, not me."

"I'd be more than happy to trade places," Mirinda said in a sing-song voice.

Dad was carrying on with Michael as though they were good friends, and Mirinda didn't seem surprised at their familiarity.

Her eyes bounced between them, but when her gaze cut toward me, she squeezed Michael's bicep and pressed her torso against his side, prompting him to smile down at her like a kid with a new red bike. "Time to draw some more numbers, baby," she said.

"Duty calls." Michael shook Dad's hand.

"Like I was saying," Dad added under his breath, "you're welcome to come out and look around the place. I can give you directions."

"I think I might"—Michael glanced at me—"know where it is."

Dad nodded. "Come by any time then."

"I'll come this week. Good to see you again, Cecily."

As they returned to the stage, Dad and I returned to our seats, but my mind was no longer focused on Mirinda and her snarky behavior. "What did all that mean?" I knew the answer even before he replied, but I couldn't quite believe it. *At all.*

"It's just business, Cess."

Dad shifted uneasily in his folding chair while I tried to find something else—anything—to look at. If I turned my head toward him, I might slap him. How could he consider selling our property to Michael, who might someday move Mirinda—Brett's sister!—in with him? The thought made me want to throw up.

Chapter
Twenty-Two

Group text from Shanty: *Your beauty should not come from outward adornment, such as elaborate hairstyles and the wearing of gold jewelry or fine clothes. Rather, it should be that of your inner self, the unfading beauty of a gentle and quiet spirit. 1 Peter 3:3-4*
Cecily: *Heard that one before.*
Shanty: *Agree or disagree??*
Cecily: *It sounds good, and I suppose I believe it, but the lies are way louder.*
Nina: *dude shanty are you a bible thumper?*

After the bingo night, Graham made it clear that I had been silly to imagine a spark between us at Shanty's barbecue. He continued to go about business as usual, treating me with professional indifference, as though I was only there to get a job done. When I walked into the office every morning, he nodded his head, smiled his tight-lipped greeting, then shuttered himself behind his office door. I only saw him briefly between clients, and if there was a lull in the schedule, he returned to his desk and worked on files.

His behavior confused me, but somewhere around Tuesday afternoon I began to get irritated. By Thursday evening, I was borderline angry.

We took a dinner break before Madam X's appointment, and after Graham inhaled his sandwich, he got up to hide in his office again.

"What's up with you?" I asked.

He paused in the doorway of the break room, frozen like a wild animal attempting to blend into the surroundings. "Um . . . what?"

"Why are you avoiding me?"

"I'm not avoi—" He pressed his fist against his mouth, cutting himself off.

"Yes, you are, and it started after Shanty's cookout."

He stared at me for three seconds, then leaned against the door frame. "Shanty's cookout was something else, wasn't it?"

I squinted.

"I mean, all that talk about society's expectations and all."

A ball of tension at the base of my neck melted, and with it, all the hope I hadn't realized I was nurturing. I nodded. "The discussion got surprisingly deep."

"Jason was a little obnoxious."

I grunted. "Quite a guy."

"He had a point, though. Sex sells, and consequently, it's everywhere."

"That doesn't make it all right."

"Of course not." He shifted his weight to his other foot and looked down at the floor. "It's just part of the lie."

"The lie?"

"The lie the world tells men. That they ought to want a certain type of woman. That they deserve that."

For the hundredth time, an image of him talking to Mirinda flashed across my brain. I crossed my arms. "And women are lied to as well. We're told we're worthless if we don't look like that."

His face contorted. "I wouldn't say worthless—"

"That's the lie, Graham," I snapped. "Absolutely. That's the lie."

His head slowly bobbed up and down. "You're right. That's the lie, but every woman is beautiful in a different way."

I smiled as brightly as my mood would allow. "The game was fun, though."

"Take a Hike?" He chuckled but his eyes didn't meet mine. "Where does she come up with these things?"

"Thanks for"—I shrugged as though my words were indifferent—"helping me not feel so awkward during the game. And for walking in with me in the first place."

He returned to his seat at the table and sat down, and I thought he sighed. "Cecily?" He rubbed forcefully at a scratch on the tabletop.

Instinctively, I leaned back in my chair—away from him—bracing myself for whatever he might say.

"You're absolutely right that I've been avoiding you, and I apologize for it. I guess I thought I was being subtle." He smiled the kind of smile a nurse gives a child just before sticking them with an immunization needle. "I enjoyed going with you to the cookout, but I hope I didn't give you the wrong impression."

I lifted my nose half an inch. "The wrong impression?"

"I just . . . I don't . . . I'm afraid you may have thought I was—"

"No." I swept my hand through my hair. "I didn't think anything." Another little lie.

"Oh, good." Then I realized how urgently he wanted me to understand.

To understand he wasn't interested in me.

I forced a smile, but my insides became jelly, shimmering and shaking with every tremor from my nerve endings. Graham hadn't wanted to give me the wrong impression, and now it was obvious he was only doing what any good counselor would do—protecting his client. But I wasn't his client, and the more I thought about it, the less I wanted to be. Imagine how I would feel if I were to sit down across from him in his office and bare my darkest secrets. I shuddered.

"You okay?" he asked.

"Yes."

His eyes held a trace of concern—or maybe it was compassion . . . or empathy—and I regretted my flippant behavior. He reached across the table and gripped my hand, a gesture I now recognized as nothing more than *touch therapy*, and his eyebrows bunched. "But, Cecily—"

He was interrupted by the beeping mechanism on the alley door, and for a fraction of a second, he only blinked. Then he seemed to remember it was Thursday night, and that I was supposed to be hidden behind closed doors for the protection of Madam X. As he stood, his chair banged against the counter, and he instinctively reached out a hand to steady it before taking long strides to the door of the break room.

But he wasn't fast enough.

Madam X paused in the doorway and smiled at him, but when she saw me, her expression changed as swiftly as a spring storm, and she visibly withdrew inside herself, a veil of forced indifference falling across her face. She flipped her hair over a shoulder, seeming to dare me to mention her presence to anyone.

I couldn't think, or speak, or move. I could only stare at the woman who had always struck me as *confident*, and try to meld her with the woman Graham had described as *wounded*.

But I couldn't do it.

Not with Mirinda Ross.

Chapter
Twenty-Three

Group text from Shanty: *TODAY'S THE DAY!!!!! WOOT!!!*
Nina: *oh crap*

On the day of Shanty's demonstration, Nina and I were far more nervous than she was. We trailed behind her, trying to match her bold strides, but when she stopped directly in front of Victoria's Secret, we positioned ourselves behind a cosmetic kiosk, practically hiding. We were all for promoting body-shame awareness, but we'd both rather do it in a way that wasn't so *visible*.

"Do you think she'll really do it?" Nina focused her phone's camera on Shanty.

"Knowing Shanty . . . she'll do it." But did I really know Shanty all that well after only two weeks?

My stomach roiled as though *I* were the one about to strip down in public, and I could only imagine what Shanty was feeling. But she didn't seem anxious at all. She wore a sweat suit and flip flops, and her long braids were pulled up onto the top of her head, falling down around her ears like a feather duster. She stood near a bench and glanced up and down the mall before kicking off her sandals. She pushed her sweatpants down to the floor and stepped out of them, then removed her zippered sweat jacket and moved away from the bench.

I had never seen Shanty in a swimsuit, but from the way Al talked I gathered that she wore it often enough in the summertime, and it showed in her stance. She held her head high as she propped a sign near her right knee, and then she slipped a sleep mask over her eyes. She held her hands in front of her with a permanent marker on each palm like some sort of offering, and then she became as still as a statue.

And she looked . . . lovely.

How she did it, I don't know. Someone her size wasn't supposed to look good in a bikini, especially standing in front of a lingerie shop where they might not even sell lacy items in her size. But Shanty's skin was flawlessly smooth and lightly chocolate, and her turquoise swimsuit and matching sleep mask accentuated her coloring. Her fingernails were strategically manicured and her toenails were tiny and bright. Even her earrings and necklace added to her put-together look. More than anything, though, her attitude was striking because the smile beneath her blindfold seemed humble, not haughty. I decided there was a lot more to Shanty Espinosa than I had imagined.

I inhaled deeply, feeling as though I might suffocate, and I noticed Nina's hands trembling.

"She's a crazy one," Nina said.

People were walking past Shanty now, some stopping to read the sign, others wrinkling their noses and turning away. A middle-aged man and woman slowed to a stop, then a group of teenagers, then a mother with a stroller, and suddenly a small group had formed, nudging each other as they peered around shoulders, trying to read Shanty's poster board explanation.

Today I stand up for women who have experienced body shaming, so that others may become aware of the pain they are causing. If you've ever been made to feel inferior because of your appearance, join me in my stand by writing your name on my body. Together, we can fight this battle and make a difference for all women . . . no matter what they look like.

The young mother, who perhaps hadn't lost all her baby weight, was the first to step forward. She took a marker and quickly wrote her name on Shanty's shoulder before scurrying away with her stroller.

The group of teenagers stood in a subdued semicircle to Shanty's left, close enough that she could probably hear them, feel their presence, instinctively know they were staring at her. One boy scratched his head and looked away, another peered at her from head to toe with a quizzical expression. Two of the girls whispered behind their hands, but another one stomped up to Shanty and grabbed a marker. She walked around her once, seemingly to find the best spot of skin, then she flamboyantly wrote her name. As she walked away, I noticed she'd included her last name too. Her two friends bounced toward Shanty and followed suit, giggling.

The middle-aged woman still stood in front of Shanty with her husband by her side. She stared at Shanty while a few more people wrote their names or rolled their eyes, and then when there was a lull in activity, she walked slowly up to her, placed a hand on each of her shoulders, and enveloped her in a hug.

At first Shanty was startled by the touch, but then she smiled broadly and hugged back. *Touch therapy.* The woman spoke into Shanty's ear, and Shanty nodded and replied, and I marveled at the way my friend seemed to be sharing her heart, not only with the hugging woman, but with every person who walked by her . . . and she couldn't even see them. Shanty would never know if she passed them later in the day, or next week, or a year from now, but they would most likely always remember the half-naked woman in the mall and recognize her on sight should they run into her again. Shanty was something else.

"How does she do it?" Nina whispered the words, more out of envy than awe. "I don't think I could ever feel good enough about myself to risk everything like that."

"No reason to." My cell phone vibrated, but now wasn't the time to check it.

"Yeah, no reason," Nina mumbled.

Nina wasn't Shanty, and I thought she shouldn't wish to be. Nina needed to be Nina, quiet and thoughtful, not bold and fearless, even though I wouldn't mind having a little of that too.

"Oh, look," she said. "There's Dr. Harper."

Sure enough, Graham was striding toward Shanty with an open-mouthed grin, his face and neck tinged with pink. Apparently he was a little embarrassed to see her half-dressed, and I was glad she was blindfolded so she wouldn't see his discomfort. He started talking to her, and laughing, when he was still two yards away. Shanty's face lit up.

She laughed outright then, and her voice traveled all the way to our hideout. "The good doctor himself? Surely not!" And then I realized the blindfold didn't matter; she knew Graham well enough to know he would be embarrassed, even if she couldn't see him blushing.

They talked for a few minutes, still laughing, but fell into a more serious conversation for the last few moments. Graham signed her arm, then patted her shoulder in a farewell gesture as someone else reached for the marker.

When he backed up to stand near the bench where Shanty's clothes lay in a pile, I studied him. He still wore the same jeans and plaid shirt he had worn at the office earlier, but his hair now stood up as though he had run his hands through it. *He was so kind to have come.* I had only worked with him for a short time, but already I could sense his professional compassion. The man had a gift.

"What's he looking for?" Nina asked.

Graham was turning in a slow circle, searching the crowd. His neck stretched as he peered into the store behind us, but then his gaze refocused, and he froze as his eyes locked with mine.

He held my gaze, and I held my breath. Neither of us smiled or waved, but as he stared at me, I felt like I could hear his thoughts. I wondered if he was regretting his words from the night before, and I wondered if he was admitting that . . . maybe . . . he had felt something at Shanty's barbecue after all.

The longer our eyes locked, the more I wanted to abandon my two friends. I wanted to go with Graham and ask him what he thought about Shanty's demonstration, tell him my concerns about Nina's tendency to copycat, pick his brain about my own problems. I wanted to hold his hand and to feel its security, the promise of Graham's protection. I wanted to get to know him, but even more surprisingly, I wanted him to get to know me. And that's what scared me.

Chapter
Twenty-Four

Group text from Nina: *that was kewl ur awesome proud to be ur friend*
Shanty: *Al's gonna have a fit when I tell him this is permanent marker!*
Nina: *he's so crazy about u he wont care*
Cecily: *I'm pumped. Feeling inspired to catch up on my homework now. ;)*

By the time we had left the mall an hour later, Shanty was covered with names, messages of encouragement, and doodle art. Among all the skin graffiti, there was only one negative scrawl—but that depended on how you interpreted it. A gray-haired gentleman had studied Shanty for ten minutes before kissing the back of her hand and writing his phone number there.

Shanty had only laughed when she saw it.

Now I sat in my car in the mall parking lot, copying the directions for the next journal entry at the top of my spiral notebook.

Write and tell yourself you are beautiful and amazing. Then tell yourself why.

I frowned at the words. Moments before, I had been filled with confidence, but now I was alone and felt removed from Shanty's contagious enthusiasm, and I was trying not to think about Graham. In the mall, he had continued to stare at me until I looked away, and after that Nina had pelted me with questions as we huddled behind the kiosk. When we peeked out again, he had disappeared.

I underlined two words in my notebook. *Beautiful* and *amazing*. For an instant, I pictured Brett wrinkling his nose at my enormous pregnant belly when he thought I wasn't looking, but I forced the memory from my mind, and I thought about my mother instead, gently telling me I was pretty. I may not have been the most beautiful woman on the planet, but I was all right. Seeing all those people write their names on Shanty's skin showed me the world is not all bad. The media may have been lying to us, but not everyone believed the lies. The shoppers at the Westgate Mall had proven that to me, so I lowered my head and started writing.

I can't say I'm beautiful. Or amazing.

This wasn't what I was supposed to be writing. I skipped a line and started over.

Okay. I suppose if you look close enough, I have a few beautiful characteristics.

I stared at the sentence, and as I did, a burning sense of shame filled my core, but not shame about my appearance. I felt shame for writing that sentence, for thinking so highly of myself, but that was silly. According to Shanty and Graham and Daddy, I wasn't supposed to tell myself I was ugly, but when I told myself I wasn't, I felt as though I were buying into the lies that told me I was supposed to think I was beautiful. I sighed and laid my head against the headrest. Good grief, this was going to have to get easier soon.

A traveling carnival had parked its numerous trailers in the back of the mall parking lot, and some of the crew members milled around their vehicles or walked toward fast food restaurants. By tomorrow morning, there would be rides set up with sticky children climbing all over them, but I had always been sort of afraid of traveling carnivals with their unsafe rides, unhealthy food, and unpredictable people. I locked my car doors and returned my focus to the notebook.

I really do have beautiful characteristics.
At least a little bit beautiful.

I shut the notebook and gripped the pen in my fist. Those words were wrong, and I could tell it by the shadows in my heart. I was holding the ballpoint pen like a dagger, and I had the urge to stab the point into my thigh. It would feel so good if I did. It would release—no, *validate*—my thoughts. It would complete them.

But slowly, my fingers loosened, and I slid the pen into my purse.

If Shanty was confident enough to stand in the Westgate Mall in her skivvies, surely I was confident enough to believe one positive sentence about myself. Even if it seemed preposterous.

Chapter
Twenty-Five

Graham's list of pros and cons for asking Cecily out on a date (neatly written on the back of an envelope in his truck):

Pros:
attractive
fun
kind
crazy about her
makes me happy
might make her happy too
admire her dad

Cons:
still emotionally fragile
could cause rumors
maybe too soon
does she even like me?

<u>I might not be good for her.</u>

Graham was nervous about talking to Cecily, but he was tired of tiptoeing around and not being honest with her, and it was getting harder and harder to hide his feelings. He had turned onto the Witherspoon's property as Dub was pulling away from the house, so now their trucks were stopped next to each other, windows down, and Graham was fielding questions.

"You think she's doing all right?" Cecily's father asked.

"I think so." Graham wished Dub wouldn't put him on the spot, but he understood his concern. "She's trying awful hard."

"She seems to enjoy working at your office."

"That's a good sign." Graham pulled on his earlobe. "Is she home?"

"Soon, I think. She was headed to Amarillo. Shopping or something."

Graham figured she'd be home by now. "How're you doing, Dub?"

"Can't complain."

"Still meeting with the group?"

"Oh, sure," he said, "probably always will."

"I know you're helping a lot of them."

"That's what keeps me going. Gives me purpose." He winked at Graham, then gestured toward the approaching gray SUV. "I best be going."

"Don't rush off on account of me."

Dub smiled knowingly. "Glad you could stop by, Graham. Real glad." He waved at Cecily as their vehicles passed.

By the time Cecily and Graham had both pulled in front of the cabin, Graham was absurdly nervous. He was with Cecily every day at the office, but now he was on her home turf, uninvited.

She eyed him skeptically. "Hey."

"Sorry to bother you at home," he took a step toward her and said the first thing that came to his mind. "My bike."

"Your bike?"

She frowned at the two-wheeler in the back of his truck, and Graham did the same, perplexed with himself. "Um . . . my handlebars are a little loose?" His handlebars were fine. "So I stopped. Thought I might borrow some tools from your dad."

She glanced down the road toward where her father's truck had disappeared, and Graham scrambled to get back on track. "But since I'm here, there's a few things I wanted to talk to you about." That was too abrupt.

Her expression cleared. "Like Mirinda?"

"Mirinda?"

"You're probably worried that I'm going to gossip about her being Madam X, but honestly, I'm not that interested in whether or not she needs counseling. Seems to me she shouldn't try to hide it."

"I wouldn't say she's trying to hide it, necessarily."

"Coming to the office under cover of darkness and requesting that your receptionist shut herself in the break room?" She gave him a pointed look. "That's not hiding?"

"I guess I just look at it from a different perspective."

"Which is . . . ?"

"She knows her limits, that's all. No need to push herself into a place that might hinder her progress."

She tilted her head to the side. "Honestly, Mirinda and her problems don't interest me."

Clearly Brett's sister interested Cecily more than she let on.

"Shanty Espinosa, on the other hand, is a mystery." Cecily softened, then grinned. She was holding a spiral notebook, but she tossed it on the front deck before gesturing toward the shed at the side of the house. "Dad's tools are out here."

Graham followed her. "Shanty's demonstration seemed to go well." Except the part where he made a fool of himself by staring at Cecily. What must she think?

"It was phenomenal. You can watch the whole thing on YouTube later. Nina recorded it."

"Maybe . . ."

"Maybe?" They were at the door of the shed now, and Cecily turned to frown at him.

He shrugged. "I don't make a habit of watching videos of women in bikinis."

"It's just Shanty."

"Why would that make a difference?"

Cecily froze with her hand on the doorknob, seeming to analyze his question along with her previous statement. Then she turned away. "Do you always have so much trouble with your bike?"

"Oh, you know . . ." He couldn't think of what to say, and the truth was out of reach.

When they entered the building, they were in a neat and tidy workshop. "What do you need?" she asked.

"A wrench."

She pointed to a pegboard on the wall. "Help yourself."

Graham was distracted by the room. Not only was there an extensive set of tools, but there were also carpentry gadgets, power saws, and neatly labeled drawers. "This is one awesome workshop. Your dad must love it."

"Actually, he doesn't spend much time out here anymore. Not since Mom passed. They used to do projects together—furniture and whatnot—but now, he doesn't seem to have it in him."

"Sorry about that," he said, feeling incompetent.

She shrugged, then glanced at the untouched tools. "Would you like to see some of their old stuff?"

When he nodded, she opened a door that led into an adjacent garage. The bulk of the space was taken up by a car, covered in a canvas tarp, but around its edges were woodworking projects, some finished, some in-process. Cecily ran her hand along the top of a three-tiered shelf, leaving fingertip trails in the dust. "They always sanded everything until it was perfectly smooth. I used to love to feel the wood grain."

"I remember them selling these years ago."

"They would set up on the side of the highway."

Graham chuckled. "My mother bought a spice rack once." His mind wandered back and forth through his memories. "These are great, Cecily. Do you think your dad will ever do carpentry work again?"

"You're the counselor."

"I'm not a fortune teller, though."

She leaned against the car and crossed her arms. "But Dad said he's talked to you before."

Graham didn't like the challenge in her eyes, but he couldn't blame her for asking. "He may never want to work in his shop again because it reminds him of your mom, but he'll probably find another interest eventually."

"A hobby." She rolled her eyes. "Shanty told me to get a hobby."

"Not bad advice."

She scrutinized him. "That was your advice to her, wasn't it?" she asked. "Oh, my goodness. Are you the reason she's a blogger now?"

His hand quivered where it rested on his thigh. "I wouldn't go that far."

"Can I ask you something else?"

"As long as—"

"It's not about a client. Not directly, anyway." She shifted her feet. "I was just wondering why you counsel Shanty and Nina, but you don't want to help me. You said I didn't need more counseling and that the support group would be enough, but if that's true, then Shanty and Nina shouldn't need more counseling either." Her voice grew heated. "It doesn't really matter. I just feel like maybe you aren't interested in my problems."

Not interested? If he was completely honest, he'd have to say he was obsessed, not merely with Cecily's problems, but with every aspect of her life—past, present, and future—but he could hardly tell her that.

He lifted his palms. "You never know about people, Cecily."

"What does that mean?"

"It means Shanty and Nina have things going on in their lives that you aren't aware of. And they may need counseling for different reasons." At least that was true.

She hugged her elbows and looked away from him.

"What kind of car is this?" he asked, his guilt driving him to shift the conversation away from his dishonesty.

Her shoulders relaxed. "It's my old Jeep. I don't know why Dad keeps it."

"No way. Is it still lemon yellow?"

"I suppose." She pulled the canvas up to reveal the bright-colored hood.

Graham whistled. "You could always see this car coming from a mile away."

"I don't know what we were thinking."

"Aw, that was just you back then." He hoped she took that the right way. "Does it still run?"

"Only one way to find out."

With one of them on each side of the Jeep, they peeled the canvas back until it landed in a pile on the concrete floor. They climbed in, Cecily in the driver's seat and Graham next to her. She rummaged through the glove box for a key, and when she didn't find it, she looked on the floorboard and on the dash, then she slumped back in her seat. "I guess we'll never know. Daddy may have lost the keys years ago."

"I doubt it." Graham imagined Dub was holding on to the bright-yellow Jeep because it reminded him of his happy daughter who disappeared.

Cecily's smile faded, and Graham wondered if she was thinking about memories of her younger self, driving around Canyon, laughing with her friends. Her forehead was furrowed, and Graham felt the urge to reach over and hug her like he had at the park.

"My dad's considering selling this place."

"Is he?" Graham already knew that, and he had probably known before Cecily did. Even though it was Dub's business to share, Graham was beginning to feel like everything he said to her was a half-truth.

"He may even sell it to Michael Divins." She gritted her teeth. "Probably as a gift for Mirinda."

This was news to him, but it wasn't surprising. Dub and Michael were good friends, and Michael had the money to pay cash for the place, but . . . *oh, no* . . . Michael buying the place for Mirinda was almost the same as Brett taking it away from her himself.

"I'm sorry," he said simply. "That can't be easy for you."

"All this time Mirinda's known the deal was in the works. She's probably been laughing at me every time I walk into that stupid coffee shop."

"Is it for sure?"

"Not yet." She bit her bottom lip. "Maybe the radio still works." She turned the knob and was instantly rewarded with music. Her head bounced gently with the beat, and Graham knew she had talked about the real estate deal as long as she could stand.

"I'm not big on rap," he admitted.

"Me neither." She punched a button to change the station, but landed on a commercial for an accident-and-injury lawyer. She punched again, and the garage was filled with piano music Graham recognized from a movie. "That's more like it," she said.

"What is that song?"

"Debussy's 'Clair de lune.'"

"Can you play it?"

"I don't know. Probably not."

Graham knew better. He figured Cecily could play anything she set her mind on.

They listened without speaking. Cecily leaned back and closed her eyes, and Graham leaned back and watched her. She was so beautiful. He shook his head, wondering how on earth she didn't know it.

"This part's good." She tapped her fingers on his knee as if she were playing the piano, her eyes still closed.

This was the Cecily he remembered, driving a bright-yellow car with blaring piano music. This was the Cecily he had been infatuated with. This was the Cecily he missed. He never would have lied to her back then.

Before the song came to a close, the battery on the old car reached the end of its life, and the music faded into nothing.

"Wouldn't you know it," she said. "We didn't get the final few chords." She continued to tap his leg, finishing the piece in her mind.

In the loud silence, Graham slowly touched her fingers, stilling her movements. With one finger, he traced a circle on the back of her hand, and she opened her eyes, calmly, as though she wasn't surprised by his touch.

She didn't move, only watched their hands, but her eyes were soft, and he thought she might not mind what he was doing. "I've been lying to you," he said. "About counseling."

"I don't like lies."

"I don't either, but I was afraid to tell you the truth."

"Are you still afraid?" she asked.

"Yes."

"Tell me anyway."

He took her hand in his, lifted it to his mouth, and rubbed his lips against her fingertips. "I can't bear to have you as a client, Cecily, restricted to weekly appointments and governed by rules and regulations. I want more than that. I want more of you." He hesitantly looked at her for a reaction. "Is that okay?"

"Yes." Her eyes were a mixture of surprise, acceptance, and something else.

Fear.

But the furrow on her forehead melted, and she leaned toward him in slow motion, stopping with her face inches from his. Her quizzical gaze slid from one of his eyes to the other, then to his hair, then to his chin as though she were looking for the answer to a question. When she shook her head, ever so slightly, Graham felt as though she were admitting to herself that the question was irrelevant. She closed her eyes.

When their lips met, Graham's insides exploded in a burst of emotions. Desire, compassion, longing, but with the good feelings came a heavy dose of guilt, and he pulled away.

"I tried to wait until you're more ready . . ."

"If you're waiting until I'm emotionally healthy enough for a relationship, you might have a really long wait." When she looked into his eyes and smiled, Graham couldn't help himself.

He pulled her close and kissed her again. Harder.

Chapter
Twenty-Six

Group text from Shanty: *No one can MAKE you feel unattractive.*
Nina: *shurrrrr they can*
Cecily: *No they can't, but sometimes it feels like it.*

Not only did I agree to go out with Graham Harper, but I also agreed to go to the carnival, of all places. In twenty-four hours, the parking lot of the Westgate Mall had been transformed into an amusement park, filled with gangly teenagers, rough-looking carnies, and flustered parents searching for one more quarter to give their children.

And then there was Graham and me.

I walked beside him, careful not to bump his elbow with mine, but when we wedged ourselves into the cocoon-like pod of the Tilt-A-Whirl, our bodies touched all the way from shoulders to knees, and for once, he wasn't fidgeting.

Our seats jerked to the left, then the pod began rotating smoothly, and I involuntarily leaned closer to him. "Sorry," I said. "Centrifugal force."

"No worries." He yelled to be heard over the organ music that grew louder every time we whirled close to a speaker. "I haven't done this in years!"

Our cocoon swung upward, and my stomach responded as though a harp had been strummed deep inside me, creating vibrations of gradually increasing pitch. I gasped in surprise, and then, feeling silly but not really caring, I laughed out loud. When our pod swung from side to side, Graham slid his arm around my shoulders and held me tight.

It happened so quickly. I didn't have time to decide if I minded, and all I could think was how the ride was better because he was there. He hooted like a cowboy riding a bronco, and then the machine began to calm, spiraling back to earth, its movements slowing until it came to a jarring halt.

A worker trudged past our car, loudly clanking the locking mechanism and hoisting the door upward, and as I clambered to the ground, I felt Graham's hand on my waist.

"Want to try the bumper cars?" he asked.

"Eww, I *hate* bumper cars."

His eyes widened. "So do I. The cars never do what you tell them to do."

"And all that banging gives me a headache."

"How about the Ferris wheel?"

I looked at the top of the ride, high above the parking lot. "I guess."

Five minutes later, we were stuck in a slow-moving line, and I crossed my arms, not knowing what to do with myself. Graham had both hands shoved in his back pockets.

"This is awkward, isn't it?" he said, and my tension eased.

"I never pictured myself going out with you," I said. When his smiled faded, I quickly added, "When we were young, I mean. Now I picture it. Obviously." I was babbling.

He gave me an I-can't-believe-I'm-about-to-tell-you-this smile. "Back in school? I thought about going out with you every single day."

His smile didn't change, but his gaze bounced away, as though he were afraid of my reaction.

"Why didn't you ask me out?"

Instead of answering, he looked me right in the eye and raised his eyebrows.

"What?" I asked.

"You just said you never pictured yourself going out with me. Why would I risk it?"

"Oh, I see. You haven't always been the confident therapist."

"Confident?"

"That's you. Confident nature boy."

He snorted. "*Nature* boy?"

"You bike in the canyon. You wear plaid shirts, *untucked*. You have a beard." I leaned toward him. "You think happy thoughts."

"But I eat processed food, I love me some air conditioning, and I couldn't live without the Internet. Clearly I'm not a nature boy."

The line stopped inching forward and music began playing. One by one, the lighted cars lifted into the air, then swung around and came back down. People were laughing and calling out to each other, pointing at things in the distance when their cars were high in the air. A couple of grade school boys rocked their car forward and backward while their parents threatened them from the car behind. A teenage boy tried to kiss the girl next to him, but she appeared to be feeling seasick and didn't pay much attention. Another couple was leaned back, the woman nestled against the man, his arm around her.

They were all just people. Normal people. And I was normal too. So often I felt just slightly insane, as though my marriage and divorce had left me in a state of mental disrepair. And maybe it had. Even now I felt crazy for going out with Graham.

"What are you thinking?" he asked.

"What makes you think I'm thinking?"

"You can tell me, you know."

I stared at the rotating cars, and after a few minutes, the ride stopped. Two little girls climbed off, then waited at the side fence until the wheel rotated further, and their parents got off. I looked at Graham. "I'm not sure why I'm here."

He nodded solemnly. "You're not sure you want to be."

"No, that's not it." A smile forced its way to my lips. "I want to be here. With you."

His eyes melted in relief. "But?"

"I have this problem with trust."

"As you should."

"Really?"

"Of course. Your trust has been breached, and it will take a while to be able to trust again."

"I'm still so angry. Brett stole seven years of my life—more than that really—and he stole my happiness. Even my sanity."

"You're not insane."

"It feels like it."

He hesitated. "What did Brett do . . . exactly?"

Seriously? He was asking me right now? In the middle of a parking lot carnival? But then I realized that was just as good a place as any. Maybe better. I took a deep breath and nodded. "It started when he was just a boy, looking at naughty pictures, but over the years, it grew worse." I swallowed. "In the end, he was doing and saying things that—" I turned my face away.

Graham didn't say anything, just reached for my hand and intertwined our fingers.

I surprised myself by resting my head against his shoulder, just for a moment, right there in the middle of the carnival, among carnies and screaming children and awkward teenagers. Among families that looked as though they never had any problems.

"Try to forgive him, Cecily," Graham said. "You'll feel better."

"Brett doesn't deserve forgiveness."

"Maybe not, but you deserve to stop letting your bitterness suffocate you."

"I've been trying to forgive him for years."

The line moved forward as people got off the ride, one car at a time, and I felt Graham's fingertips run up my arm. "I'm glad you stopped covering up your tattoo," he said lightly. "That's a sign that you're healing, don't you think?"

He didn't say he liked it. "Yeah, it was time to stop hiding. This is me, and I might as well accept it."

He moved to stand in front of me so he could look me in the eye. "The tattoo was Brett's idea?"

"One of many."

"But . . . he didn't like it?"

I shrugged. "Not really."

"How does that make you feel?"

Clearly he had slipped back into his role as *Dr. Harper*. "I felt marred. And ugly. And eventually . . . unwanted."

"And how do you feel now?"

"Now?" My gaze swept upward, and I was surprised to see a clear sky full of stars. "Now I tend to feel the same things, but I'm convincing myself it's not true." I shook my head. "And there's this persistent voice inside my head that reminds me of the things Brett said."

"But Brett was lying." Graham's voice was so soft I could barely hear him over the sounds of the carnival.

"Everyone's lying."

"But you don't have to believe the lies."

"Don't I?" My words popped like a coiled whip, but then I regretted my tone. "Okay, no. You're right. I don't have to believe them."

"And . . . there's no time like the present to confront the past."

I laughed. "Did you read that on a greeting card?"

"A Facebook meme."

"What's it got to do with me?"

He took a deep breath. "Brett is coming back to Canyon for our high school reunion."

I squinted. "I bet Mirinda told you that. She knew you would tell me."

"Well . . . yes."

Graham and I settled into our seats on the Ferris wheel, and he slipped his arm around me. His nearness should have been a comfort, but as we began to rise into the air, I couldn't feel the warm glow of security he usually gave me. Or maybe it was still there, but it wasn't strong enough to melt the iciness that always crept into my veins whenever I thought about Brett. I would see my ex-husband at the reunion, and I knew he would act like nothing happened, and I would have to go along with it. Again. I'd keep forgiving him every time I remembered the pain. Not because I wanted to, but because that was the right thing to do. My in-patient counselor had said so. Graham said so. Even Shanty and Nina had told me so.

And now Graham said I needed to stop believing the lies Brett had told me.

But none of them knew how convincing the lies were.

Chapter Twenty-Seven

THE MEN OF THE CONGREGATION ARE INVITED TO ATTEND A SATURDAY
SEMINAR DISCUSSING THE BOOK

*EVERY MAN'S BATTLE: WINNING THE WAR ON SEXUAL TEMPTATION ONE
VICTORY AT A TIME*
BY STEPHEN ARTERBURN AND FRED STOEKER.

10:00 AM IN THE FELLOWSHIP HALL. BARBECUE LUNCH TO FOLLOW.

The man was a liar. He knew it, and he was lying to the one person who
meant more to him than anyone else. Not blatantly telling her things
that weren't true, but lying by omission. Not telling her everything.

He cursed himself.

The first time had been an accident, and he recalled that the second
time had been surprisingly easy, but the next hundred times weren't by
choice. They were by compulsion, something he couldn't control and
didn't want, and he hated—*despised*—being out of control.

And he despised himself.

He sat on the cushioned pew, near the back, trying to remember how to pray. His parents had taken him to church a few times when he was a kid, maybe more than a few, because he remembered the feeling of it. And the good people. He glanced around him at husbands and wives and children, teenagers and old people. Did any of them have problems? They didn't seem to.

He stared at his hands, which were clenched tightly in his lap, then rubbed his thumb across his knuckles. The voices in his head seemed louder than the microphone at the front of the chapel. They seemed louder than just about everything. Even now, he had the urge to pull out his phone and look at a few pictures, maybe a video, but that was heinous. In a church of all places.

His eyes squinted closed. *Hello, God?*

A child behind him whined loudly, something about his apple juice.

God? I'm in over my head, and I don't know what to do. If she ever finds out, it will kill her.

A tap on his shoulder caused him to open his eyes, and he worried that someone had thought he was sleeping.

"Could you hand it to me?" A woman behind him, the child's mother, pointed to the sippy cup that had rolled down the sloped floor and now rested against the edge of the carpet near his foot.

He reached down and grasped the sticky plastic, handing it back. He looked over his shoulder and nodded at the woman, and as he did so he caught a glimpse of her bare leg. A lot of leg. All the way up to her thigh. He turned back around, rigidly staring at the back of the bald head in front of him, but still seeing that young mother's curves. Her legs had been crossed at the knees, and she was tanned. The kind of tan that, for whatever reason, reminded him of toasted almonds. He had seen that skin color on a girl in a picture recently, only she had on fewer clothes. He remembered it clearly.

He shifted in the pew as he imagined the woman behind him in fewer clothes. Would she look as good as the toasted almond picture?

162

Was she tanned all over? He ran both hands through his hair, then gripped the back of his neck. One minute he was trying to pray for help, the next minute he was lusting after someone's mother.

He returned his gaze to his fists.

He had thought church would be different. That he would somehow be protected from himself and his thoughts and the pictures in his mind, but it was no different here. *He* was no different. He was still out of control, spiraling downward into a pit that he couldn't climb out of. He was still disgusted with himself.

And still lying.

Chapter
Twenty-Eight

Sunday afternoon, I sat on the counter in the garage, watching Dad work under the hood of the Jeep and getting more and more impatient with him. "How do you even know Michael Divins? Everybody acts like the two of you are such good friends."

He paused in his work but didn't raise his head. "We're in a group together."

"What kind of group?"

"Just a group, Cess."

"Like Texas Hold'em?"

He straightened then, but kept his back to me. "Naw, like Shanty's, only different."

His words didn't make sense. Not that men weren't in support groups, but still . . . *my dad*? "For low self-esteem?" I asked.

"Nothing like that. We're just under a lot of stress." He leaned over the engine again.

I was getting fed up with secrecy. "How many men are in it? I mean . . . they are *men*, right? Or are there stressed women in it too?"

"Just men. Usually three or four."

He didn't offer any other information, and I huffed and crossed my arms, knowing I was pouting—but I didn't care.

"It's just a group for guys in recovery, Cess. For some of them it's recovery from an addiction, or depression, or grief. They're just trying to get control of their lives."

Well, I could relate to that.

He continued to fiddle with the engine. "Why are you asking about my friendship with Michael anyway?"

"Why do you think? You're about to sell my home out from under me."

"Your home?"

The question sliced like a blade. "Is this not my home?"

Daddy leaned heavily against the Jeep. "I mean, sure, it's your home . . . *now* . . . but even a year ago, you didn't want much to do with the place."

"That's not true. Just because Brett and I didn't visit often doesn't mean I wasn't interested in our home." *Or you.* "The thought of losing it makes me feel lost."

"I know what you mean." He stepped to the counter, selected a few tools, and walked lazily back to the car. He hesitated with his palms on the frame, but then reached for a ratchet.

I watched him for a while. He was wearing a solid white T-shirt— what I called an old man's undershirt, probably because my old man wore them under his uniforms. I smiled. Dad was just so . . . Dad. Out here in the shed, with his workshop and garage, he was like a wild animal in his natural habitat, working, fiddling, repairing. He was a doer, and he had always had a lot of doing that needed to be done on our property. I couldn't picture him anywhere else. Would he get a house in town? With a little yard and a cement driveway? Would he get an apartment? I shuddered.

"I can't picture Mirinda in our cabin," I said, forcing my mind in that direction because the thought of Mirinda living in our home was less painful than the thought of my dad living anywhere else. "She doesn't belong here. I know you're going to say you're selling it to Michael, not Mirinda, but they'll probably get married." I picked at a hangnail on my thumb.

Daddy didn't respond. He continued working, but perhaps he was working a little more aggressively. No, not aggressively . . . absentmindedly.

I crossed my legs beneath me, feeling relieved—even cleansed—by the statement I had made, as though verbalizing my frustrations had released them from my thoughts and had lessened my bitterness. I hated to admit it, but with the medical bills, I supposed he had no other choice. I studied him, bent over the hood, and thought about what I'd just said to him. *Mirinda doesn't belong here.*

My head sunk between my shoulders. Of course Mirinda didn't belong in our cabin. Only my mother belonged there. Would I ever stop thinking of myself? "Oh, Daddy. I'm sorry."

He leaned with his palms on the frame and winked at me. "Nothing I haven't already told myself."

"I miss her too," I said. "Sometimes I wish I could talk to her. She had a way of making me feel better about myself."

He didn't answer, didn't nod his head, didn't move.

"She always told me how pretty I was, you know?"

Dad rubbed his wrist with the opposite thumb. "Your mom and I disagreed on some things . . . when it came to you."

"Like what?"

"Like telling you all the time how beautiful you are."

"I'm not following. You didn't want her to tell me I was pretty?"

"I didn't want her to put so much emphasis on it." He sounded a little angry, and a wave of defensiveness swelled inside me.

"She didn't put emphasis on it."

"Yes, she did." He straightened and walked two paces away, stopping with his back to me. "Ever since you were tiny. She dressed you up in lace and bows, teaching you that you needed all that in order to make something of yourself, but she could never see the damage she was doing. She just—"

"That's *ridiculous*." I slid from the counter. "Mom loved me."

"Of course she loved you." His voice was low. "She loved you more than anything in the world." His gaze drifted away from me. "Sometimes I think she loved you more than was good for her."

What was he saying? I planted myself in front of him so he couldn't look away. "What does that mean?"

"Your mother was insecure about herself. Always had been, and the two of us had to work through a lot of things regarding her self-esteem, but when it came to you, we didn't see eye to eye. We were both intent on you being strong and confident, but we disagreed on how to get you there. She thought the answer was to praise you and do things to help you feel pretty," he said, "because those things made *her* feel more confident."

"She wasn't like that." His description of my mother caused me physical pain. "She wasn't the type of woman to flaunt herself and wear fancy clothes and jewelry. She was beautiful without all that."

"*Yes.*" He took a deep breath. "She was beautiful, inside and out, but she relied on clothes and makeup to boost her self-esteem. She didn't overdo it, but she couldn't do without it either. Ever. I wanted to teach you to find value inside yourself for more than just your appearance. I should have made her listen to me."

I peered at the Jeep, then crossed my arms. My parents were the last ounce of goodness in my crazy world, and in one conversation, Daddy had thrown a bucket of ice water over my memories.

He lifted his hands in the air. "Let's let this rest for a while. Talk about it later."

He was right, of course. We were too heated, but who was he kidding? Both of us knew *talk about it later* was code for *let's never discuss this awkward topic again as long as we live.* And that seemed just fine with me.

"Okay," I said.

When Daddy picked up a wrench and thoughtfully stared at it for a few moments before tightening something under the hood, I wanted to wrap my arms around him and lay my head on his shoulder. I wanted to tell him I was more like Mom than he knew, and I wanted him to remind me—like he had reminded her so many times—that I was beautiful on the inside and out. But, of course . . . that wasn't our way.

Chapter
Twenty-Nine

Text from Graham to Cecily: *Would love to see you tonight. How about dinner at my place? Maybe a picnic in the backyard.*
Cecily (thirty-one minutes later): *I'm not quite ready for dinner at your place.*
Graham: *No worries. The park then?*
Cecily (twenty-four minutes later): *My house. We can hike down to our family campsite on the floor of the canyon.*
Graham: *Sounds perfect. If you'll bring candles and a mirror, I'll bring everything else.*
Cecily: *A mirror? What for?*

I didn't know why the thought of a candlelit dinner made me nervous. Maybe because it was Graham. Maybe because candles, in my mind, seemed to take the relationship to the next level. I had felt safe inviting him to my place since Dad would be home, putting a damper on any romance Graham may have been planning, but a quarter of an hour before he was set to arrive, Dad had showered and left the house. *Of course.*

He claimed he had a meeting, but I figured he was trying to play the matchmaker. I made a mental note to drop a few more subtle hints about Olivia. Maybe even *to* Olivia. This matchmaker thing could work two ways.

"How far is it to the campsite?" Graham was following me down a steep incline, carrying a picnic bundle in a backpack.

"Less than ten minutes. It's actually only forty feet from our deck if we could just jump down to it."

The campsite reminded me of my childhood. A fire pit, a picnic table, and a few cleared areas where we used to set up tents. Not very romantic, but at the moment it seemed just right.

"Do you and your dad camp down here?" Graham said, setting his pack on the table.

I glanced at the overgrown spot where my tent had typically been pitched when I was a little girl. "Not since my mom died, but we used to come down here almost every weekend. We didn't always camp, but we'd picnic here during the warm months and roast marshmallows during the cold ones."

After setting my own small bag on the bench, I withdrew two votive candles and a bandanna table cloth, but opted not to remove the handheld mirror I had snatched on the way out of the house.

"What's for dinner?" I asked as I spread the cloth over the weathered wood.

"Don't get your hopes up." He opened his bag and withdrew a small takeout box of Asian food. "It's just Soccer Mom's. I've been craving it."

"Yum. Did you happen to get teriyaki chicken?"

"*Score.*" He grinned widely. "I wasn't sure what you liked, so I got a variety. Beef broccoli, sweet-and-sour pork, and teriyaki chicken." He continued to pull small boxes from his backpack, setting them on the table like a miniature village.

"Suddenly I'm very hungry."

He set paper napkins and plastic forks next to the village, then opened two canned soft drinks. "Did you bring a lighter for the candles?"

"But it's barely dark yet."

"It's the mood we're going for." Graham chuckled as he lit them, setting them among the boxes. Two streetlamps on the village square.

We sat down and passed boxes back and forth as we tried each dish, not caring about germs or etiquette or manners, and as my stomach filled, my nerves relaxed.

"This is my first candlelit dinner," Graham said. "Not exactly a traditional one, but I like it."

"This is definitely not my first." I laughed self-consciously. "But I agree that the venue is better than most." I almost started jabbering about Brett's obsession with exquisite candlelit dinners at fine restaurants, but I was determined not to allow his memory to invade this date. The sun had set, and Graham's face now glowed above the flickering light of the flames. When his eyes met mine, I smiled mischievously. "So if you never had a candlelit dinner, what kind of dates have you been on?"

His mouth fell open in a grin. "Your turn to ask the personal questions, is it?"

"Long overdue, if you ask me."

"Okay, let's see. I once took Lindsay Timms to a Trace Adkins concert at the Tri-State Fair."

"You did not. Lindsay Timms was a friend of mine, and I would've heard about it."

"No, really. It was after you left for college. And . . . let's see, there was the time I took what's-her-name-who-you-don't-know to Red Lobster and then to the Amarillo Community Theatre."

"Really? That doesn't sound like your thing."

"It was *her* thing. Needless to say, that relationship didn't last long."

I was leaning forward with my elbows on the table, and Graham's hands were near mine. When he touched the tips of his fingers to my palm, I responded with a gentle touch, and for a few moments we stopped talking and focused our attention on our fingers as we explored each other's hands. Such a simple, innocent thing to do, but warmth spread up and down my spine, and I found myself wanting to reach past his hands to his arms, then up to his shoulders. I wanted to explore the muscles on his chest. I wanted him to explore me.

I straightened and pulled my hands away.

Graham acted like he didn't notice, and he stood, picked up his bag, and started loading empty containers into it. Then he reached into the bottom of his bag. "I almost forgot. I brought an after-dinner activity. Not quite as fancy as dinner theater, but I think it will make you laugh." He set something down on the table. "And I love it when you laugh. Did you bring the mirror?"

My gaze fell to the tabletop, and when I saw a roll of Wint O Green Lifesavers, confusion clouded my thoughts. "Um . . . what are we doing?"

"My mom calls it *sparking*."

It was his mom's idea? "And we need a mirror?"

"Don't look so worried." He tore the wrapper away and popped a Lifesaver in his mouth. "If you bite them hard enough, they spark. You just have to be in a really dark place." He peered over his head at the now dark sky.

"Show me," I challenged, moving to stand in front of him.

His laugh sounded uneasy. "I can't believe I'm doing this, but here goes." He kept his mouth open for my inspection, and obnoxious chewing sounds rattled across the canyon.

I smiled at his absurd facial expression. "I didn't see a thing."

"No? Probably not dark enough." He bent down and blew out the candles, leaving us in pitch blackness.

I heard the wrapper tear again, and then his chewing, and his nearness sent goose bumps down my arms. "You sound like a cow." Then I saw it—a tiny spark. "Oh, my goodness. There really are sparks in your mouth. Sort of blue. Or green."

"Told you." He tore more of the wrapper.

"Do it again, but bend down so I can see you better." In the darkness, I sensed that he leaned against the end of the table and moved his feet on either side of me. I put my hands on his shoulders to keep my bearings, and our faces were almost level so that when he crunched again, I had a better view of the sparks. "Your mother does this?"

"She puts on a show for the little kids she babysits. But only if they're good."

"Can I try?"

"Please do. I'm getting a stomachache." He fumbled for my hand and palmed me a mint.

"Now I see why you wanted a mirror." I reached for my bag but tripped over his feet, falling against his chest.

"Whoa there."

Graham's arms encircled me as I regained my balance, and when I stood back up, his cheek brushed mine. "You okay now?"

When I felt his breath on my ear, I turned my head and brushed my lips against his. "Couldn't be better."

He chuckled brusquely. "Let's see if you can spark then." He scooted back to sit on the table, and I stood between his knees, holding the mirror above his right shoulder.

My first try didn't work.

"Can I try it again?"

His hand traveled up my body, and his fingers tapped my neck and chin until he found my mouth. Then he slipped a mint between my teeth. "This time, really crunch hard, and keep your mouth wide open."

His hands moved down to grip my waist, and I bit down so hard I thought I might dislodge a filling. "That's it. Three sparks in a row."

I giggled, and he gave me more candy, but this time when I chewed, I could hear him snickering. "What are you laughing at? It sparked. I saw it."

"Oh, it's sparking all right, but listen to yourself. You're humming when you chew." He laughed again.

"Hush up." The next time I consciously tried not to hum, but I couldn't chomp hard enough that way.

"I guess humming gives you extra power." He paused dramatically. "One Lifesaver left . . . and I think it should be mine since—"

"No way, I get the last one." I groped for his hand, and we scuffled briefly, and when he shoved the candy in his mouth, I laughed once again at the sparks shooting in the darkness.

"I love it when you laugh, Cecily," he said quietly. "It makes me laugh too."

"Well, Dr. Harper, you know what they say . . . laughter is good therapy."

He was still laughing when he pulled me toward him and covered my mouth with his.

It felt strange when I kissed him back, smiling, but I decided it was a good strangeness. To be happy with a man seemed right and healthy, and to be happy with Graham seemed natural. And complete.

The mintiness of the Lifesavers gave my tongue a tingling sensation, and his kisses felt different from before, new and exciting. My hands went to either side of his face, as though to keep him from pulling away. His fingers dug into the curve of my back, and both of us stopped smiling. My carefree mood had been replaced with something deeper and more base, instinctive. This man, Graham Harper, cared more about my happiness than anyone I had ever known, maybe even more than *I* did, and that knowledge was swiftly intoxicating my senses.

When one of his hands left my body momentarily, I heard the votive candles clattering to the ground. Then his arms surrounded me, and he pulled me roughly against his chest before he lay back on the table, and I giggled one last time as my feet came off the ground.

Chapter Thirty

Group text from Shanty: *Don't forget to love yourself. (That's a quote from my blog!!!)*
Cecily: *I'm pretty sure I think about myself too much already.*
Shanty: *There's a difference between selfishly THINKING about ourselves too often and LOVING ourselves. It's a balance.*
Cecily: *Not sure I'm following you, but whatever.*

The three members of the support group climbed onto tall chairs around a counter-height table near the front windows of the shop. It was an uncharacteristic choice, but it was also the only available option. Apparently the high school had had some sort of banquet, and half the student body decided they needed coffee afterward. Hopefully the boisterous voices would drown out our sensitive conversation.

"Girlfriends," said Shanty, "I'm still pumped about the mall, and I've still got black marker in a few places." She leaned toward us and whispered. "Al don't seem to mind it too much. He kinda likes to run his fingers across the names, if you know what I mean."

I dropped my forehead into my hands and moaned, and Nina stifled a laugh.

"Spare us the details," I said. "But the demonstration was awesome. Did you see it in the paper yesterday?"

"Sure did. And the YouTube video already has over two thousand hits."

Nina shuddered. "How can you stand it? If it was me, I'd feel so . . . exposed."

"Aw, sweet girl, I'm a crazy one." She slapped her palms against the tabletop. "But how's your journaling going? Were you able to write down the reasons you're beautiful and amazing?"

"See, I can't even do that," Nina said.

"Tell me what happened."

"I'm teasing you. I wrote down a few reasons, but the hard part is believing them."

"I agree," I said. "I found myself writing things I knew I was supposed to write."

"But you wrote them down." Shanty said. "Good for you, because now that you've done it, your subconscious can work on the idea. Keep writing things down, or just sit and think them with your eyes shut—*meditate on them*—and eventually your mind will begin to believe what your hand has been writing. I know it's weird, but it works."

A group of teenagers near us erupted in laughter. A girl was sitting in a boy's lap, running her fingers through his hair dramatically while their friends hooted. She kissed his cheek and the others cheered.

Shanty glared at them with her hand on her hip even though none of them were paying attention. "Anyhoo." She turned back toward us. "Tonight, I want you to compliment yourself." She folded her hands and gave us a tight smile. "Right now. Out loud. Just for me." She looked back and forth between the two of us and must have decided I was the least appalled. "You first, Cecily."

"Compliment myself?"

She nodded.

"Um . . . I . . . have good hair?" My fingers instinctively pulled at the long side.

"Excellent! See? That wasn't so hard. How about you, Nina?"

Nina leaned on one elbow. "I have good hair too."

I thought she'd cheated a little, but Shanty beamed at her. "You sure do, hon! You both have beautiful hair." She squeezed our hands, and her palms were soft and warm. "How does that make you feel?"

Since I had gone first with the compliment, I felt it was only fair for Nina to go first with the analysis, but she only sipped her coffee and lifted her eyebrows in a my-lips-are-zipped sort of way.

"Actually, my hair is one of the things I wrote down in my journal," I admitted.

"That's all right." Shanty nodded, but Nina snapped at her.

"But neither one of us believe what we've written."

Shanty smiled faintly and focused on me. "Cecily, why do you think you don't believe you're beautiful?"

I didn't even have to think about my answer. "Because of Brett. His words and actions told me otherwise so many times over the years, and since he was the only one who truly mattered, it sunk in deep. Even now, when I hear his voice, it makes me feel bad about myself. And when I feel bad about myself, that voice inside my head tells me I'm unattractive."

Shanty rolled her eyes. "You're not still listening to that phone message, are you?" She snatched my cell from the tabletop where it rested near my elbow. "Girl! We're deleting that stinking thing right here and now. You don't need any more of Brett Ross's discouragement in your life."

"But he didn't even say anything. Not like that."

"It doesn't matter," Nina said. "You're still allowing him to hurt you whether he means to or not."

"There." Shanty set the phone in the middle of the table, and we all peered down at it for a few moments like three cranky school teachers disciplining a wayward child.

"It works better if you turn it on." Mirinda stood next to our table, tilting to one side, mocking us.

For a few long seconds, none of us said anything, even Shanty. And right then I knew that Shanty and Nina had my back. We may have only known each other a few weeks, but they weren't about to let Brett's little sister rankle me the way Brett had.

Shanty's shoulders shook with laughter. "Now that's ironic, Mirinda. We were just deleting your brother from Cecily's phone."

Maybe Shanty didn't have my back after all.

"You may be able to delete him from your phone"—Mirinda looked at me—"but you can't delete him from your life. No matter how many dates you have with your *therapist*." She gave Shanty and Nina a lazy grin before turning away.

When had she seen me with Graham? I wanted to crawl under the table. No, I wanted to strangle Mirinda, then crawl under the table. No, I wanted to tell Shanty and Nina that Mirinda was Madam X and had her own hidden insecurities, then strangle her, then crawl under the table.

"You're dating Dr. Harper?" Nina spoke first. "He could lose his license for that."

Shanty puckered her lips. "Clearly you've put some thought into the notion." When Nina's hand fluttered in indifference, Shanty studied me. "You okay?"

It seemed like a peculiar question, and I didn't know how to answer. "I'm not sure."

She nodded. "I know Graham well enough to know he's not breaking the law, but I don't know him well enough to know if he's up to something. Men are cockroaches."

"Oh, good grief," snapped Nina. "*Your Al* is not a cockroach. You're happily married."

Shanty's face grew quizzical, but right then the teenagers next to us stood as if on cue and banged and bumped their way past our table, finally leaving. Nina's gaze followed them out the door, and I wondered if she had been happy in high school. Somehow I doubted it.

"So how can you say that?" Nina's question came out in a whine, but she was clearly sincere. "Not all men are bad, are they?"

"Naw, they're not all bad, and when I say they're cockroaches, I don't mean it in a bad way. They're just not always good for us. Or they could be, but we don't always let them. We expect them to be something they're not, or something they can never be, or something they're not willing to be. If we just accept them for who they are, then we'll be all right. Besides, without cockroaches, the world's ecosystem would be overrun with problems."

"I have no idea what you're talking about," I said. "Are they cockroaches, or not?"

"Okay, just forget the cockroach comment." Shanty stared at the corner of the ceiling, thinking. "It's all about how we look at them, right? And what I'm afraid you girls are doing is making them out to be your savior, as if men can make you feel pretty, make you feel good about yourselves, make you live happily ever after. But that's not realistic. If that's what you're about, then it would do you well to think less of them. Maybe not rank them as low as cockroaches, but at least take them off the pedestal . . . if that's where you placed them."

"I had Brett on a pedestal," I admitted, "but now I readily agree that he's a cockroach."

"What about Graham?" Nina countered. "Is he a cockroach?"

I bit my lip. "I don't think so? I hope not. But I'd be wise to proceed with caution." I squinted at Shanty. "That's what you're telling us, isn't it?"

"I think you're hearing me now."

Nina's head moved back and forth in slow motion. "I'm not sure I need a man right now. Dr. Harper suggested a book called *Boundaries in Dating*, and it's made me look at things differently." She giggled. "The other day I was reading it on my Kindle, and I almost bumped into a bulletin board in the JBK. But anyway, I don't think I can be with a man right now without putting him on a pedestal where he doesn't belong.

I think I need to get healthier first." She laughed softly and looked over her shoulder toward the bar where Michael usually worked.

Mirinda was there instead, watching us.

"Maybe we shouldn't meet here for a while," Shanty said. "For several reasons. I'll be in touch when I work something out." She took a long swig of coffee, finishing her drink. "But of course I have homework for you between now and then."

"I get enough homework at school," Nina teased.

"But this is an easy assignment."

"That's what you always say," I argued. "Easy smeasy."

Shanty's long fingernail swept back and forth in front of our noses. "Do something that makes you happy."

We just looked at her.

"You mean—"

"Anything. Just do something that makes you happy."

"Happy," Nina said.

"Mmhmm. You remember *happy*? That good feeling you get?"

Nina smiled as she stood. "*Used* to get."

I followed them to the door, tossing my trash on the way, but then I stopped. *Do something that makes you happy.* Maybe I would do just that. Right here. Right now. And then my homework would be done for the week.

"You know what?" I held the door open for them to walk through. "I've got to make a pit stop before I leave. That coffee went straight through."

Shanty and Nina said their goodbyes and went to their cars. I turned around and peered into the back corner of the shop, but not toward the restrooms. I steeled myself, gathering up the confidence it would take. And finally, I headed in that direction.

Chapter
Thirty-One

The piano in the back of Midnight Oil was an old upright with no bench, and when I dragged a chair up to it and sat down, it didn't feel right. The seat was too low, and my forearms and elbows made an uncomfortable angle when I rested my fingertips on the keys, but somehow the awkwardness seemed appropriate.

My thumb pressed middle C, and a smoky tone filled the room— the hollow, reverberating sound that could only be made by an old instrument crafted long ago. It mimicked the sound of the first full-sized piano I'd played on, a spinet, back when I took lessons from Mrs. Stewart in the choir's practice room at the Episcopal church. Quietly, I played a simple treble chord, then added the left hand and played a rapid scale before resting my hands in my lap.

Did I really want to do this?

Only a handful of coffee drinkers remained in the shop, so it wasn't as if I had an intimidating audience, and the ones that did remain continued their chatting, paying little attention to me and my echoing notes. As it should be. There was a time for music to be front and center, and there was a time for it to be background noise, subtly adding to the atmosphere, and guiding people's moods on an almost subconscious level.

Someone muted the television—Mirinda maybe—and with the TV stilled, the voices in the room amplified more clearly, and I could hear snippets of conversations, even from the far corner. And if I could hear them, if I felt vulnerable and exposed from the decrease in volume, then I knew others did too. They needed the background noise. They needed the music.

I began with Johann Pachelbel. His "Canon in D" would be familiar enough among the general population, and its well-known melody would ease tense muscles and pacify day-long worries. The woman at the side booth would be reminded either of her best friend's wedding or her own. The two teenagers at the bar would wonder where they had heard it and finally decide it was on a commercial. Someone in the room would replay a movie scene in their head, probably a love story.

When I finished, stilted applause stumbled across the room, and the teenagers whooped, but I didn't pause. It wasn't about me, it was about my gift to them, so I went right into Yiruma's "River Flows in You." His simple, repetitive, magical melody coursed down my arms and through my hands to the keyboard where it floated up and out and around the room.

Next came Beethoven, then Tchaikovsky, then Mom's favorite, Floyd Cramer, followed by Dad's, Scott Joplin. And somewhere in there, I decided Shanty was a lot smarter than I gave her credit for. She had told me to do something that makes me happy, and even though it sounded shallow and oversimplified and *corny* . . . it worked. Playing the piano had almost always made me happy, and it was something I needed to be doing.

If I wanted to stop wallowing.

"I've heard that last song before. What's it called?" Mirinda leaned on the side of the tall piano, letting her arm fall lazily along its top, and behind her, a green broom rested against the bathroom door. Her eyes seemed to be daring me to speak.

My back was to the shop, and I glanced over my shoulder, surprised to see it deserted other than the two of us. Even the chairs were turned over and resting on tabletops. I scratched my chin. "The Entertainer."

She nodded. "You played that song at a talent show years ago. I was ten or eleven. I thought you were übertalented." She rolled her eyes, and then shook her head, like a nonverbal *yeah, whatever.* "Anyway, I'm closing up the shop now."

"Sorry. I wasn't paying attention."

Her hips shifted from side to side, and she seemed to still them by shoving her fist against her waist. "What's that group you meet with here? Shanty and that other girl?" Her mouth wrinkled into that unattractive smirk she seemed to save just for me.

"Just a support group."

"Like, for divorce, or what? Cause Shanty's not divorced, and that other girl looks too young."

"Nothing like that. It's just for self—" Oh, great. I was breaking the first rule of the group: that blasted confidentiality. "It's sort of personal, you know?" And besides, if she had a problem with low self-esteem, Graham would have recommended she join us. *Maybe.*

The tight lips returned, but this time she added the chest thrust. "Of course."

I didn't care if she got snippy. I wasn't going to reveal anything about Shanty and Nina without getting their approval first, and odds were they wouldn't give it. Not for Mirinda. Not for a Barbie doll.

She reached for her broom, but just then, the front door opened. She glanced past me and flinched, and the broom handle slid down the wall and clattered against the floor. She bent and reached for it but missed. Finally, she grabbed it with unnecessary force. When she stood, her face was flushed, either from bending over or from embarrassment, and her gaze flitted from the piano to the front door to the kitchen, then back to the broom handle that was now firmly anchored in her hand.

I smiled a little, though I knew I shouldn't relish anyone else's discomfort, but it was a tremendous comfort to know even a woman as confident as Mirinda could get flustered under the right circumstances. Now her role as supershy Madam X was beginning to make sense. The only thing left to wonder was who on earth could put her into such a state. I glanced over my shoulder at the man standing just inside the door, and I felt as though my heart had fallen to the floor along with the green broom. It was Graham.

Chapter Thirty-Two

He stood there, frozen, with his hand resting on the handle of the door, and I thought he might turn and bolt back to the parking lot. Mirinda swept her way to the counter, calling with forced nonchalance, "We're closing, Dr. Harper, and I've already cleaned the machines."

"No worries." He bounced on his heels. "I just came by to see . . . Cecily." His palm swiped his lips, and I was beginning to think that simple movement was a tell—a neon sign flashing an alert every time the good doctor told a fib. "I noticed your car outside." He stood in front of me now, cocking his head toward the parking lot.

"Did you?"

He studied me and glanced at Mirinda, who was wiping the counter with her back to us. Then he smiled as though he had been caught with his hand in the bank bag at a garage sale. "Can we talk? Outside?"

I wasn't sure I wanted to talk to him. Earlier, I had wanted to. I had thought I might die if I didn't see him soon, but now? With Mirinda all flustered and dropping the broom? No, not really.

I walked to the door without looking back at either of them.

Graham bumped into a chair that was perched on the top of a table by the door. It banged as he grabbed it to prevent it from falling to the floor.

Then we stood on the sidewalk with our backs to the door of Midnight Oil, staring at the old courthouse across the street. I wanted to accuse him of something, but I didn't know what. There was no code of ethics against therapists buying lattes from their clients.

"Did you come here for coffee?" There was a punch to my voice, but I didn't care. "Or did you honestly just happen to be driving by"—I turned from side to side, searching the shops on the square—"even though most everything has closed for the night?"

His shoulders slumped. "Okay, no. I didn't just happen to be here. I was checking on Mirinda."

"Checking on her."

"She's a little rickety right now. Got a lot going on in her life. And in her mind." He gestured down the sidewalk. "Let's walk."

I heard the key turn in the lock behind us, then the street fell into darkness as Mirinda flipped a switch inside. I fought the urge to turn and look at her.

Graham didn't.

Brett had taught me how difficult it was for men to keep from staring at women like Mirinda. Especially when they all but begged for the attention. Graham wasn't like Brett—at least I didn't think so—but he was still a man.

We walked down the cracked sidewalk, passing a string of small shops. One appeared to be a consignment boutique, and the market-savvy shop owner had left a single light shining inside, illuminating the makeshift window dressings. I planted my feet and inspected a distressed farmhouse table, set with bright-colored Fiestaware and rustic iron accents.

"So." I spoke louder than necessary. "Do you always check on your clients at their workplaces?" A simple question with a complicated underlying meaning: *Are you infatuated with Mirinda, pushing the law, messing with my fragile heart? Are you tired of my plainness?*

He wasn't looking at the shop display. Instead, he faced me solidly. "Only the tough cases."

The tough cases. His words fell on my ears, inched into my brain, then seeped into understanding. I turned and continued walking. Graham didn't say anything else, just walked next to me, and I began to wonder about something. "Is that why you took me to the park for lunch that day?"

He stopped abruptly, his shoes gritting against the cement of the sidewalk.

"No," he said firmly. "I admit, some of my conversations are strategically planned, but not because you're a tough case. You're not."

"I'm not?"

He chuckled. "I just want to be with you because I like you."

"You like me?"

"I thought I made that pretty clear last night at the campsite."

My thoughts turned from logic to emotional mush. I glanced back. Fifty yards away, Michael Divins's Corvette pulled up in front of Midnight Oil. Mirinda loped out, but Graham didn't turn around this time.

I was so silly. So insecure.

We started walking again, past a chiropractic office and then an empty shop whose windows were covered with "For Lease" signs, but it wasn't until we'd walked all the way to the other side of the square, to the dark and silent windows of Soccer Mom's, that Graham slipped his hand into mine. And I was glad.

In fact, I squeezed it. Just like I had done all those years ago at the prom. Just like at the carnival. He had squeezed back both of those times too, firmly but not hard enough to hurt.

"Graham?"

"Hmm?"

"Do remember that time in high school—"

"Of course."

I stopped again. "You don't even know what I was going to say."

"Sure, I do." He lifted my hand to his lips and kissed my knuckles. "The time we held hands in your car. It was after senior prom. Or during, really. You were having a hard time."

That was an understatement. It was the anniversary of Mom's death, and I had let Brett talk me into going to the prom anyway. "It'll do you good," he had said. But it hadn't. It had only reminded me how much I missed her. I ended up feeling as though I had betrayed her memory—or worse. It felt as though I had smeared dirt on it. Brett had been crowned prom king, and someone else—maybe Zoe Gomez—had been crowned queen.

"Nobody ever thought Brett and I were right for each other," I mumbled.

"Do you think you were?"

"At the time I thought so." I snickered, a hard, bitter sound. "But I was a fool."

"That's harsh."

I gave his hand a tug toward the courthouse lawn, lit by the glow of old-fashioned streetlamps. "Okay, so maybe I wasn't a fool."

"You were in mourning that night at the prom. You were grieving the fact that your mother had missed your entire high school career, and you were still in mourning when you left for college. Maybe even when you married Brett."

"But it had been *years* since she died."

"Grief takes time, Cecily."

"Well, why didn't somebody stop me from going away to college with Brett? Why didn't my dad?"

"He was in worse shape than you." I could hear a smile in his next words. "And I was just a kid with a crush. I wanted to talk you out of leaving, but I thought my reasons were selfish. They *were* selfish. I didn't know enough about anything back then."

"I always thought you were high that night."

"Understandable mistake." He sounded sad. "But I wasn't. I was right there with you, one hundred percent." He led me to a bench, and I snuggled against his side as he put his arm around me.

It felt good. And right. And real.

His fingertips brushed my wrist, up my arm, to my neck, and he nudged my chin until I was looking into his eyes, which were shadowed because he was lit from behind. When we kissed, it wasn't anything like it had been the night before. It was gentle. Purposeful. As though we were trying to undo the regrets in our past and to prove to ourselves that we were who we wanted to be now.

I let my lips part, inviting him to kiss me more intimately, and when he responded, I felt myself getting lost in his touch. He leaned over me, blocking the light, blocking the sounds in the distance, blocking the entire world. And I was safe, sheltered, and *desirable*.

He pulled away, settling against the back of the bench, calming himself. Then he reached up, and with his fingertip, he tucked the long side of my hair behind my ear. "I'm falling for you, Cecily Witherspoon." He used my maiden name, maybe accidentally and maybe because he didn't want to remember that I had ever been Brett's wife. "I'm falling hard."

His voice was gruff, and I became ever so aware that Graham wasn't a teenager anymore. He wasn't a drug user. He wasn't fumbling for my hand in the parking lot outside the prom, wishing he had been my date. He was *here*. He was *now*. And I was falling for him too.

Chapter
Thirty-Three

*Write about a mistake you made and how it impacted your life in a posi-
tive way.*

For crying out loud. Where did Shanty come up with this stuff? The
question seemed to be directed straight at me. But no, that was silly.
Everyone makes mistakes that turn out for the better.

I sat cross-legged on the hood of my Jeep, which was still undrivable
and was parked in the garage. Dad said he'd fix it as soon as possible,
but I didn't see a need to rush. It was only a car. I smiled. It was only a
car, but it was also the place Graham and I had kissed for the first time.

I gripped my pen tightly and continued to write in my notebook.

*Well, there's no doubt about the mistake I made. My problem is
seeing how it's affected my life in a positive way. That's probably Shanty's goal for this entire journal entry. For me to see
it as a positive instead of a negative. Not sure I'll ever be able
to do that. Maybe I will . . . I don't know. For now, I think I'll
stick with trying not to view it as a horrible thing.*

I've been dwelling on my past mistakes for way too long. No, not just dwelling on them, I've been nurturing them until they're about to take over my life. Okay, let's get real. They DID take over my life, but that was the old me. Now I'm thinking differently.
But ... ugh. Why do I still feel crazy?

I slid off of the hood and climbed into the driver's seat, where I punched the radio on, glad that my dad had charged the battery. I tuned the dial to a classical station and was immediately rewarded with Rachmaninoff's second piano concerto.

Shanty would probably tell me I'm defining myself by Brett's actions (duh) and that I'm subconsciously keeping myself locked in bitterness. She must be right because when I stop to think about it, I can actually feel the prison bars. I'm beginning to wonder if that's due to the lack of forgiveness that everyone keeps telling me I need to work on.

The sound of the pen against the paper had become scratchy, the handwriting pointed and sharp. I traced over the word *forgiveness*, then traced it again and again until it darkened so much it was almost unrecognizable.

I firmly believe Brett doesn't deserve forgiveness, but he's not the only one it affects. Graham said I would feel better if I forgave him. Am I driving myself insane because I can't forgive my ex-husband? Am I holding myself hostage to these negative feelings?

I rested the notebook against the steering wheel and stared at the closed garage door until I worked up the nerve to write my next thought.

Is it my own voice I hear when I look in the mirror?

I paused with the pen suspended above the paper, trying to decide if I should scribble out the question. But of course it was my own voice. Who else would it be? Sometimes I told myself I was remembering things Brett had said to me. Sometimes I told myself it was a demon. Sometimes I simply blamed it on my low self-esteem. But that was a crutch.

Maybe I need to forgive myself as much as I need to forgive Brett. Is it even possible for a person to forgive herself? Maybe not so much forgive myself as get over myself. Give myself a break for not being what Brett wanted, or what I wanted, or whatever I think society wants. If I really tried . . . I could stop caring about all that.
I could be me. And I could like me.
I really could.
At least . . . I THINK I COULD.

My cell phone shrilled loudly, causing me to jump, and I scrambled for it in the passenger seat. I was surprised to see it was Shanty. When I answered, she didn't even give me time to say *hello*.

"Cecily, I need you and Nina."

"Okay . . ." Shanty never called me, just texted. "Should we meet at Midnight Oil? I can be there in thirty minutes or so."

"No. Not there." Her voice sounded funny. *Flat.*

Slowly, I shut my notebook. "We can come to your place then. I'll call Nina."

"That would be good."

"Is . . . everything all right?"

"No."

I wanted her to tell me more, but for once, she wasn't talking. "Are you sick? Are the kids all right? Did something happen?"

There was silence on the other end of the line, then Shanty's clipped answer. "It's Al."

Those two words sent a ripple of apprehension through me. She could have meant any number of things, but my mind automatically rested on the worst. I closed my eyes and asked one more question. "Is Al . . . sick or something?"

"No." Her simple answer was slow in coming, and filled with an implied explanation. "Al's not anything."

Chapter
Thirty-Four

Shanty was almost unrecognizable. I had never seen her look so small—in a way that had nothing to do with her weight. She had turned inside herself, folding her spirit into a tiny ball of despair, her trademark smile completely wiped from her face. The beaded braids that normally bounced around her shoulders now lay on the floor near the end of the couch. Apparently she had cut the extensions from her natural hair, which stuck out in tufts around her head.

She wasn't crying.

Nina and I sat on either side of her on a brown sectional sofa, the kind with an oversized ottoman at the end that created a cushioned lounge as big as a full-size bed. Two baby dolls had been put to sleep there, neatly covered with a crocheted blanket and then forgotten.

Shanty stared through the picture window overlooking the backyard. Her kids were out there, two of them climbing on the fort and another one sitting in the sandbox, slowly pouring sand from a plastic Solo cup onto her own shoulders. But the oldest child, a boy, sat cross-legged in the middle of the yard, elbows resting on his knees, head bent. He should have been in school.

"Gage saw him do it." Shanty's voice was sharp, unforgiving. "He saw his daddy kiss that girl. Right here in the living room." She sobbed once, then stifled it. "I never should've hired a babysitter in the first place. I never should have allowed another woman into my home. No, not a *woman*. She's a *child*. Barely eighteen." She stood and stomped to the kitchen.

I stared after her, stunned.

Nina picked up a sippy cup from the floor, set it on the coffee table, then peered around the disheveled room. She slid to her knees and started picking up wooden puzzle pieces and Legos.

That was smart. Helpful. If we straightened Shanty's house, maybe her mind would be less cluttered as well. She would have room to organize her thoughts and make sense of her situation. Maybe. It would help at least.

But we couldn't both clean house and avoid our friend. I stood.

When I entered the kitchen, Shanty instinctively turned away from me.

"I already saw the Snickers wrappers on the coffee table," I said. "Too late to hide it."

She took a bite and talked around the chocolate. "I've moved on to Twix now."

"Whatever works."

"My Weight Watchers mentor wouldn't think so."

"Your Weight Watchers mentor didn't just find out her husband's cheating on her."

"He's not cheating. It was just a kiss." She frowned defensively, but then her face lost all expression.

A kiss. An affair. It was all the same to me, but I didn't say so. Probably I had said too much already. Just because Brett had had multiple affairs didn't mean Al was doing the same thing. "Sorry, Shanty. My bitterness is showing."

"How did you ever survive this, Cecily? The pain I'm feeling is worse than anything I've ever felt in my life."

I reached for a candy bar. "I know."

We ate in silence for a few minutes, then Shanty pulled two glasses out of the cabinet. "Milk?"

"Do you have chocolate syrup?"

"Smart thinking. Go for the hard stuff." She opened the refrigerator and then cursed, which was uncharacteristic. "I've only got strawberry."

Nina called from the living room, "Umm . . . Shanty? What do you do with these soiled diapers?"

Shanty ran her palm across her face. "Diaper Genie's in the first bedroom on the right. Want some strawberry milk, Nina?"

"In a minute."

"Bless her," Shanty mumbled as she pulled another glass from the cabinet.

"Where is he now?" I asked.

"At work." She squinted. "I wonder if that girl uses his pharmacy. Do you think he's kissed her there too?"

I couldn't fathom Al kissing any woman except Shanty, let alone a teenage girl. My mind whirled back to the first day I'd met him, when I was buying bandages. He had told me how beautiful and wonderful Shanty was. "I don't think he's like that."

"I don't know what he's like any more. Or if I ever knew him at all."

"How did you find out?"

Shanty was pouring milk, and she sloshed it on the counter when I asked the question. "Gage told me. Said it happened last night when I was at a writers' event. The babysitter had put the kids to sleep an hour before, but Gage stayed awake, reading *Hank the Cowdog* under his sheets with a flashlight. When he heard his daddy come home, he wanted to tell him goodnight." She laughed and it sounded acidic. "He didn't want the girl to get mad at him for getting up, so he waited long enough for her to be gone." She froze, the strawberry syrup in one hand.

"Does Al know Gage saw?"

"No."

I was trying to piece together the bits and pieces she was giving me, but it wasn't adding up. "Then how does he think you found out?"

"He doesn't know yet."

My insides tightened. "He's at work, and he doesn't know you know?"

"And he doesn't know Gage knows. He doesn't know his son is devastated. He doesn't know his wife is shattered. He doesn't know any of it, and for all I know, he doesn't care." She shuddered. "This morning he kissed me goodbye, just like he always does. Like nothing had happened."

A dull ache settled in my stomach. "When did Gage tell you?"

"After Al left for work." She looked out the back window at Gage, who was now slumped in a swing, one foot on the ground, slowly swiveling back and forth. "Gage is a timid one, always worried about being good. But it's funny because he always *is*—good, I mean—but he's sensitive." She wiped a tear from her cheek. "This isn't good for him."

"It's not good for any of you."

The ache in my stomach swelled, and I crossed my arms over my waist. If Al Espinosa could cheat on a wife he adored, then my shaky perception of men in general was seriously in danger of toppling. But maybe Shanty was right. Maybe he had only *kissed* the babysitter. Maybe it had only been a slip. I wanted desperately for Al to be innocent, but the ache didn't ease.

Nina came into the kitchen just as Shanty finished swirling a spoon in each glass, and the three of us somberly held our glasses at waist height.

Nina raised hers. "To the possibility that there are good men left in the world."

I lifted my glass and so did Shanty.

"Cheers," I whispered.

After that we sat on the kitchen floor, leaning against the cabinets, drinking our milk while Shanty told us about their marriage problems—though she had never thought of them as problems until now. She supposed they were too busy with the children, and she was too busy with her blog, and Al was always at the pharmacy. Both of them tended to be workaholics.

"I hate that about myself," she said. "My dad worked too much, and I never felt like he had time for me." She bumped her head against the cabinet door. "Surely Al doesn't feel that way. Surely he knows I love him even though I'm busy. Surely I haven't done to him what my dad did to me."

The sliding glass door opened on the other side of the bar, and the house filled with the sounds of preschoolers crying. Gage came around the corner, carrying one sister and dragging the other while his brother toddled behind them, a dismal parade. When Gage saw us on the kitchen floor, his eyes widened, but he delivered his news without pausing. "They're fighting again, Mama."

Shanty's children were incredibly beautiful, even screaming, even with their eyes wide in fear and uncertainty. Their creamy caramel skin and black hair were the perfect blend of Shanty's African and Asian roots and Al's Hispanic heritage. As I admired them, I imagined them spending every other weekend with Al and two weeks in the summer.

Shanty waved them toward her. "Bring 'em over here, Gage." She took the younger one out of his arms and handed Gage her milk. "You and Aaron finish this for me, hon, and help yourself to a candy bar."

"For real? Even before lunch?"

"Today's not a normal day, baby."

The girls settled as Shanty bounced one on each knee, comforting them with kisses and low humming sounds. "You two better stop your fighting. That won't solve anything, now, will it?" She frowned at her own words as the preschoolers scrambled off her lap and scurried after their brothers, no doubt wanting their share of candy.

The three of us stood as well.

"What do I do?" Shanty asked.

"Talk to him," I said. "Find out what's going on. Don't kill him."

"It's probably just an innocent kiss." Shanty bit her lip.

"There's no such thing," Nina said, and her boldness surprised me.

Shanty handed each of us a Twix bar, and we took them obligingly, then followed her to the large doorway leading into the living room, now straightened. "Nina, thanks for doing that."

"It's the least I could do."

Shanty seemed paralyzed in the doorway, staring at the living room as though it were an intricate problem that needed solving.

A metallic screech alerted us that the exterior glass door had been opened, and when we heard a key slide into the lock, Shanty gripped her candy bar in a fist. "That'll be Al coming home for lunch."

Nina gasped.

My stomach tied itself into a pretzel.

And the door opened.

At first Al's face was all grins when he saw us, but when he registered that we weren't smiling back, his expression blanked. Without the smile on his face, without the love in his eyes, he didn't look like the same person. "Hey, Nina." He ducked his head. "Cecily. What are you guys doing here?" He peered at Shanty. "Everything all right?"

I prayed everything would be all right. I silently begged God in heaven to make things right. To make Al a good man after all. If only just to prove that every marriage didn't end in adultery.

Shanty's right foot stepped forward, but then she seemed frozen again, unable to move another inch closer to her husband. "Gage saw you kissing Lauren last night."

Al's face paled instantly.

"That's all it was, right?" Shanty's voice fell so that she could barely be heard over the children clamoring down the hall. "It was just a kiss, right, Al?"

His gaze bounced immediately to the sectional sofa where the dolls had been, then he looked at the floor, seemingly unable to meet Shanty's eyes.

But he didn't have to. All three of us knew the truth.

Whatever happened with the babysitter . . . it had been a lot more than a kiss.

Suddenly all the emotional growth I had accomplished since I'd been back in Canyon seemed to hinge on the good men in my life—men like Daddy . . . Graham . . . Al—who had shown me that not every male of the species was like Brett. The ache in my stomach finally made sense when I realized I wasn't merely hurting for Shanty. I was hurting for myself. For the possibility that men weren't what I had decided they were after all.

But Daddy was good.

Graham was good.

Al had to be good too. This kissing the babysitter thing probably just caught him by surprise. Surely he never meant for it to happen.

Chapter Thirty-Five

WEEKEND SALE!
The Sexy Shortie 2/$40—Your new must-have!

The man told himself the same thing over and over: *I didn't mean for this to happen.* He repeated that truth in his mind, trying to believe it, reminding himself that he wasn't evil. Sure, he had fallen mindlessly into a trap, but he was conquering the demon.

He walked through the Westgate Mall, searching for just the right gift for her, to make up for everything. The way their relationship had been going lately, he would need something perfect. Because he was ready, finally, to tell her the truth. She deserved an explanation, now more than ever.

About what he did, what he looked at, the way he spent his time when he was alone. As he passed Victoria's Secret, a ten-foot poster caught his eye—a curvy woman in lace shorts. He forced his eyes away, focusing his gaze on the Dillard's sign far down the corridor. He didn't need to look at the poster to feel good about himself. He knew that now.

"Something special for the woman in your life?"

An auburn-haired woman held up a bottle of perfume as she took two steps away from her kiosk, following him as though hungry for a potential sale.

He paused, wondering if perfume might be just the thing he needed to smooth things over.

"Smell?" She held the bottle toward him and tilted her head to the side. "Don't I know you?"

The woman—a girl really—was small and fragile looking, and her hair fell in waves, almost to her waist. She smiled at him and swept the locks over one shoulder, lifting her chin and baring her neck as though to display all she had to offer. She looked to be a college student. Young.

He didn't smile back, just gazed above her head and stepped away. "Not what I'm looking for, thanks."

She protested, but he didn't look back.

Women were all the same, he thought, flaunting their bodies in some sort of primitive, animalistic instinct to mate, to catch the attention of the male of the species, to procreate. He was attracted to them and repulsed at the same time. He slowed, then stopped, staring at a six-foot potted plant.

No.

No, that was wrong thinking. Women were not all the same, any more than men were all the same. They were no more animalistic than men, though men had a much worse reputation for that sort of behavior. Like him with his pursuit of picture after picture, video after video. But he had installed blockers on his phone and protection on his laptop, he had joined an accountability group, he was looking the other way when he saw things. And he saw them *everywhere*. Sometimes he felt like he was going insane, knowing he needed to squelch his thoughts but unable to escape from the problem. There was no rest.

The preacher said it was Satan, and if that was the truth, then Satan was very, very good at what he was doing. Maybe it was Satan and maybe not. He hadn't yet decided about God, but church seemed a safer place than most.

He turned in a slow circle, looking at the stores within sight. Gap, Verizon, Disney, Dillard's, and in the next open space, the food court. Everywhere he looked there were images that triggered him. Why was he even here? If he was serious about changing his habits, he should protect himself from this sort of place. But for crying out loud, it was a *mall*. Just a mall.

Maybe he would give her roses. Or daisies. Love or happiness? He should give her both.

But how would she react? He had thought the truth would send her into a nervous breakdown, but the other guys said he needed to tell her anyway. Relationships are built on truth, transparency, trust. The three Ts. He shook his head. The three Ts seemed unattainable, but he was determined to tell her the truth, and when he did, an enormous burden would be lifted from his shoulders . . . and Satan—or whatever it was that gripped him so tightly—would lose a little power over him.

Chapter Thirty-Six

Graham's list of things to do on Saturday (as entered into the Notes app on his phone):

1. *Borrow bike for Cecily.*
2. *Look through high school yearbook.*
3. *Check on Shanty? No, better wait on that.*
4. *Make Cecily smile.*

As usual, Graham felt minuscule standing next to the grandeur of the canyon, and with Cecily by his side, he felt even smaller. He wondered if she felt the same way.

"Who'd you borrow this bike from?" She straddled the seat with her feet on the ground, tightening the strap on a bright red helmet.

"It's my mom's," Graham said.

"Your mom is a biker dude?"

He chuckled. "Not anymore, but she used to ride with me some. She hurt her knee in a fender bender, though, so she can't do as much now."

"And your dad?" She asked.

"He's more of a video game guy. The two of us have had some late-night Halo wars."

"Halo?"

"Guns, aliens, dual controllers on the Xbox."

"Ah." She gripped the handlebars. "I haven't ridden much in . . . well, ever. Can you take it easy on me?"

"I'll try to hold back."

"No edge-of-the-cliff curves? No sudden drop-offs?" she asked.

"And absolutely no airborne jumps. None of the fun stuff. We'll keep all wheels on the ground."

They had decided to take an afternoon bike ride after Cecily admitted how nervous she was about seeing Brett again. Graham had offered to keep her distracted for a few hours, but she made him promise to have her home with plenty of time to shower for the reunion that night.

"I'll lead on the trail," he said, "but if you need me to stop, just holler."

"Okay, I'll be sure and *holler*." She put one foot on a pedal. "I like the way you talk."

Her giggle made him smile as he shoved off with one foot. "Follow close."

He led her down a curving trail at medium speed. He didn't want to go off and leave her, but he also didn't want to go so slowly that she ran up on him. He could hear her tires grinding against the sand behind him, but when he glanced over his shoulder, she seemed to be doing all right.

She had talked to him after work yesterday, telling him just enough about Shanty's drama for him to know there was a lot she wasn't telling him. But that seemed right. It was Shanty's to tell, when she was ready. But Cecily had clearly been shaken. Whatever was happening with the Espinosas had rattled Cecily's confidence, and unless it was his imagination, she seemed to have withdrawn a little from him as well.

He called back to her. "You doing all right?"

"Never better." There was a tremor in her voice from the rough terrain, and she sounded winded already, so Graham eased to a stop.

"Ready for a drink of water?"

"Are you kidding? We just started."

He uncapped his water bottle. "I don't want to push you too hard."

She grinned and kept riding past him. "I'm good! But you rest as long as you need to."

Graham chuckled as she bumped down the trail, then his gaze settled on her backside. He snapped his water bottle back onto the frame of his bike and followed her, trying to keep his eyes on the path.

He hummed as a distraction. How could she possibly see herself as anything but gorgeous? Even if she hadn't been physically attractive—which she was—the woman was beautiful from the inside out. She was still a shadow of the girl he knew in high school, but he was beginning to get glimpses of the real Cecily, and those glimpses made him crazy.

They rode for thirty more minutes, taking turns leading, following the Paseo del Rio trail through the floor of the canyon and continuing on the Rojo Grande trail. They avoided the roughest spots, and when they finally stopped for water, they were both sweating.

"Now I see why you bike all the time," she said as she drank, and Graham watched a trickle of water leak from the corner of her mouth and slide down her throat.

"It's addictive," he said. "The view, the sun, the ups and downs of the terrain. The *speed*, and not knowing exactly what's over the next rise."

She laughed, and the sound was swallowed up by the canyon. "I'm not sure I've experienced the speed you're talking about."

"You'll get faster each time you come out here."

"What makes you think I'll come again?" Her smiled teased him.

"Like I said, riding the canyon is addictive."

"But I live on the canyon. I could ride at my place."

"Oh, I don't know." He frowned, a sudden urgency stealing across his chest. "Riding on unmarked trails isn't the same. I mean, sure, it's fun—a rush even—but your place is on the surface, and it might be easy to forget you're on the edge of a hundred-foot drop-off."

She squinted, nodded, shrugged. "You're right. It's safe here."

"*Safer,*" he said, not wanting to mention the hikers who had fallen.

Cecily grew silent, and Graham figured she was thinking about them anyway.

"I'd like to try rappelling sometime." He hoped to shift her thoughts.

"Sure." She was staring at the opposite wall of the canyon, a jagged decline, spotted with boulders and cedars that made a mottled design as the ground gradually fell away from itself, cascading downward in a brown, green, and red waterfall to the canyon floor. But Cecily wasn't looking at that part. Instead, she was focused on a short but sheer drop-off to their right. Her gaze seemed foggy. "Do you think that guy did it on purpose?" she asked.

"Who?"

"The man who fell to his death years ago. Do you think it was suicide?"

Suddenly he felt as though he and Cecily were standing, figuratively, on their own cliff. "No . . . ," he said carefully. "Seems like the papers said they didn't have any reason to believe it was deliberate. They think he just got too close and lost his footing."

Her head turned from side to side as though she were looking for other areas in the canyon. "But haven't there been suicides out here?"

"You know? As long as I've lived here, I don't remember any." She was beginning to scare him.

"Yeah, I suppose there are easier ways to kill yourself. Where's my house from here? Can you see it?"

"Not from here, but you can see it from the far end of the park. Barely. It's just a little speck deep in the canyon." He welcomed the lighter topic, and he walked his bike forward until he was next to her. The light breeze was blowing her hair out of her eyes, and her face was flushed.

She smiled and glanced toward him. "You seem to know exactly where my house is."

Graham's face heated ten degrees in two seconds. "Wait a minute, now. I can also point out any number of other landmarks."

She squinted, but her eyes didn't leave his. "You don't have binoculars, do you?"

Graham guffawed in surprise. "Of course not." His laughter settled into a chuckle. "But now that you mention it, that might not be a bad idea."

"So if we went to the far end of the park, could I see Dad if he was standing on the deck?"

"Only if he was wearing something bright. A red shirt or something."

"Not that you would know, though."

"No, not that I would know." His words came out in a near whisper.

Their bikes were side by side, and Cecily hooked her index finger on the collar of his shirt and tugged until he bent down, his face just in front of hers. "How long have you been watching my house from miles away across a huge gorge in the earth?"

He looked from one of her eyes to the other, then to her lips, ringed with tiny beads of sweat, then he glanced toward the far side of the canyon and shrugged. "It seemed like a safe distance." When he turned back to smile at her, Cecily's mouth covered his, and Graham swayed on his bike. She still had hold of his shirt, and she clenched it in her fist, wadding the fabric and pressing it against his chest. With her other hand, she gripped the back of his neck, but Graham left his hands on his handlebars, living out a dream he had imagined every time he'd taken a bike ride since Cecily had come back to town.

When she pulled away, they both exhaled.

"Can we go a little faster now?" She nodded toward the trail.

Her question held a double meaning to Graham, but he wasn't sure she intended it that way.

"You're quite the daredevil," he said.

"This makes me feel alive, you know?" She walked her bike forward three feet. "Makes me realize how *bored* I've been."

"Okay, then follow me. There's a soft little bump up here that I think you can handle, but when you get to the big rock, go to the right, not the left."

"What's to the left?"

"A bigger bump."

"Gotcha."

Graham steered his bike back onto the trail, and Cecily followed close behind. He increased his speed, just enough to give her a thrill but not enough to leave her behind. The rise in the trail was minimal, but just beyond it the ground gave way unexpectedly. It only scooped down a few feet, but that was enough to leave a new rider's stomach in the air. Graham passed over it easily, and Cecily followed. She cackled, a high-pitched and gleeful sound, and when he approached the big rock, he sped up and veered to the right.

The drop was more abrupt here, with a curve in the middle, and he whooped as his bike tires gripped the trail and pulled him past. He came to a stop on the rise just beyond, and turned to watch Cecily come around the rock.

But she never came.

Instead, he heard metal against stone and the sickening thump of a soft body slamming into the boulder. In one swift movement, Graham was off his bike and running.

Chapter Thirty-Seven

Group text from Nina: *might get a tat maybe even a sleeve :)*
Shanty: *Seriously? That would be cool. As long as it's you being you.*
Nina: *huh?*
Shanty: *I mean don't do it just cause Cecily has ink.*
Nina: *im not!!*
Nina (forty-seven minutes later): *ok maybe/maybe not. cecily did it hurt real bad?*

"Cecily, I'm so sorry."

I was seeing a side of Graham I hadn't seen before. Nervous and panicky.

"I shouldn't have brought you on this trail," he said.

"I shouldn't have steered straight into a boulder."

"It was a rough stretch. Probably your front tire hit a rock."

I sat flat on my bottom in the dirt with Graham's mother's bike curled around me, and I gingerly touched the lump that was rising on the side of my head. "Now you're just making excuses." I inspected my arms, flexing them to make sure they still worked properly, but other than two bad scrapes on my left elbow, they seemed all right. Graham hesitantly laid his hands across my shoulders, pressing gently as he searched for hurt spots.

"Anything tender?"

I leaned my head from side to side. "It feels like an elephant sat on me."

"Well, that's appropriate."

He slid his hands down to my sides. "Ribs all right?"

"That tickles." I clasped his hands against my sides with my elbows. A reflex.

"Good sign." He chuckled, but his laughter turned into a gasp. "Cecily, your *legs*."

For a split second, I didn't know what he meant. My legs weren't hurting any more than the rest of my body, but as I looked down, I saw that my knee-length shorts had inched up to expose my scarred thighs. A fresh scrape had broken the skin on one of the old cuts, and it was now oozing watery blood. "Oh . . ." I started to say something—anything—but there were no words.

Oh, it's nothing. Just self-inflicted wounds from an emotional meltdown I had three weeks ago. Nothing to worry about.

I tugged at the hem of my shorts, instinctively trying to pull them down to cover my shame.

"No." Graham's voice was gentle as he touched my wrists with his fingertips. "Roll them up so the fabric won't rub."

I wondered if he recognized the cuts for what they were. He was a counselor, after all. For crying out loud, he probably saw crazy women and their self-abusive behavior every day.

He stood, gripped the bike frame, and carefully lifted it away. After setting it to the side of the trail, he removed my water bottle and squatted next to me. "Here, take a drink." He watched as I obliged and then suggested I lean against the boulder for a few minutes. He gripped my right elbow and helped me scoot over. "Anything else hurt?"

I looked away from him, feeling exposed, on display, scrutinized. "Really, I'm fine."

"You need ice on that bump. I could go for help."

"You are not leaving me here." I frowned. "I'll be able to ride in a few minutes."

"Not on that bike."

"Then I can push it back to the car."

He settled onto the ground next to me, his weight on one hip with a knee bent. His gaze traveled from the knot on my head to my scraped elbows, and then to my thighs. He looked away.

My eyes pinched shut and I leaned my head against the rock. Graham wouldn't want me now that he could see what I was. Now that he knew what he was dealing with. My thumb traveled across a scar just below my rolled-up shorts, and even with my eyes closed, I could see how ugly my skin looked. Probably my face was blotchy from exertion too, and I could feel a film of dirt in the crease of my neck.

"What are you thinking?" he asked.

I didn't open my eyes, just told him the correct answer. "Happy thoughts."

"I'm serious, Cecily." He sounded stern.

I squinted one eye. "I don't want to tell you what I'm thinking."

His expression held a trace of hurt. "Is it all right if I tell you what *I'm* thinking?"

I shrugged.

"I'm thinking how amazing you are."

My head jerked to the left as though he had slapped me, and I had the overwhelming urge to hide myself. I shook my head twice before willing it to stop.

"Yes, Cecily." He moved closer to me. "You're a beautiful woman, inside and out, and those marks on your legs don't change that fact. If anything, they prove how strong your emotions are, and when you learn to manage them, you'll have a huge amount of love to share with others."

"What?" I was following along until that last part. "Love for myself, you mean." I spat the words out. "*Wallowing in self-pity* doesn't begin to describe these scars."

"You're not wallowing in self-pity. You're fighting a battle, and you're winning. You're passionate about life, about relationships, about your loved ones, but you're getting things set in their proper order." He looked me in the eye. "Those scars on your legs prove you *feel*, Cecily. Three weeks ago, you were feeling pain, but even this short time later, you've made tremendous headway in this battle, and now you're beginning to feel other emotions. You're allowing people—like your dad and me—to get close to you. You're trusting us with your problems, and you're channeling your passion outward instead of inward." He nodded. "You're making it, Cecily. You are."

"But why do I hurt myself?"

He squinted. "It's called cognitive distortion." When I frowned, he explained. "We're made in such a way that our emotions are a direct response to our thoughts, but sometimes our thoughts get a little screwed up. Our minds conjure up lies, but we view them as fact, and since our emotions are a response to our thoughts . . . our emotions go berserk."

"And when my emotions go berserk, that triggers more negative thoughts."

"It's a crazy mixed-up cycle, but once you identify the lies in your thoughts, and how you react to them, you can start to move forward." He looked as though he didn't want to say the next sentence. "In your case, recognizing the cognitive distortion will help you deal with the crux of your negative body image."

I didn't want him to know I had a problem with body image, but of course he did. Still, I hated this conversation. "What I think about myself affects how I act toward myself."

"In fact, the human brain actually forms grooves from the pathways created by thoughts and reactions." He smiled. "But here's the good news: we can train our brains to process thoughts differently. And make new grooves."

I tried to make sense of everything he was telling me. "So, you're saying . . . I'm groovy."

He chortled. "I'm saying your brain is in the process of forming new pathways, so yes, you're groovy, Cecily. And all the work you've been doing is starting to pay off."

I pulled his hand into my lap, then looked down at our fingers—interlocked like puzzle pieces—and I knew a few of the pieces to my life's puzzle had just snapped into place. Edge pieces, too, that would outline the boundary for the rest. I was getting there. But still. "It doesn't always feel like it."

"Of course not." With his other hand he pulled me toward him so that my head was resting on his shoulder, and I relaxed against him, only tensing when his free hand accidentally brushed the bump on my head. "Oops," he mumbled. "My bad."

We sat that way for ten minutes, not saying anything, not needing to. But then I felt compelled to remove a load I had been carrying in my heart. The one I never mentioned to anyone. The heaviest burden of all.

"I lost a baby."

Graham didn't say anything right away, and I knew he was choosing his words carefully. "Was it a miscarriage?"

"No." I sat up and rested my elbows on my knees. "She died when she was six weeks old."

He looked at me but didn't touch, and I was glad. "How long ago?"

"Five years." I rolled the leg of my shorts one more time. "That's when our problems started."

He nodded silently, and I figured I knew what he was thinking.

"Actually, our problems started before that, but that's when I acknowledged them. Brett didn't want a baby in the first place. Or actually—he didn't want a wife who had a baby."

"He's not the 'father' type."

"No, but it was more than that." My teeth gritted. "He always wanted me to look a certain way—hair, makeup, clothes—and when my body started changing, things were different between us." I shrugged. "He didn't want me anymore. I mean, physically. He still wanted me around to be his little wife, but he didn't want to touch me anymore."

I paused and then decided to keep going. "I thought it would change once the baby was born and I was slim again, but it was only worse. Apparently stretch marks and saggy skin were worse than being fat . . . in his eyes anyway. After that he spent more time looking at pictures and videos online. He'd always done that, but after the baby, he didn't hide it anymore. I think he felt justified."

"And then the baby died?"

"She went to sleep in her crib one afternoon and didn't wake up." A nervous chuckle slipped past my lips, a crass attempt to mask my feelings.

I expected Graham to say he was *so sorry, Cecily* and look at me with the same sad eyes I'd seen on other people's faces. But Graham did none of that. Instead, he leaned forward and nodded once, slowly, never breaking eye contact. I felt as though he had hold of a single thread that spiraled around my pain. In his silence, he gently tugged on that thread, and I could feel my memories loosening and beginning to unwrap themselves from my heart.

"Sometimes I feel like she slipped away because I didn't love her enough." I wiped a tear from my cheek, not wanting to cry, not wanting to reveal everything.

"You loved her deeply. I can see that."

"I did." I could hear the insistent tone in my voice, and I realized I was trying to convince myself, had been trying to convince myself for years. I nodded. "I did love her, but I always felt as though I wasn't a good wife to Brett after she was born. Things were never the same."

"You were busy with the baby. It's normal for a husband to feel left out."

"But he never wanted kids in the first place."

Graham was silent for a moment, then he asked, "Did you plan the pregnancy?"

I surprised myself by laughing. "No, but Brett thought I did it on purpose. He probably still thinks so."

The wind whooshed past us, and Graham squeezed my hand. "You grieved alone then, more or less."

"And I went just a little bit loony, to tell you the truth." I blinked rapidly, trying to dry the wetness around my eyes. "That was the first time I went to counseling, trying to make sense of losing the baby, and trying to accept Brett for who he was, and trying to hang on to my sanity at the same time."

Graham's thumb rubbed the back of my hand, twice clockwise, twice counterclockwise, over and over. He stared across the canyon, but it wasn't as though he were contemplating what I'd said. Instead, he seemed peaceful, and I wondered what on earth he was thinking.

He cocked his head to the side. "What was her name?" he asked.

"The baby?" I smiled. "Ava. Ava Denise Ross."

Graham returned my smile. "Denise was your mother's name."

"That's right." I looked away from him then, not wanting to admit what I was about to say but knowing it might help me if I did. "For a little while . . . at first . . . I was glad she died." I held my breath.

"That's understandable."

My gaze snapped to his. "What?"

He shrugged. "That only makes sense. It's not that you didn't love Ava, and it's not that you actually wanted her gone. The truth is that your husband was emotionally abusing you, and you thought her death might stop his behavior. You wanted the love of your husband as well as the love of your child, but the two couldn't happen at the same time."

I'd been told that before, but this time it seemed to sink in a little deeper and to make some sense of the craziness. I reached my arms around Graham's waist and held onto him like a lifeline. He pulled my head down to his shoulder and ran his fingers through my hair, and I felt more peace than I'd felt in a long time. Maybe in my entire life. A burden had been lifted from my shoulders, and my heart finally felt light.

I chuckled. "I guess your exercise idea worked. It ended up being counseling."

"I meant it more as therapy all on its own, but I guess what needed to happen happened."

"Slamming into a boulder?"

"Not that part." Graham kissed the top of my head. "But all the other parts."

Chapter
Thirty-Eight

Group text from Cecily: *Shanty, you holding up all right?*
Nina: *wuz afraid 2 txt. u killed al yet?*
Cecily (fifty-eight minutes later): *Shanty, let us know how you're doing.*
Nina: *i can come over :*
Cecily (one hour and twenty-four minutes later): *Shanty, come on now . . . let us know you're all right.*
Shanty: *Been better. Will survive.*

Our ten-year class reunion was held in a banquet hall on the university campus. I thought the senior class officers could at least have rented a room at the Amarillo Country Club, but what did I know? I needed to remember where I'd landed and stop looking for Los Angeles.

Brett hadn't shown up yet, but with Graham by my side, I had the confidence I'd need to help me get through the evening. We sat at a round table covered with butcher paper and draped with purple and white streamers. When I wondered aloud who was on the decorating committee and what had motivated them to treat us like eighteen-year-olds, Graham said, "It's meant to bring back memories of school."

"It's definitely working." My insides were experiencing the same loop-on-a-roller-coaster queasiness they'd had for most of my high school career.

Graham fingered the crinkled crepe paper. "I guess you're thinking about Brett."

"Since he's about to walk into the room, and I haven't seen him in over a year? Yes. I'm thinking about him."

"Relax, Cecily."

"Don't patronize me."

"Don't treat me as though I'm the one at fault."

His words slapped me in the face, causing my spite to soften.

"I'm not Brett," he said softly.

"I know."

"And I'm not Al."

"Okay." I verbally agreed, but my heart had its doubts.

The reunion band, former classmates who had pulled out their dusty instruments, played John Philip Sousa march tunes as people filtered into the building. Sousa was a favorite of mine, but under the circumstances, I would have preferred the tranquility of Jim Brickman's piano playing. When I thought of the instrument waiting for me in the living room of the cabin, I longed for home. I really should start playing more. Dad would probably enjoy it.

Zoe Gomez, who had actually squeezed into her cheerleader uniform, bounced from table to table, pinning name tags on shirt fronts while her husband watched tolerantly from a corner. I didn't recognize him from my school days, and I got the feeling he wasn't impressed with the evening. Elliot Emerson approached Graham and subtly asked if he had any goods for sale, and from the looks of it, I'd say Elliot hadn't gone a day without drugs in the past ten years. Graham assured him he was out of the business, then gave him the number for a detox center. Lindsay Timms, a girl I had run with, stopped at our table, greeted me, and asked where Brett was. When she discovered I was not only divorced, but at the reunion with Graham Cracker, she sidestepped to the snack table, glancing at me over her shoulder as she whispered to her date.

I was about to suggest we leave before the party started when Mirinda slipped into the seat next to Graham.

My surprise must have shown on my face because she shot me a quick explanation. "Michael is the keynote speaker."

Well, of course he was. Our little school couldn't pass up the opportunity for such a big-name guest, and naturally Brett's little sister would come with him. To my high school reunion. And sit next to my boyfriend.

My *boyfriend*. Is that what Graham was? I supposed so, but it sounded tacky, and suddenly I didn't blame Lindsay Timms for turning up her nose. Divorced, with a boyfriend. That certainly hadn't been my ten-year goal at graduation.

"Have you seen Brett?" I assumed Mirinda was directing her question to me, but her eyes were trained on Graham.

"Not a sign of him. You sure he's coming?"

"Mom and Dad haven't heard from him." Mirinda pulled at a lock of her hair, wrapping it around her index finger. "But I figure he'll show up. With the other woman, right?" Now she looked at me.

I didn't answer.

Brett would definitely bring a woman with him. There had been many back then, but he seemed to have settled on one in the end. *Kate.* I'd once walked in on the two of them, half-dressed on our white sofa. Brett had merely sat up and looked at me, not even trying to cover himself, or shield the woman, or explain his actions. He only stared at me, his face impassive and tolerant, until I fled to the bedroom and took refuge in the closet.

For a split second, I wasn't at my class reunion; I was in that lonely walk-in, scooting deep against the back wall beneath the hanging clothes and curling myself tightly into a ball so I couldn't see myself in the floor-length mirror. I had stayed hidden in the closet for hours that day, but Brett never came.

Across the room, Zoe Gomez squealed, and every head turned toward her as she threw her arms around my ex-husband. Brett had barely made it through the doorway, and already, there was a crowd around him. He had that effect on people, like a magnet. Or a virus.

"I take it he just walked into the room." Graham sat with his back to the hubbub, not making any movement to turn and look.

Mirinda settled back in her padded chair and took a deep breath, overreacting. So she hadn't seen her brother in a while. Big deal.

I leaned to the left, brushing Graham's shoulder, and finally saw the woman Brett had brought. It *was* Kate. Her hair had grown longer over the past year, and she looked bustier than I remembered. Brett had probably paid for that. He always wanted me to have surgery, but I refused. Now I asked myself why. If that woman had gone under the knife for him, maybe I should have done the same thing. It seemed like a simple request now, here, among all these people who had dressed in their best so they could look good in front of old friends they hadn't seen in ten years and wouldn't see again for another ten.

I rested my elbows on the table, reminding myself—again—that it didn't matter what people thought of me. It didn't matter what I looked like. Even Mirinda appeared dowdy when that woman was in the room. Kate. If Mirinda was a Barbie, Kate was a Bratz doll, big-eyed and sexy. Exotic.

Mirinda felt it too, I could tell. She had her fingers laced together in her lap as though she were praying.

And then Brett and Kate appeared in front of us, tilting their heads to the side and looking down at us as though we had come to the event just to see them. And maybe we had. I certainly hadn't come to see anyone else in my class, and I didn't really care about any of them seeing me.

"Kate?" Brett put his hand on her waist. "You remember Cecily, my high school sweetheart—"

Was that what I was?

"—and this is my . . . little sister." He gestured to Mirinda with raised eyebrows. "Who, it seems, has no apparent reason for being here." He motioned to Graham with a flick of his wrist and a frown. "And if I'm not mistaken, this is Graham *Cracker* himself, the boy who almost got me kicked out of athletics my senior year."

Graham stood and forced a laugh. "I can't take full credit. You had a little to do with it too."

They were talking about drugs, of course. Several other people in the room could've said the same thing to Graham, though none of them had.

"I wouldn't say that, but it's in the past." Brett looked away from Graham, dismissing him along with the accusation he had laid at Graham's feet. "Cecily, you're looking . . . wonderful." His grin sliced me. "Don't you think she looks wonderful, Kate?"

"Just *beautiful*."

I couldn't know for sure if Brett intended to rub salt on the wounds to my self-esteem, but he was giving me the same tiny bread crumbs of praise he had given me in the past, and now he was pulling Kate into the madness, and doing it in front of Graham.

"Beautiful as always." He shook his head with a tiny shrug as though to say, *Why in the world did you ever think otherwise?* Then he spotted someone on the far side of the room and lifted his hand.

I was nothing to him. Of course, I already knew that, but now it was solidified like drying concrete, and my feet were stuck firmly in it, just waiting for someone to toss me over the edge of the canyon. For the life of me, I couldn't figure out why I cared.

"So you guys are together?" Brett's index finger swung from me to Graham and back again, as though he were scolding us—*uh, uh, uh . . . no you don't*—and then he laughed a little. "Well, I didn't see that one coming. Cecily, you're doing"—his smile pulled down at the corners in the facial equivalent of a shrug—"good for yourself. I suppose."

His condescension acted as a trigger, and I felt myself falling into the shadowy place. Just that afternoon, on the bike ride, I had been happy with Graham, but now I felt as though I had settled for someone inferior. But as quickly as my insecurity reared its head, it morphed into anger, and I wanted to upturn the purple-and-white table, to yank out handfuls of Kate's lovely long hair, and to punch my thumbnails into Brett's eyes. I wanted to hurt him.

Actually, I wanted Graham to do it. Like a knight in shining armor, I wanted him to come to my rescue. Brett had insulted both of us, and if Graham would retaliate, then I would be vindicated. I would have the better man, the one who fought for me because I was worth it. But Graham didn't even appear to be angry. In fact, instead of coming to my defense, he was listening intently as Brett continued to speak, blubbering to Mirinda, something about her being a cute kid. The three of them seemed set apart, their bodies turned away from me, as though I weren't important.

Then Graham walked away and left me there.

He ushered Mirinda to the hallway leading to the restrooms, his hand hovering near the small of her back, not quite touching her, and I was left standing with Brett and his girlfriend or lover or whore. I hated Kate. Maybe I hated Brett too, but at the moment, I was more concerned with whether I hated Graham.

Brett's neck briefly disappeared into his shoulders in a mock cringe. "Looks like Graham Cracker may have his eye on greener pastures, Cecily."

That was absurd. Graham may have enjoyed looking at Mirinda's body, but he was too smart to think he stood a chance against Michael.

Speak of the devil. Michael was standing two tables over, watching us. He lifted his chin in greeting to me, then walked in a slow arc behind Brett, coming to a stop by his side. He extended his hand. "I don't think we've met. I'm Michael Divins."

"Michael—" Brett laughed through an open-mouthed smile. *"Michael Divins?"* He pumped the athlete's hand, and I thought he might start drooling. "It's good to meet you." Brett straightened to his full height, scoping the room as if to see who might be watching the exchange, but he seemed oblivious to Michael's body language: shoulders back, right foot forward, arms bent. "What brings you here, Michael?"

The athlete's smile was tight. "I'm dating your sister. She's told me a lot about you."

"Has she?" Brett shrank. "Well, you can't trust everything the girl says."

Michael squinted at Brett, then turned to me and smiled robotically. "Do you know where she is?"

Brett didn't give me time to answer. "She was here a second ago, but she left with Graham Cracker."

"Graham . . . *Cracker*?" A vein in Michael's neck twitched.

Brett pointed, and when I followed his gaze, my knees quivered.

Graham and Mirinda were standing a few yards down the hallway, talking with their heads close together. Then Mirinda pressed herself against Graham, and he put his arm around her shoulders.

Brett snickered. "I see she hasn't changed much."

As I turned back toward Brett, it was evident that Mirinda had plenty of people to come to her rescue, to tell her she was worth it, to clamor for her attention. Not only was Graham comforting her in the hallway, Michael was fighting for her honor. He reared back and punched Brett square in the face, laying him out on the floor of the banquet hall.

Chapter
Thirty-Nine

I sat in front of my closet door, staring at the plastic brackets that had once held the mirror. Even without the silver glass, I could see my image from memory. Tear streaked, makeup smudged, slouched posture, frumpy. No wonder Graham left me alone with Brett.

I felt myself spiraling downward. What had Graham called it? Cognitive distortion. That's what I was doing now, and that's what I was feeling. Negative thoughts about myself, which led to crappy feelings, which led to a bad, bad, dangerously bad mood, which led to more negative thoughts that felt like the ugly truth. Those horrid grooves in my brain.

But Graham said those thoughts were lies. So did Shanty. They certainly didn't feel like lies, but I guess that was the point. I wasn't supposed to pay attention to what the lies *felt* like. That was the distortion, the pinch. My bad feelings didn't make my thoughts true. Lies were lies no matter what I felt, and truth was truth, no strings attached. Somehow, I needed to break the cycle, see the lies for what they were, and start talking to myself with someone else's voice.

Think happy thoughts was an oversimplification of the entire process, but it had become my internal, never-ending, not-quite-enough mantra. I would form new grooves if it killed me.

I was kneeling on the floor with my feet tucked beneath me and my hands resting on my thighs. Those stupid thighs of mine, wide, dimpled, and now scarred. My thumb rubbed against my jeans, and even as I thought my thoughts, I knew I was giving in to my emotions. The nail of my thumb dug into my thigh, causing more pain to my cuticle than to my leg, and that angered me. I reached for the nearest object, a tennis shoe I had last worn at the canyon, with Graham. I gripped it in my fist, raised it over my head, and brought the heel down hard against my leg, just above the knee.

But only three times.

After the third hit, my logic outweighed my emotions, and I threw the shoe into the corner of the room, where it landed with a thud, the toe leaning precariously against the wall before sliding to the floor. I stared at the lifeless piece of footwear, thinking how meaningless everything seemed, and how damaged I still was, and how far I had left to go before I would be healthy.

I was so exhausted from it all.

Lying down on the shag carpet, I pressed my cheek against the floor and asked myself for the millionth time if I even wanted to try anymore.

Chapter Forty

Group text from Nina to Shanty and Cecily: *im doing it! blindfolded demonstration in the jbk this morning 10 am will let you know how it goes so excited! shanty how long does it take for the marker to wear off?! :)*

When I read Nina's message, I didn't panic. Nina knew what she was doing, and even though I wouldn't have taken my clothes off in a public place for a million dollars, Nina had a point to prove, not only to the student body but also to herself. Then I stopped to think about it. Sure, Nina had something to prove, just like Shanty, but Nina *wasn't* just like Shanty. Bold, daring, *loud*. If anything, she was hesitant, like me, so the thought of her holding a demonstration rubbed me the wrong way. The more I thought about it, the more I became convinced that Nina, bless her heart, was a follower. And she followed in the footsteps of those she admired.

As I sat at the receptionist's desk in Graham's office on Monday morning, I realized, with alarm, that Nina was only doing a demonstration because Shanty had done one. She idolized Shanty. Good grief, we both did, and who wouldn't? Funny that I should say that after being so disdainful of her only a few weeks ago, but now she seemed so strong, and such a leader, that I found myself wanting to be like her.

Not a bad idea. But not a good one either.

I nibbled a hangnail. Tapped a pencil against the appointment book. Wiped dust from the phone. Read the text again.

Nina sounded so positive, hopeful, uncharacteristically upbeat. No need to worry.

My phone dinged.

Text from Shanty to Cecily: *Oh, my goodness! SHE'S DOING IT!!! I shouldn't take off but she needs my support. Gotta take Gage's forgotten lunch up to the elementary, then I'm heading to the Student Center. Will Dr H let you leave for a while?*

Would he? Did I even care? The reunion had become a fiasco when Michael punched Brett. Zoe Gomez had screamed, Lindsay Timms had called the police, and Kate, interestingly, had stood back from the commotion, patiently waiting to take Brett away with her. They had left almost immediately.

After the reunion, Graham and Mirinda's actions seemed forgotten by everyone except me, and I didn't want to confront him. I'm not sure why. Maybe I didn't want to sound like a whiny, insecure nutcase, and maybe I didn't want to know the truth. Now we were two appointments into our day, and we had barely spoken. I glanced down the hallway at his closed office door. He swore he needed me in the waiting room for propriety's sake, but propriety hadn't stopped him from hugging Madam X at our class reunion.

Text from Cecily to Shanty: *Pick me up at the office. We can talk about Nina on the way.*

The JBK Student Center was packed, so I figured Nina had deliberately chosen a crowded time of day. All the feelings of insecurity that had suffocated me when I was in college now came flooding back. Brett had been my anchor, boosting my ego when we walked around campus together, but when I was alone, I'd felt as if a million pairs of eyes were scrutinizing my every move.

When I dressed that morning, I had put on a long-sleeved shirt over my blouse as a loose cover-up, and now I pulled it tightly around myself, hiding oh-so-much more than my tattoo. I lifted my chin, ignoring the bustling college students as I followed Shanty through the dense crowd that seemed to be anything but a typical cross section of the student population. Surely there were nerds somewhere, academics, holy rollers—but they certainly weren't in the JBK. Shanty and I were surrounded by sorority and fraternity kids, fashionistas in designer jeans, and preppy types with trendy haircuts.

No wonder Nina never wanted to walk through this place.

Nina, with her all-American good looks and down-to-earth humility, didn't fit in with this crowd. I cringed. Nina probably wanted to fit in just as badly as I had wanted to at UCLA.

"Lord almighty!" Shanty stopped and stood with her hands on her hips, turning in a circle in front of a Quiznos and peering around her with the concerned look of a mother trying to figure out which child to scold first. "This explains a lot about sweet Nina, don't it?"

"If I had to come in here every day, I'd probably kill myself."

"Ah, girl, don't even joke about that."

"I'm not."

She met my eyes. "Yeah. I know."

A girl bumped into Shanty, then gave her a put-out expression and didn't offer an apology. She mumbled something to her friend about *old people*, and they both kept walking.

"Where do you suppose she is?" I asked.

"Let's just keep trekking through the jungle till we find her." This time Shanty's intimidating stance didn't begin to part the waters.

"I don't mean to be unsupportive," I said, "but do you think we should try to talk her out of it?"

"Yes."

Shanty's instant answer surprised me but also verified my own thoughts.

"There she is." I pointed at a huddle of students near the post office. I could just see Nina's black ponytail between the shoulders of two boys. She was standing in front of a nook of post office boxes, and above her head hung an advertisement for Priority Mail. The group around her seemed tame compared to the rest of the building, and my nerves calmed. A short distance away, I noticed a small pile of Nina's clothes, a spiral notebook, and her Kindle. Did she ever go anywhere without something to read?

A girl took a marker and gently wrote something on Nina's cheek. "People are good down deep, aren't they?" I asked as we stopped at a bulletin board plastered with announcements and flyers. "Even on this crazy campus, people are good."

The girl touched Nina's wrist with her fingertip, letting her know she was handing the marker back. A boy had the other marker and was carefully drawing something on Nina's back, then he stuck a finger in the side of her bikini bottoms and snapped the marker on her hip. I frowned, ready to step forward, but Shanty held up a hand to stop me. "I think it's all right. They're hormonal teenagers, right? That one looked like a freshman. Probably don't know any better."

"I suppose." I rested my weight on one foot, unable to find a position that seemed natural. In a weird way, I was imagining myself as Nina, standing in this horrible place and wearing next to nothing. I could feel the marker on my skin, its wetness leaving trails that tickled and maybe stung a little. I even felt that boy's finger pulling at the elastic of my bottoms and the plastic marker cold against my hip. But stronger than that, I felt the crowd around me, moving and shifting, three students walking past me, two others stopping, a girl and a boy standing so close behind me that I could feel their breath on my neck as they read the words on my skin. Then one of them snickered.

Shanty took one step.

Three boys were standing in front of Nina. They had a girl with them, but she stood back a few paces, watching with apparent disinterest. One of the boys wore a T-shirt with the arms cut off. He took a marker and bent down on one knee as though he were proposing, and then he began to write and draw just below her belly button. His friend had decided to write something on her foot. From where I stood, it looked like he was drawing an ankle bracelet.

Shanty took two more steps, and I followed her. We were closer to Nina now, but still far enough away that we didn't hinder the demonstration.

The boy kneeling in front of her stood up and surveyed his artwork. He turned to the girl next to him and she shrugged. The other boy looked at it and guffawed before stepping behind Nina.

Shanty stomped forward. Three dark, bold words stretched across Nina's abdomen, and a thick arrow pointed downward. *F— me here.*

Shanty's hand came back, and her palm caught the boy on the back of the head.

Just as his friend unhooked Nina's bikini top.

Chapter Forty-One

Nina hardly had an inch of skin that wasn't covered with profanity. Shanty and I got her out of the student center as quickly as possible, but even then, kids stared and pointed. Our hasty exit might have been worse for her than the actual demonstration since she was no longer blindfolded and could see the reactions of the students around her.

By the time I left the campus, I had a circus of emotions tangling inside me, vying for position, and I couldn't quite make sense of them or identify which one was going to end up at the forefront of my mood. Anger at the college students who had been so cruel to my friend. Irritation at Nina for doing it in the first place, without asking our advice. Disgust for her because she was such a follower. Shame for women in general, and hatred for men. Hatred was probably the emotion that would rise to the top.

I slipped into Graham's office and sat down at my desk, and it was almost as though I hadn't left. His door was closed, and I could hear muted voices on the other side. Had he even noticed I was gone? I opened the Solitaire app on my phone, but immediately pushed the device away and stood. I paced to the front window, then to the back of the room, then repeated the action. Over and over, willing my heart to calm. Willing my mind to erase the images of Nina's skin.

When she had been blindfolded, she held her head high, probably thinking about Shanty's demonstration and imagining herself in the same situation. But when her bikini top came off, she had instantly crumpled, scrambling to cover herself with one arm while she clawed at the blindfold with the other hand. Her eyes had widened when she saw Shanty and me—Shanty swatting at college boys like they were horseflies, and me, yanking off my overshirt to throw it around her shoulders.

We had taken her back to her dorm room, where her roommate looked on with distant interest. Shanty had held Nina while she cried, and I had scrubbed at the words with fingernail polish remover and Dove soap, reading each phrase as though they were entries in an urban dictionary.

Slut.
Whore.
Ugliest thing I've seen all semester.
555-915-0143 Call any time.

There was a messy drawing that I assumed was meant to be a penis. And on a different part of her body, another of the same that was perfectly drawn, as though the artist had been there a while, laboring over every detail, savoring the moment. Had the artist's friends been watching, nodding, jeering? And scrawled on her inner wrist,

Jesus loves you.

As I scrubbed at that one, I noticed scars there that I should have noticed before. *Jesus loves you.* In tiny, messy handwriting, as though the writer had been hurrying to get away, and not at all confident in his own words.

Where had that guy been in the end?

I stomped my foot, and the voices in Graham's office paused for a moment before continuing. I was only imagining *males* writing on Nina's body because most of the students I'd seen near her were boys, but I had witnessed at least one girl write something. And several of the comments were written in neat, girlish handwriting with loops and curls. One phrase I remembered well: *Get a life*. Written just above Nina's heart.

Shanty had taken Nina home with her. To comfort her and feed her and love on her.

I had come back here. To the office. To Graham.

I craved his reassurance, but after thinking about Nina and her ordeal, a small part of my neediness was beginning to chip away. She had been so vulnerable, and I wanted to be strong.

Graham's door opened, and a moody-looking teenage boy walked through, passing me without acknowledgment and yanking the glass door so hard it slammed against the magazine rack. I watched him from where I stood at the back wall, feeling nothing. Even if the kid had broken the door, what would it matter?

"You're back." Graham stood next to me, his eyebrows raised. "Everything all right?"

What could I say? Where should I begin?

I shook my head.

"What is it?"

"Nina." I whispered, and whatever minuscule amount of strength I had evaporated.

Graham pulled me toward his office, and I willingly followed, allowing him to sit me down on the sofa and nestle me in the crook of his arm. He didn't say anything, didn't ask questions, just ran his fingers through my hair and waited.

I closed my eyes and waited too. I waited for the peace I knew would come from being close to him. Because it always came. He was like a healing tonic, calming and soothing.

"She did a demonstration like Shanty did," I said.

"Not in a bikini."

"Yes. In the Student Center."

He tensed. "In the JBK? Should I call her?"

"She's with Shanty now."

He relaxed. "Was it very bad?"

"They were awful to her. People are terrible everywhere, aren't they?"

"Hmm. Sort of."

"I don't know how to handle this."

He pressed his cheek against my forehead. "Your heart is full of love for Nina, and disgust for the people who hurt her, but still . . . you need to pay attention to what's happening in there." He tapped my chest. "Respect your feelings."

"Do you ever stop giving counseling advice?"

He shrugged. "That's what I do."

"I'm not sure that's what I need you to do right now."

He nodded, but didn't answer. "Sometimes Mirinda says the same thing."

My spine stiffened. "Mirinda?" I settled an elbow on the armrest on the far side of the couch. "I thought you couldn't talk about your clients." My voice held a challenge.

"Yes," he said cautiously, "but I don't think she would mind. Have you ever considered befriending her?"

"Befriending my ex-husband's sister?"

He pulled at his earlobe. "She could probably help you work through this. And Nina and Shanty too. She could help all three of you."

"You seem to have put a lot of thought into it."

He studied me. "It's my job, right?"

"That seems to be your explanation for a lot of things."

He stood slowly, then trailed his fingertips across his desk as he stepped around it. I could physically feel the distance he placed between us as he sat down in his chair and began swiveling back and forth, once again making us the counselor and the client.

My fingernails dug into the couch cushion, and I gritted my teeth to keep from snarling. How dare he? Was I just another client now? I remembered his expression when I wrecked on the bike. He had glanced at my thighs, then looked away from me. Now I understood. Everything had changed when he realized what a mess I was.

"Saturday night, at the reunion," he said, "you saw me with Mirinda." His lips pressed together.

"A lot of people did." Like Brett. And Michael. And Mirinda had seen me see them.

"It wasn't what it looked like."

I pressed my palms against each other, then squeezed them between my knees. "I wanted to believe that. I mean, for two days, you've said nothing, and I decided to believe it wasn't anything. You've always said she wasn't your type."

"Cecily, it wouldn't matter if she was . . . Men don't fall victim to every woman they're attracted to."

"So you're attracted to her?"

"That's not what I meant. I don't know. Sure, she's attractive, but I don't think of her that way."

"What way do you think of her?"

"As a client."

"A client you like to look at."

He rubbed a palm over his beard. "You're making more out of this than you should."

I thought of Nina, standing in her bikini with black scribble covering her body. She hadn't meant anything to those people who'd hurt her. She had been a source of curiosity, a joke, and for some of them—possibly—a reminder of their own pain.

I swallowed. "Mirinda is one of the most beautiful women I've ever met, Graham."

He eyed me skeptically, wisely keeping his mouth shut.

"And she uses her beauty to manipulate people around her. Our world is a crazy mixed-up mess, and men are pigs—some of them—but Mirinda is the type of woman who supports everything our culture throws at women. Not only does she believe the lies . . . she makes them true."

"She's working through a lot of that."

"And you're *there for her.*"

He sighed. "Cecily, I'm not interested in Mirinda, I'm interested in you, and I find you incredibly attractive, but I can't force you to believe that. I can encourage you, but you're the only one in control of your feelings."

"What about your control?" I snapped, anger rising in my gut. "You're the one letting her press her body against yours right there in front of everyone in our senior class. In front of Brett. He was laughing at me. And probably laughing at you too for being blind to her slutty ways."

Graham clenched his teeth before he spoke. "You despise being judged by your outer shell. You *detest* it. Yet you continue to judge Mirinda—partially, at least—by her appearance."

"Maybe you're doing the same thing."

"No. Actually, I'm not." He shook his head just as his cell phone chirped. When he pulled it out of his pocket, he flinched, then read a text. "I have to go."

"You're not eating lunch here?"

"Not today." He stepped to the door. "I'll talk to you later?"

He waited a few seconds, but when I didn't answer, he opened the door and walked away.

My heart followed him down the hall and out the front door, and I was left with emptiness. The office suddenly felt like a vacuum, sucking the air out of my lungs, and without thinking, I walked to the window, thirsty for one last glimpse of him and hungry for the feel of sunshine on my cheeks, any kind of light to shine on my shadow, but what I saw only made my darkness more complete. Black and blinding.

Mirinda was getting into Graham's truck, and they were leaving together.

Chapter
Forty-Two

I left the office unattended again and didn't go back. Even though it was irresponsible of me, I couldn't find it in my heart to care. If Graham could leave with Mirinda, then I could spend the afternoon sitting on the edge of the canyon, wishing the earth would swallow up all the feelings that were running rampant through my soul. I squinted at the enormous gorge before me and speculated if it would be large enough to hold them all.

I flipped my spiral notebook to a blank page and wrote Shanty's latest challenge at the top. Then I grunted at the irony.

Make a list of people who have committed offenses against you. Then forgive them.

Shanty and Graham had both insisted I needed to forgive everyone on the planet, as well as myself—whatever that meant—but at the moment I wasn't in a forgiving mood. On the other hand, I was definitely in a make-a-list-of-those-who-had-offended-me mood. No problem. This could easily be the simplest journal entry yet.

Graham.

Maybe I shouldn't have written his name first, but he was at the forefront of my mind. I had thought he was different than other men, but now I couldn't be sure.

Next to his name, I wrote,

not what I expected.

He was much more primal than I had thought. A stereotypical man, driven by hormones, chasing after long legs, tanned skin.

I squeezed my eyes shut momentarily, then scribbled in my note-book again.

Mirinda, for being herself, and making the lies true.
Brett, for obvious reasons.

I stopped there, and a tear slid down my cheek. Brett had hurt me so many times. So thoroughly, indifferently, callously. More than once he had loomed over me as I lay naked on our bed. By then, he had stopped making eye contact. Instead, he held his phone in one hand, his face illuminated by the lighted screen as he watched some other woman he found titillating. When he needed his hands free to support his weight, he tossed the phone on the pillow next to my ear and continued to watch. Until he was finished with me.

I slammed the notebook shut and pulled my knees up to my chin. Shanty's assignment was completed.

My fist closed around the pen, and I held it in front of my eyes, clicking the end repeatedly and watching the roller thrust out of the casing, then back in. Click-click. Click-click. My thighs were pressed against my chest, but I shifted them far enough away so that I could run the pen forcefully from my kneecap to my hip. Then I did it again, harder. The pen was safely inside the casing, and the action caused minimal pain and left no visible marks on my jeans, and probably none on my flesh beneath. It was pitiful really. Self-pity and wallowing. I held the pen behind my head and hurled it into the abyss, watching as it sailed through the air, turning end over end as it arced into the canyon, disturbing a branch on a mesquite tree before it bounced to the ground.

I snickered. I had wanted to throw the object far away from me, letting the expanse of the canyon swallow it up dramatically, but it hadn't gone more than twenty feet, though it seemed a little farther because of the slope. My arms had little strength, but I had gotten the pen—a weapon at the moment—away from my legs and out of my hands. I may have been offended by Graham and Brett and Mirinda, but I was sick and tired of the emotional spiral that always ended with me hurting myself.

Then I wished I had the pen back, partly because I didn't want to mar the beauty of the canyon with trash, but mostly because I realized I should've written my mother's name. I loved her more than I could express, but I was beginning to realize I was offended by her death. Even though she couldn't help it, and her disease had nothing to do with me, my hurt feelings hadn't recovered from the loss.

And then I thought of Ava, and a sob caught in my throat. I hardly ever thought of my baby. Why was that? Whatever the reason, Graham would tell me it was normal. To be expected.

I hugged my knees tightly, realizing I needed to forgive my sweet girl. Was that even the right terminology? I couldn't forgive her for an action she didn't intentionally commit, but I could release my bitterness toward the situation itself. I could *let it go*. I could allow myself to live life, *happily*, without her. I could stop tormenting myself with all the guilty thoughts that swirled around her memory.

Daddy's truck hummed into the yard behind me, and I wondered why he was home so early, but I didn't move from my spot. He would go in the house, fix himself a sweet tea, and eventually mosey onto the back deck and see me thirty yards away. And that would be all right. So far Daddy hadn't made it onto my list of offenders.

"There you are." The voice came from the side of the house, hesitant and hopeful, but my nerves pulled as tight as the nylon rope when I rappelled off the cliff. It wasn't Daddy after all.

It was Graham.

Chapter
Forty-Three

I didn't want to talk to Graham. I didn't want his counseling advice. I didn't want his questions. I didn't want his hugs and kisses.

"You ran off again." His voice held a hint of a reprimand, but his facial expression added a question mark. "Twice in one day."

It seemed like a week ago I had watched Nina being publicly humiliated. It seemed like a year. Was it really just this morning?

"Sorry," I said. He waited for an explanation, but surely he knew that walking away from me in the middle of a difficult conversation to run after another woman wouldn't have a positive effect on our relationship . . . or my mental health.

My mental health. I sighed, so exhausted from thinking about my mental health. So tired of trying to get better.

"Can we walk a while?"

Why was he even there when he had clients scheduled? "Did you have a cancellation?"

He took a few steps. "You could say that."

"What does that mean?" I followed him.

"It means I canceled a few appointments so I could come talk to you."

Was I supposed to feel bad about that? We were walking toward the cliff where Daddy and I rappelled, and I remembered Graham saying he'd like to try it together sometime. Now I thought we probably never would.

"What did you want to talk about?" I asked.

He turned away from me so that he was looking over the edge of the canyon. "I've been thinking about those scars on your legs, and I'm worried about you."

"I'm fine now."

"But that was only a few weeks ago, Cecily. You need to work through some of your emotional pain, and I'm not helping. I was wrong to try to date you. You're not ready."

I inhaled deeply to rid myself of a drowning feeling. "What are you saying?"

"I'm saying we shouldn't be dating. Not now."

My pride curled into a tight ball.

Even though I had been considering breaking things off with him, more than considering it, I was planning it . . . even then, his words cut deeper than any shard of glass ever could. He didn't want me after all. "It's because of Mirinda, isn't it?"

He spun on his heel. "No. Why on earth would you say that?"

"She calls and texts. She manipulates you in order to be alone with you every Thursday night. She touches you. Not that her hugs mean anything, she presses her body against every man she knows."

"*Cecily.*" He stared at me like he hadn't truly seen me before. "You don't even know her."

"I was married to her brother for seven years. I think I know her."

"You know what Brett told you about her."

"We really don't need to talk about this," I said.

"So you're saying you want to take a break too?"

"I'm saying I agree with you. We never should've gotten together in the first place."

He stared at me with hard eyes, but then he blinked and softened, nodding as though accepting a sentence for a crime he'd committed. "Okay," he mumbled. "You're right." He took two steps away from me, heading back toward the house, but then he stopped and turned around.

He glanced at the anchor, then into the canyon depths. "You'll be all right?"

"I'm not going to cut myself, if that's what you mean."

"You'll call me if you get to that point?"

I would call Shanty or Nina or Daddy. I had any number of people in my life who could help me and would do it without leading me on. I pointed my face into the wind so that my hair swept out of my eyes. "No, Graham. I won't call you."

I wouldn't even think about him.

Or would I? Would I let his memory shout negative thoughts at me? When I looked in the mirror, would I see Mirinda standing next to me? Would I continue to compare my body with hers and others like hers, and tell myself it was no wonder Graham had rejected me? I shivered.

After a few long moments, dry grass crunched beneath Graham's feet as he walked away.

I stood motionless until I heard his truck leaving, and then I trudged back to the house. I wanted to look in the mirror and remind myself, once and for all, who I was. Not Brett's pitiful wife, not Graham's damaged girlfriend, not society's reject. But the mirror wasn't a safe place for me because of those stinking *grooves* of mine. I might listen to the lies, I might spiral into a dark place, I might act on my negative thoughts.

Instead of hurting myself, I did the only other thing that came naturally to me. I sat down at the piano. I intended to play a soft melody, a lullaby, but that was not the music that worked its way from my heart to my fingertips. Instead, I produced Prokofiev's Piano Concerto no. 3, frantic and aggressive, and the muscles beneath my barbed wire tattoo flexed and quivered. Frustration welled inside me as I pounded on the instrument, my hands traveling up and down the keys in a frenzy. I played faster and faster, wishing I had never come back to Canyon, wishing I had never talked to Graham Harper, wishing I could disappear along with my reflection.

Chapter
Forty-Four

Group text from Shanty: *I've found a way we can vent our frustrations. Can I pick you up after lunch?*
Nina: *i guess so*
Cecily: *Whatever it is, I'm in. Been a l-o-n-g week, and I really really need to vent.*
Shanty: *Anything in particular? Or just everything?*
Cecily: *Nothing monumental. Graham and I have decided to take a break for a while.*
Nina: *not monumental? thats GINORMOUS*
Shanty: *I have just what you need.*

For five days, I went through the motions of my new and improved life while toxic feelings surged from my insides—emotions that reminded me of my life with Brett, back when I acted like everything was fine. I felt the same now. Empty. Hollow. Fraudulent.

But I couldn't fake it at work and neither could Graham.

He stayed in his office between appointments, and I left every day for lunch when the last client walked out the door, casually chatting with them as we walked to our cars, so as not to leave a spare moment alone with Graham. But it was hell. Thursday night was the worst of all—I hid in the break room, knowing he was with Mirinda.

When Shanty texted me on Saturday, I didn't care what she had in mind—I was willing to try. Now I stood in the middle of Rudy's Pick-a-Part with her and Nina. We were surrounded by dead cars, so a more appropriate name might have been *Rudy's Auto Cemetery*, or maybe even *Wrecking Yard*. I'd seen it on the edge of Amarillo for years and driven past it without a thought other than what an eyesore it was. Now I looked around me at the rusted cars and felt strangely at home.

Nina carried a Walmart bag, twisting it around two fingers and then letting it spin free. She cleared her throat. "Um . . . why are we here?"

She stood a few steps behind me, and I stood a few steps behind Shanty, and Shanty stood with her hands on her hips, staring at an old Chevy as though she despised the poor car.

"What we're doing here"—Shanty spun to face us—"is releasing some of our pent-up anger. Dr. Harper is always telling me to let my emotions go, and right now I'm feeling RAGE." Her face reddened, but then she smiled sweetly. "And I need a safe place to vent it."

A man in coveralls walked toward us, and *scruffy* was too high-class a word to describe him. He carried two three-foot sledgehammers, and as he sauntered toward us, Nina made a low whining sound.

Instinctively, I stepped toward her. "Shanty?"

Shanty's eyes widened, but not in fear of the man—in surprise at our reaction. "You guys, that's only Earl Ray, Al's cousin. He said we could come here. It was his idea. He's as fed up with Al as I am." Her eyebrows scrunched. "The Espinosas don't hold to cheating on their women."

"Yo, Shanty." Earl Ray had a nasally voice and a deep accent, and the combination made me like him. He tossed one sledgehammer on the ground where it thumped against the earth, then handed the other one to Shanty. He nodded at Nina and me. "Ladies."

Shanty held the hammer in two hands like a shotgun. "Earl Ray, this is Cecily and Nina. They're not exactly in the same shape I'm in, but we've all gotten ourselves into a bit of a tizzy the past few days."

He motioned to the Chevy. "Old Blue here ought to do just fine for you." He grinned. "If you need me, I'll be in the trailer."

I watched him saunter away, and I began to understand.

Shanty turned to Nina. "You bring the spray paint?"

Nina opened the Walmart bag and pulled out two cans, one red and one black.

Shanty reached for the black, changed her mind, and grabbed the other one. "Blood red," she said. "That'll do just fine." She stomped to the hood of the Chevy, shaking the can noisily as she went, then she paused a moment, having trouble removing the cap. She growled until it finally broke free. Then, leaning over the hood of the car, she painted a large capital *A* followed by an *L*. Then she stood back and surveyed her handiwork and carefully set the paint can on the gravel at her feet. She hoisted the sledgehammer to her shoulder, but then seemed to have second thoughts and lowered it to the ground again. This time when she painted on the hood, she used neat cursive lettering, adding the word *cockroach* beneath her husband's name.

The sun felt warm on my scalp, and a bead of sweat slid down my side. I wasn't sure what I was about to witness, but already, I could feel that it might be the best therapy I'd had in years.

When Shanty slammed the hammer into the center of the *A*, she howled like a rabid animal, and her anger continued with the second and third hits, until *AL* was obliterated, and *cockroach* was dented beyond recognition, but then her rage softened and she was crying, and with every hit, a sob wrenched through her body, until finally, once the hood was nothing more than a pulverized hunk of tin foil, she stopped for breath.

She looked at Nina, who was still holding the black spray paint, and tilted her head toward the back of the car. Then Shanty let the sledgehammer drop to the ground, and she slumped, exhausted and spent, against the hood. She gave *AL* one last slap with the palm of her hand as though she were spanking one of her children.

Nina covered the back of the car with her own graffiti. Her head was tilted to the side like she was creating a studied piece of artwork, but her expression was cold and calculating, as though she were planning a murder.

Hesitantly, I reached for the red paint and stepped to the driver's side. The front and rear doors were both intact and perfectly smooth with windows removed. Suddenly I had the ridiculous sense that I had just been given tickets to the fair, where scary carnies and dangerous rides would give me a thrill of power, the feeling that I could risk everything and still survive.

As Nina began to pound the car—with surprising force for someone so small—I wrote a bold *B* on the driver's door. I didn't write the rest of Brett's name, only sprayed over it two more times until the paint ran down the sides of the car like a fresh wound. Shanty had been right. Blood red would do just fine. I almost reached for a sledgehammer, but I stopped myself, realizing I wasn't finished. I added a *G* next to Brett. Even though Graham hadn't treated me like Brett had—Graham was better than that—the good doctor had hurt me. Or maybe *hurt* was the wrong word. He had *disappointed* me. Even more than Brett had, because I had expected more from Graham. I stared at the two letters while Nina pounded the rear end of the car and Shanty added more graffiti to the hood.

Then I added one more letter.

If this was meant to be a purging session, then I wanted to be sure and get it all out at once. I wasn't holding anything back, and when I slammed the hammer against the door the first time, it surprised me that I dented the last letter first. The *B* had been my target, but I'd never been a very good aim. The paint wasn't yet dry, and the hammer smeared a streak all the way down the door, but when I reared back again, the hammer hit the *B* dead center, and I felt an overwhelming sense of satisfaction.

Hurriedly, I sprayed a smiley face above the *B*. Brett had always smiled at me, even when he was saying horrible things. Even when he was looking at pictures on his phone, standing over me as I hid beneath the covers, waiting until he was ready. Even then, he had smiled. A soft, gentle smile of anticipation before he tossed the phone to the floor, leaving the room in darkness so he wouldn't have to see my body. Now, I envisioned a three-dimensional image above my smiley and pounded it with the iron hammer three, four, five times—screaming with each exertion until I stalled, exhausted, my face burning from anger.

My body was not repulsive.

And if I had to beat this stupid car all day long, until it was a flattened pile of metal and fiberglass, I would do it. I would pound that *B* until it was unrecognizable. I would pound all three of them . . . for making me feel less than I should have. For lying to me.

"No more lies!" I shouted the words and Shanty howled her approval.

"We're not putting up with it anymore." She had the other hammer now, working on whatever else she had painted.

"No! More! LIES!" I hit the door with each yell, but I felt my anger seeping through my pores, running down my sides with the sweat, to puddle on the ground at my feet. And with each yell, my rage turned into sadness, and my sadness turned into self-pity, and my self-pity turned into a thick shadow that sent me falling to the ground.

Nina and Shanty left me alone, partly because they knew I needed the space and partly because they were dealing with their own demons. And I cried. I sobbed. I howled and whimpered. But I did not hurt myself.

Afterward, I stared at the sand and pebbles on the ground in front of me, and I rested, breathing deeply and thoroughly. My anger had evaporated, and in its place lay a bundle of raw emotions I hadn't noticed before. Until now, they had been buried beneath the rage and injustice, but now, as I sat crumpled in the gravel lot of a wrecking yard, I discovered the root of my problems.

Venting my anger had opened my eyes to the reality of my pain, and my pile of life's puzzle pieces had taken on a clarity I hadn't expected. All this time, I had only been holding *one puzzle piece* tightly in the palm of my hand, and not even attempting to fit it in with the rest. That puzzle piece was *self-image*. Of course. I had been holding it so long that it was warped and bent and might never lay flat alongside the other pieces.

Lifting my head, I looked at the dented *M* in front of me. It represented Mirinda, and every other woman I had ever compared myself to. Other than that first misplaced hit, I had only deliberately hit that letter a handful of times. The *B*, on the other hand, I had pounded into oblivion.

But I stared at the *G* between them. Other than being pressed back due to the damage to the other letters, Graham's letter hadn't taken a direct hit at all, and at first I thought I needed to fix that. As though I had missed an opportunity to vent and I might not ever get another one, but then, after I studied it for a while, I realized I was done. All my anger had been released, and I held no animosity toward Dr. Graham Harper. I had no strength left in me to pick up the hammer, much less slam it into the capital *G*.

Instead, I swiped my palm across it, wishing I could erase the paint, regretting I had ever painted it in the first place. And hoping I would someday be able to forget him.

Chapter Forty-Five

Group text from Shanty: *Think thyself happy if thou hast one true friend; never think of finding another.—Thomas Fuller*
Cecily: *And I've got TWO!*
Nina: *shanty suddenly I'm hearing thy voice with a british accent rofl*
Shanty: *Hey, can y'all meet Sunday night instead of Monday this week? Al's got a thing.*
Nina: *sure no prob let's meet at MO i like it there*
Cecily: *How's 9 pm?*

Dad could tell something was different with me. I knew he could tell, and he could tell I knew, but I didn't mention my split with Graham, and he didn't ask. That wasn't our way. If Mom had been there, she would have boldly asked what was up, and pestered me until I told her all about Graham, and the reunion, and Mirinda. I would've told her about Shanty's marriage troubles and Nina's bikini disaster.

And Mom would have talked me through it. She would have understood how excruciating it felt going to the office every day with Graham. And how I couldn't believe Mirinda had showed up for her appointment on Thursday night. And Mom would've enjoyed hearing about Brett getting punched in the jaw at the reunion.

Now I just had Dad, but Dad was enough.

It was Sunday afternoon, and he and I had just rappelled into the canyon.

"You ready to say goodbye to this place?" he asked.

A pinprick of irritation itched at me. "Well, no."

"Yeah, me neither." He fiddled with the rappelling gear, but then shoved it away. "You want to walk down to the campsite?"

"You mean like . . . a farewell walk?"

He sighed.

"Okay," I added quickly. "You know I do."

I followed him deeper into the canyon, and as the ground sloped downward, my mood tilted. This could well be one of the last times I hiked on our property. Anger festered inside me, but I had run out of people to be angry at. Dad was only doing what he had to do in order to pay off his debts. Mom had accumulated the debts in the first place, but it wasn't as if she had any control over her cancer and all the medical bills it caused. Michael was buying the place, but I couldn't blame him for doing so. Even though Mirinda's attitude was snooty, she literally had nothing to do with its sale; she didn't have two dimes to rub together.

Dad stopped at the campsite, and I noticed the two votive candles on the ground next to the picnic table. My heart felt numb.

I glanced at my dad. "Remember when we brought that table down?"

He laughed. "I can't believe we got it here in one piece."

I gently rubbed my hand across a corner where the wood was splintered. "Barely did."

"When you were away, I'd come down here sometimes, build a fire, sit and think, usually at nighttime." He shrugged. "There's something peaceful about a campfire under the stars."

"I'm sorry I wasn't here."

He made a sound like an old man in a western movie. *Pshaw.*

I giggled and moved to sit on top of the table, stretching my legs across its surface in the afternoon sunshine. "You didn't rappel by yourself, surely."

"Course not. I took the trail down."

He sat on the bench near my feet, and it creaked beneath him.

"You seem different." He picked at a splinter in the table. "Better."

"Yeah."

"Shanty Espinosa?"

I chuckled. "Who would have thought?"

"Graham." He squinted at the top edge of the canyon, and I knew he was watching the shadows of the canyon walls as they slowly crept across the floor. The shadows were six feet from the table. In another five minutes, we would be sitting in shade. "He's a good judge of character, and he uses his resources wisely, especially people."

"I suppose."

He rubbed his chin. "You two having a tiff?"

A tiff. "You could say that."

"Hmm."

I waited for him to ask for details, but he didn't. I waited for him to ask about Shanty's support group, but he didn't. I waited for him to mention the property sale again, but he didn't.

"Cecily?"

I hummed in response.

"I need to tell you something."

"Okay then, shoot."

"It's not that easy."

I waited in silence, puzzled.

Dad rested one elbow on the tabletop. "You know how I told you I lead a support group? A kind of recovery group?"

"Yes."

"Well . . . I had trouble after your mother died."

What did that mean? "Okay."

"I suffered from depression for a while." He inhaled deeply and finished his explanation on the exhale. "I even took medication on and off."

He was turned so I could only see the side of his face, and now the shadow fell across him, but not me, leaving my eyes unable to focus on him. "That's what your support group is about," I said.

"Yep. Graham set me up with a few guys, and somehow I'm encouraging to them because of what I went through back then. I just thought it was right I should tell you."

A beetle toiled across the ground, rolling a ball of mud or something else. "You've conquered it?"

"Yes, that's part of the reason for the accountability group. We're all struggling or recovering from some sort of addiction, and we check on each other, make sure we're doing all right."

"Depression isn't an addiction, though."

He shifted on the bench. "I'm not so sure about that. I think I was addicted to grief, to not allowing myself to get on with life."

Well, I could certainly relate. "That explains all the meetings," I said.

The shadow continued across the bottom of the canyon floor, inching onto my shoulder, then sliding down my side to the rocky ground.

Daddy cleared his throat. "I'm sorry Brett caused you to doubt yourself."

Everyone was sorry about that, but not as sorry as I was.

"And I'm sorry I wasn't a better father."

My heart fluttered. "Wh—What?"

He watched as three dragonflies danced circles above our heads. "There were some things I wasn't very good at. You were left without a mother, and I thought I could be both mother and father after she died. I hoped I could. But I couldn't do everything."

My dad was a wonderful father, and I wanted to argue with him, to demand that he look at things from my perspective, but when I started to speak, he lifted a hand to stop me.

"Let me explain," he said.

I nodded.

"I'm sorry for not being there for you, Cess. For not telling you how important you were to me, and for not letting you know how pretty you are, both inside and out."

I had never thought about needing that from my dad, but now, his tender words stirred my emotions, creating a halo of peace around my fractured self-esteem. A tear slid down my cheek and dropped to my arm.

"I want to make up for lost time." Daddy stood and took a step toward me so that he was looking me right in the eye, something he didn't do often. "You're a beautiful woman, and any man would be lucky to have you, but you're not only beautiful on the outside, your heart is lovely as well. You're a good person, Cecily. And I'm proud of you."

I tried to speak but was only able to make a humming sound until I swallowed. "Thanks, Daddy." Another tear leaked from my eye, and I swiped at it. "That means a lot to me."

"I should've told you that a long time ago. I should've told your mother more often too."

"So . . . Mom and I? We were alike in that way too."

He didn't have to verbally agree with me. Our similarities were abundantly obvious now.

Daddy leaned over and hugged me, not seeming to know what to do with his arms. I didn't mind his bumbling, though, and the *touch therapy* felt marvelous.

When he pulled away, his eyes were moist, but he was smiling. "Ready to hike back up now? Maybe make a sandwich?"

"No." I chuckled at his clear attempt to get things back to normal. "I'll be there in a while."

I watched as he climbed out of the canyon. When he got to the surface, he coiled the rappelling lines, sorted the gear, and carried it all back to the cabin. Soon, he would fix us two sandwiches, and later, he would probably act like this discussion had never happened. For a while at least. He may have been on the tail-end of his recovery from grief, but talking about Mom was still difficult for him. I could respect that. And my mother would have too.

Once Mom had sat on the side of my bed, running her fingers through my hair as I cried into my pillow. Who knows why I had been crying. She had told me the sadness would end soon. She had used the analogy of clouds in the sky, blocking out the sun, and she said the shadows were only temporary, and that I would always be able to find a way through my pain.

She had been right about that, even if she'd transferred some of her own problems with self-worth onto my shoulders. I would act on that advice instead of the advice I had been telling myself for the past decade. I would climb out of this enormous hole in the ground and into the sunshine. I would stand on the side of the canyon, peer into its depths, and find myself. I would get rid of the pain in my heart . . . once and for all.

I pushed away from the picnic table.

Chapter
Forty-Six

Graham's letter of apology to Cecily (as scrawled on printer paper just before he wadded it up and threw it in the wastebasket under his desk):

> *Cecily,*
>
> ~~*I just wanted to apologize again for the way our conversation ended the other day.*~~ *I'm sorry. My words* ~~*didn't do the situation justice*~~ *came out wrong when we talked. Please know that (no matter how it seems) I really do* ~~*have your best interests at heart*~~ *care.* ~~*You said we never should've gotten together in the first place, but I disagree.*~~ *I hope, eventually, you'll consider spending time with me again.* ~~*Even though I don't consider myself worthy of*~~

Graham couldn't ride his bike fast enough or far enough to escape the pain in his heart. Tomorrow would make a week since he and Cecily had broken things off, and it had been a week of torture. He had been polite to her at the office, and she had done the same, but there was a huge elephant in the room—an elephant larger than Palo Duro Canyon itself—and he longed to have things back like they were. Lunches in the park, laughter between appointments, kisses.

He took the Rock Garden trail, winding up from the bottomland in a steep ascent, keeping his gaze focused intently on the path. On impulse, he veered to the right, deciding to bushwhack his way cross-country. It was late Sunday afternoon, not typically a busy time at the park, but he desperately needed solitude, time away from any hikers and tourists he might encounter with their water bottles in tow.

His mind drifted back to Cecily and their bike date. She had been so hesitant to ride, but then her confidence had grown, and they'd had a fun time together. Until she wrecked and hurt herself. That seemed to be her habit, hurting herself.

He wanted to curse. Not only did she habitually hurt herself, she allowed herself to be hurt by others—whether or not their actions were intentional. Somehow her brain created pain where there didn't have to be any.

He sped around a cedar, then jerked his handlebars upward for greater lift when he reached the top of an incline. For two seconds, he was airborne, his wheels off the ground and his bike sailing weightlessly, and part of his tension blew away with the freedom. He landed with a jerk and turned his wheel toward the next curve, speeding up even more, trying to outrun his memories. He had never wanted anything as badly as he wanted Cecily Ross in his life.

If their lives had been simple, he could have kept dating her. Maybe even married her someday. They could have had a life together. He increased his speed even more, his back tire sliding as he rounded a dusty curve. Not only did he want Cecily in every way a man wants a woman, but he also wanted the best for her, and that was where his pain lay. He had no right to be with her when everything he did hurt her. Not until she could see life clearly did he have a right to distract her from her number one mission, which was to become a healthy and whole person.

He grunted as he took the next jump, and this time when his bike sailed through the air, the unhindered feeling brought tears to his eyes as he thought of the look on her face when he told her he wanted to take a break. She had been just as torn as he had. Salty sweat trickled into his eyes and he blinked, and in that split second, he lost control. He tried to correct, but it only made matters worse, and he missed the next jump. Instead of weightlessly floating, his bike took a nosedive, pitching forward and dropping two feet into a ravine below the trail. His front tire slammed against a rock formation, and he was slung onto the rough ground.

Lying on his back, he stared at the sky, breathing heavily. Clouds, wispy from the wind, mocked him, as though he were a tiny little man in such a great big world, nothing compared to life and all its pain.

He chuckled. "Stop wallowing, Dr. Harper." He pushed himself up, tilting his head from side to side and rotating his shoulders. He hadn't taken a spill in months, but this one wasn't as bad as some of the others. He wasn't even bleeding. He stood, arched his back, then hobbled over to check on the bike. He might need to add some air to the front tire later, but it was rideable. Removing his helmet, he let the wind blow through his sweaty hair, and then he took a long drink from his water bottle and peered up the sides of the canyon walls, trying to decide which part of the canyon he liked more, the floor or the surface.

Probably the surface, because that was where Cecily usually was.

Maybe the fall had shaken a little sense into him. Gone were his negative thoughts, and in their place was the very vivid feeling that he couldn't live without the girl. He smiled. Maybe she wasn't healthy enough for a relationship at the moment, but he could wait. He had waited this long for the right woman—what was a few more months? Or years? Eventually she would work through her feelings of jealousy and inadequacy—she had already overcome a ton of insecurity—and underneath all that messiness was a precious heart Graham wanted to embrace.

His gaze swept the rim above his head. She was up there some-where, probably fretting about something, probably angry at him, but she would get over it eventually, and Graham would be there when she did.

Something caught his eye in the distance. A hiker probably. Was that the hiking trail, or was it farther around the canyon on private property? Wait—it was a woman, and he recognized her. She was standing right on the edge, too close, staring—not at the expanse, but straight down to the ground below. She took a tiny step forward, hug-ging herself.

Graham's water bottle fell to the ground as he started running. He shouted her name, but she didn't turn his way, didn't hear, probably wouldn't have acknowledged him even if she had. The wind swished through the cedars, blowing Graham's voice in the opposite direction, and his shouts swept down the canyon like a trickle of water. He yelled anyway, running faster and faster, cursing his awkward cycling shoes that prevented him from sprinting. If only she could see him out of the corner of her eye, maybe then she would stop, maybe she would step back to safety, maybe she would want to figure out her life and heal. Maybe it would be worth it all.

Graham clenched his fists, bellowing at the top of his lungs, des-perately willing her to look up. But he had been willing her to look up long before this, and she still hadn't managed to do it.

She took one last step, and as she fell there was no sound except the wind.

Chapter
Forty-Seven

Group text from Cecily: *Well, if this isn't us, I don't know what is: "It is one of the blessings of old friends that you can afford to be stupid with them." Ralph Waldo*
Cecily (twenty-seven minutes later): *I honestly thought I'd get a response now that I finally found an Emerson quote to share. Not to mention the fact that it's all friendship-y and whatnot. Lol.*
Cecily (twelve minutes later): *Okay, so anyway . . . I'll see you at Midnight Oil at 9 pm.*

"Hey, Cecily." Michael reached for a cup in the size I typically ordered. "You and the girls haven't been here in a while."

"No . . ."

"Been meeting somewhere else?"

I almost felt guilty. "Most recently we met at a junk yard in Amarillo."

"Why a junk yard?" he chuckled.

"Let's just say we had a lot of pent-up anger we needed to unleash on an old wreck."

He stared at the cup in his hands, then shoved it under a spigot.

"Sledgehammers," I added.

"Ah." The cup almost overflowed, but he caught it in time and poured out a small amount of the coffee. He added flavoring and snapped on a lid, but then he left the cup sitting in his work station as he came to stand in front of me. "So . . . are Shanty and Nina meeting you tonight?"

"They are, but they should be here by now."

He peered toward the front windows, scanning the dark street, and I turned to look as well. In the middle of the shop, an elderly man stood stock-still, staring at the television mounted on the side wall, his mouth hanging open slightly.

Curious, I looked over at the TV and saw a still shot of the canyon and a news-release ribbon scrolling across the bottom of the screen. Next came a female reporter standing by the entrance sign of the state park, microphone in hand. "Something's happened out at the park." I turned back to Michael, but he was already coming around the counter with the remote control, turning up the volume.

We stood next to the old man, gaping at the screen as the reporter told us a woman had fallen to her death on one of the park's most popular hiking trails. As of yet, she was unidentified, and authorities had not ruled out foul play. Behind the reporter, flashing lights swept through the gates.

I couldn't move. Could barely breathe. Where were my friends? Both of them were charged with raw emotions at the moment, and both suffered from low self-esteem and flashes of depression. Shanty was upset about Al, and Nina was upset about the incident at the student center. Would either of them take their own life? I hadn't thought so—hadn't even considered it—but now the fear crept into my thoughts like a festering storm. *Nina had those scars on her wrists.*

My hands were shaking as I pulled my phone from my purse, blinking to see the screen clearly. I tried to open my messages but accidentally tapped the icon for settings instead. Then I shook my head, returned to the main menu, and concentrated on finding the correct icon. When I finally had it opened, I stared at the options, unable to remember how to spell either of their names. A sob jerked through me, and I tapped back to saved messages to click on the group text I had used earlier. My fingers moved in slow motion as I typed. *Where are you guys?*

I stared at the screen and waited for a reply. Nothing. I looked around me, frantically scanning the street for either of my friends and searching the shop for any encouragement.

Michael stared at the television. His feet were planted shoulder width apart, and he was bent at the waist as though he had a bad stomachache. The old man shook his head and sat down with his coffee, but Michael and I stared dutifully at the television as it showed an aerial view of the canyon taken from a helicopter. Emergency vehicles could be seen parked haphazardly in one of the parking lots. Then the screen cut to a shot of the hiking trail on the surface where first responders were rappelling into the canyon.

My phone vibrated in my hand, and I jerked, but it was only a text from Pizza Hut. A coupon. How could the world function normally right now? I returned to my group text. *Please answer me.*

The text was so misspelled it would be a wonder if they could read it, and I suddenly had an overwhelming fear that it wouldn't matter if they could read it or not.

The door of the shop opened with such force it slammed against the trash can, and Shanty barreled in. Her eyes were wide, and her hair stuck out in all directions. She looked first at me, then Michael, then all around the shop. Her face crumpled and she wailed. "Thank God you're all right, but where's Nina?"

"Where have you been?" It was a senseless thing to say.

"Coming home from Amarillo. There was a wreck on the interstate, backed up for miles, and my cell's dead." She hugged me tightly and didn't let go. "I was stuck there," she whispered, "listening to it on the radio. Oh, Cecily, do you think it's our sweet girl?"

It had to be.

I pulled away from Shanty and looked her in the eye. "She hasn't answered my texts."

Michael lowered himself to a chair.

"I should have kept a closer eye on her," Shanty said.

"I should have checked on her more often."

"Maybe it's not her." Shanty said the words forcefully, willing us to believe it. "Maybe one of her classes ran late, and the professor doesn't allow phones."

"Maybe she forgot we were meeting."

"Maybe her battery is dead too."

Michael stood and took a step toward the windows.

We followed his gaze to see Nina—quiet, timid, weak little Nina—walking slowly toward the door while she read a book on her Kindle. She paused with her hand on the door handle, finishing a paragraph, then opened the door and came in. Even then her gaze remained on the book, and she didn't look up until she almost bumped into us.

Michael slipped away, moved behind the counter, and slumped against the side wall.

"Thank God you're here." Shanty gripped Nina by the shoulders, engulfing her in a hug.

I wrapped my arms around both of them, burying my head in Nina's hair. "Where were you? What took you so long?"

When we pulled away from her, Nina looked stunned. "You said meet at nine thirty, right?"

"No, I said nine."

"Oh . . ." She looked back and forth between us, clearly confused by our reactions. "I'm sorry."

"Why didn't you answer my text?" I wiped my eyes.

"I had my phone turned off while I was reading." She frowned. "What's going on?"

I motioned to the television, and as we watched the news story unfold, we moved closer together, linking our arms around each other, in disbelief at what was happening so near us at the canyon, and so relieved that we were separated from it. The channel had been repeatedly showing the same footage, but now they cut back to the reporter. She still stood by the state park sign, but there was a flurry of activity around her.

"This is Brandi Villarreal, reporting live from the Palo Duro Canyon State Park, where just this evening a hiker fell to her death. It has not yet been determined if there was foul play involved, but we've just received word on the victim, a long-time resident of Canyon—"

She went on to state the woman's name and background information, but I was no longer listening. A photograph—which looked to be an old high school yearbook picture—filled the entire screen. It was of a beautiful blond teenager.

It was Mirinda.

Chapter
Forty-Eight

We stood arm in arm in front of the television until one of the baristas nudged us to a table in the back corner. She brought each of us a cup of coffee, then stood silently by our table for a few minutes. The other employee had gone with Michael, driving him to the canyon, or the hospital, or the morgue—I could only imagine—and this barista was left alone in the shop, clearly dazed. "Y'all let me know if you need anything else."

"Will do, hon," said Shanty.

I didn't take my eyes off the lid of my cup. Why were coffee lids shaped like that? All hard and bulky on the edges? Why couldn't they be smooth?

"Life is so complicated," I said.

"Why did she do it?" Nina's eyes were wet.

Shanty's weren't. I got the feeling that in the past week Shanty had cried all the tears her body could generate. "For the same reason we've all considered it at one time or other." She shrugged. "To stop the pain."

"But she had everything." Nina frowned.

"Apparently not," Shanty said.

I fiddled with the lid of my cup. "Even though I was married to her brother, I don't think I ever really saw her as a real person with feelings. I thought of her as a Barbie doll, and I was jealous of her. I should've been more kind."

"Considering the circumstances, you weren't unkind," said Shanty.

"I could have helped her."

Shanty shook her head. "Just because she's dead doesn't mean you need to go painting her as a saint. She was snarky to you because of Brett, or maybe because of Michael, but you didn't do anything wrong."

"My thoughts were wrong," I said quickly.

"But she didn't know your thoughts." Shanty's gaze bore into me. "You were way too close to her as it is."

"What does that mean?"

"You were emotionally connected because of your history. The two of you were both so prickly, you couldn't get close enough to help each other."

Nina's eyes grew wide. "Are you saying you and I should have reached out to her? I could have, but I didn't."

"No, sweetie, I'm not saying that either. Sure, we could all beat ourselves up right now with the what-ifs, but we mustn't take on the responsibility for what happened. *We* did not do this to Mirinda. She did it to herself. Even if we can see things clearly now, that doesn't make it our responsibility."

"But we could have made a difference," I said.

"Maybe," she said, "but we don't know that."

Nina shuddered. "You sound so heartless."

Shanty's posture melted. "I'm not heartless. I'm feeling all the things you're feeling right now, but I've been down this road before, and I know it doesn't help anyone if I blame myself."

"You've been through this?"

Nina interrupted before Shanty could answer. "But she had *everything*."

"What do you mean by *everything*?" Shanty's voice was calm.

"Well, in the first place, she's gorgeous—" Nina's face went pale as she realized what she'd said. Then her voice softened. "She *was*. And she had an amazing boyfriend who was famous and wealthy, and he was obviously crazy about her. She even had a fun job . . . not that she would need it after she married Michael Divins."

I thought back to my own marriage and the way Brett had hurt me in ways nobody else could see. "Shanty's saying things aren't always as they seem."

We fell silent then, each lost in our own thoughts, and the mood in the entire shop felt quiet and subdued. The barista stood at the cash register, as if there were a line of customers, but there were none.

I moved my chair to the piano but didn't play. Instead, my palms merely rested on the keys, maybe absorbing strength from their potential, maybe releasing my pain into them. Trying to feel their serenity. I imagined Mirinda standing on the side of the canyon. Probably her emotions had desensitized her until she couldn't recognize her own fear.

I had been there before, anesthetized to the point I couldn't feel anything but the pain. Fear would have paled in comparison. Once, after Mom died, I had stood on the edge of the canyon, looking down at the drop, and I had considered doing exactly what Mirinda had done, but it seemed too messy, too complicated, too public. Even after Ava died, I wouldn't have done it that way. I would have taken pills. Or started my car in the garage with the door down. Or—and I hated to admit this, even to myself—I might have killed myself with a shard of glass, or a knife, or some other object during one of my darker periods.

In front of a mirror, no doubt.

Had Mirinda had a mirror with her? I bet she didn't have the same obsession. Surely she liked the reflection she saw when she peered into the glass. But no. I had already forgotten what I'd said to Nina not ten minutes earlier. *Things are not always as they seem.* Mirinda hadn't thought she was good enough, but that didn't mean her pain had anything to do with her appearance. I wondered if she simply hadn't been able to find herself beneath all that beauty. What was it Graham had said? *Every woman is beautiful in a different way.* What had blinded Mirinda to that truth?

Nina had a point. "It does seem like she had everything," I said as I turned away from the piano to look at my friends.

"Yet it wasn't enough," Nina said.

Shanty was looking away from us, and she didn't comment.

"Once Graham told me I need to look at myself for what I am," I said, "not for what I'm not."

"He told all of us that." Shanty seemed a little angry.

"I haven't been doing a good job of allowing myself to be me."

"What do you mean?" asked Nina.

"I still put too much emphasis on my looks." I sighed, then gritted my teeth. "But looks aren't the only valuable characteristic I have. I also have a knack for music, and I'm a good friend and daughter. There's more to me, and I need to think of myself in those terms."

Nina's eyes grew wide, then she nodded as I continued.

"Instead of thinking positive thoughts about my appearance—*I'm a pretty person. I like myself*—I need to give myself permission to be me, and then believe it's important. I'm worth something because of who I am, not who I am not." I shook my head, wondering why it had taken me so long to figure this out. "I need to be thinking, *I'm talented and kind. I'm worth something because of who I am.*"

Shanty didn't lift her eyes from the table. "It's not about us anyway. There's always a higher power that's way more important."

"Yes." I laughed lightly. "It's not about us at all." It seemed so clear now. As though I had just figured out the solution to world peace. I wanted to stand on the chair or on top of the piano and shout it to everyone in hearing distance, but I could already feel my smile slipping. These were the same words everyone had been telling me for over a year. Graham, Dad, Shanty, my counselor in California. Even Brett . . . way back . . . though he clearly hadn't believed his own words. All those people had told me, and still, I had to get to this point on my own.

It took Mirinda killing herself for me to feel the truth.

"I'm a nice person." Nina seemed to be staring at nothing. I wasn't sure she even knew she was speaking out loud. "And I'm good at literature analysis. I think I might even be a writer someday." She blinked and looked at me, startled. "I'd be a good writer. Everyone says so."

I nodded.

"And some people say I have a knack for art." Her gaze bounced to Shanty.

She was getting it too. Somehow Mirinda's tragedy had pushed us out of our self-pity and into a healthier place. Maybe because we were afraid that we'd end up like her.

Shanty sighed. "Lately, I tell myself all the good things I have going for me, but it doesn't seem to be enough."

Just then there was a clamor at the front of the shop, and Al rushed through the door. He was carrying one of the kids, and the other three trailed behind him. When he saw Shanty, his face crumpled. "I heard about Mirinda. I'm so sorry, baby."

They looked at each other for a long time. Was Al sorry for Mirinda's death? Was he sorry for what he had done to his wife? Was he sorry Shanty had lost a sort-of friend? He seemed to be apologizing for all of it.

When Shanty wilted, Al took four large steps and dropped to his knees by the table. He hugged her, smashing the toddler between them while the other kids looked on. They seemed awkwardly conscious that their parents were making a display in a public place, but at the same time, their half smiles held a tinge of relief. Things were returning to normal.

"It's all right, Al." Shanty pulled away. "The girls and me? We've decided to stop wallowing."

Her words caused the habitual swell of defensiveness inside me, but then I turned back around on the chair. I rested my fingertips on the piano keys, caressed them for a few seconds, then began playing Brahms. Sweet. Soft. Gentle. I was almost to the end of the piece when I realized what I was doing.

My soul was apologizing to Mirinda.

Chapter
Forty-Nine

Group text from Shanty to Cecily and Nina: *Al and I had a long talk when we got home. Healing happened. *sigh* We've got an uphill journey ahead of us, but I think we're gonna make it.*

It was late when I left Midnight Oil, but I didn't want to go home. Shanty had left an hour earlier with Al and the kids, and Nina and I had sat in the back booth, talking, staring, scratching our heads. It seemed impossible. Mirinda couldn't have killed herself. Even though I'd made peace with my own problems, it would take a while for me to get my head around hers. Maybe I would never understand.

I unlocked my car but didn't get in. Instead, I watched Nina as she drove past the old courthouse, and I remembered the night I had sat there with Graham. The bench near the sidewalk pulled at me as if a tether had been strapped around my waist, because the last time I sat on that bench, I had been happy and my thoughts had been balanced.

The bench seemed harder tonight. The paint was clumped and bumpy from being painted and repainted over the years, and I hadn't noticed that before. Things were certainly not always as they seemed. I took a deep breath.

In the past few hours, the shadows had lifted from my mind, and I was left feeling refreshed. I didn't want to hurt myself anymore, or allow others to hurt me. I finally accepted the fact that I was worth more than the unrealistic expectations I placed on myself.

My life was worth living, and I was the only one who could live it.

A shiver went up my spine as I thought of Mirinda, but my next thought sent a wave of ice water through my veins.

I could have been her.

I *had been* her—so consumed with myself that I couldn't see what was happening around me. I couldn't see the good in my world. In my life. Graham had helped pull me out of that funk.

My hands slowly covered my face as I thought about my last few conversations with him. Clearly he had been trying to help Mirinda work through her problems. *He was her therapist!* And I had thought of nothing but myself and accused him of lusting after her. How self-absorbed could I possibly be?

My heart settled as peace washed over me. Graham had been telling me the truth about Mirinda all along, which meant he had been telling me the truth about *myself* all along. I smiled. Graham and I would still be friends.

As I settled back on the bench, my hands fell to my lap, sending a dull pain across my thighs. Graham had been so loving when he saw my scars. He had encouraged me and comforted me, even praised me for my progress. He had made me feel better about myself.

He was extremely gifted at his job. Probably because he couldn't rest until he figured out how to help someone. He almost cared to a fault.

A quiver of dread inched into my thoughts. What was it? My emotions had dipped, but I couldn't think why. Maybe it was just another cognitive distortion, but it didn't feel the same. It was something about Graham.

My spine straightened as it came to me. *Oh, my goodness.*

Would I ever overcome my selfishness? Even as I sat on that stupid bench, working through my problems and reveling in my emotional success—even then . . . I was still thinking about myself.

I could have been Mirinda.

I was becoming more emotionally healthy.

I would be able to smooth things over with Graham.

But what about Graham? He cared just as much about Mirinda's emotional health as he did about any of his other clients. He had been texting her, spending extra time with her for additional counseling sessions, even putting his personal life on hold while he helped her grapple with suicidal thoughts.

My heart shattered when I thought about what he must be feeling.

Slowly, I stood and walked to my car, but as thoughts of Graham spiraled through my mind, I increased my speed, taking a few quick steps before breaking into a trot. Then I started running.

Chapter Fifty

I found Graham at his office, swiveling slowly in his desk chair as he stared at the wall.

I wanted to tell him I was sorry, that I had been a silly fool, that I understood now. But none of that mattered anymore. For the first time in a long, long time, I could truly say, *This is not about me.* Sure, I had been involved, but right now, in this office, Graham was the one hurting.

As I moved to stand next to him, he looked up, and the exhaustion in his eyes saddened me. One of his ankles was crossed over a knee, and when he shifted it to the floor, his biking shoe brushed my leg. He had on shorts, and dust and bits of grass clung to his leg hairs. He wore a T-shirt, and his hair was messy with a ridge around his head that had been left by his bike helmet. He looked haggard and worn-out.

Oh, dear God. "You were there," I whispered. *He had seen her jump.* He closed his eyes.

"Graham, I'm so sorry."

"It's all right." He sounded defeated. "I wasn't with her. Not exactly." Graham shuddered but then seemed to steel himself against whatever emotions were coursing through his mind. He sat up a little straighter. "I had been trying to help her. And Michael. I tried to help both of them. And so did your dad."

"It doesn't matter." He wasn't making sense, and I leaned toward him, wanting to comfort him, to hold him, to take away some of his pain, but he raised his palm.

"There are things you don't know." His eyes were focused on the desktop. "I can talk about it now."

"No, Graham, later."

"You need to know." The urgency in his voice convinced me that he needed to talk about it as much as I needed to hear it.

"Okay." I settled on the edge of the desk, our knees brushing.

Instinct told me to touch him, to massage his shoulders and ease the tension, but he sat on the edge of the chair as though he might explode.

"Michael Divins is addicted to pornography," Graham said, "but he's beating it. Your dad's recovery group is helping him get control of his life, but he still has so much guilt. He wanted to come clean with Mirinda, and I—I encouraged him to tell her the truth, so the burden would be lifted from his shoulders."

I felt nauseated until I closed my eyes and took a deep breath. *No, Cecily. Not all men are the same.* I reached down and squeezed Graham's hand, surprised by its iciness, but then a chill went across my shoulders that had nothing to do with Graham's body temperature and everything to do with Mirinda. Michael had told her about his addiction, and I knew firsthand how she might have felt. Insufficient, unwanted, ugly. I had been there before.

"Michael killed her." As I said it I realized that I didn't really mean it, but the compassion I suddenly felt for Mirinda compelled me to state the accusation in her defense.

"Actually, it may have had more to do with Brett."

I blinked, then refocused my eyes and noticed Graham's clenched jaw. I was almost afraid to breathe. And definitely afraid to ask. "How?"

Graham spoke quickly, as though the words had been torturing him for months and he was now able to spew them from his mouth. "He molested her. When she was young."

Rage bubbled inside me, but just as quickly, it dispersed, and I wondered if my body could no longer generate strong feelings—even when provoked by something so repulsive—for Brett Ross. Gradually, the clues began to piece together. Mirinda struggled with self-esteem even though she was beautiful, she hadn't joined in family gatherings for years, and she had become incredibly nervous just before Brett came home for the reunion. "How old was she when it happened?"

Graham looked up at me then, and even though his eyes were dry, they were rimmed with redness. "It was when you were pregnant."

My ears filled with sounds I had heard over the years. Memories. Ava's first cry, the tinkling of a mobile above her bed, the angry voice of my husband, my own desperate cries of sadness and insecurity. My eyes slowly closed. "What did he do to her? Mirinda was just a child at the time. Maybe twelve."

Graham's voice grew calmer and soft. "He touched her, but he didn't sleep with her. But as far as I know, Brett isn't into kids."

"She developed early." My eyes opened. "He was attracted to her as a woman, not as a child." It made so much sense now. "From the moment she matured physically, she began to lose the people that mattered."

"Yes." Graham sounded so tired. "When Brett told her he was coming home, Mirinda's insecurity snowballed, and at the reunion, his indifference put her on the brink of suicide. I wanted to tell you, but I couldn't, and she appeared to be handling it." His chest seemed to collapse. "Now I know she wasn't being completely honest with me, and at the last, she manipulated me so she could accomplish what she wanted. If I had known how bad she was feeling, I would have had her hospitalized."

I lifted his hand and held it in mine, stroking his fingers.

He nodded once, and a tear slid down his cheek. "I failed, Cecily."

"No." I knelt before him. "You didn't fail."

He looked at me then, peering into my eyes as though desperately searching for confirmation of the horrific place in which he had found himself. The nightmare. My heart hurt in a way it had never hurt before, and I slipped my arm around his back and patted his shoulder, then gripped it, digging my fingers into the muscles. My other hand went to his ear, where his hair was matted with dried sweat, and I gently pulled his head down to my shoulder. I held him, rubbing his back and stroking his hair and crooning words of comfort.

At first his muscles were stiff, but then he nestled into the crook of my neck, and inhaled deeply, his body relaxing against mine. He said nothing, but he didn't have to.

I kissed the top of his head as he buried his face in my chest and sobbed.

Epilogue

Text from Shanty to Cecily: *Those who look to him are radiant; their faces are never covered with shame. Psalm 34:5*
Cecily: *Nina was right. You're a Bible-thumper.*

After the accident—everyone was calling it an accident—I continued my unofficial counseling with Graham, and several months later we settled into a comfortable friendship. And somehow . . . it was enough for me. Gradually, I learned to focus my life on something greater than myself—which, of course, was the key all along. Everyone had always told me I was fearfully and wonderfully made, but it wasn't until I broke the cycle of my negative thoughts and emotions that I could finally rest in that knowledge.

And rest I did.

It had been a full year since I sat in the kitchen, talking to Dad over bacon and eggs. Now I sat in the same chair, but this time, it was pulled up next to the piano where Gage Espinosa dutifully played the C major scale.

He smiled up at me. "Is that good, Miss Ross?"

I wasn't *Miss* Ross, but I didn't correct him because I wasn't quite *Mrs.* Ross either. "That's perfect, Gage."

Really, I was just *Cecily*—but Shanty wouldn't allow Gage to call me that.

He opened his book and began picking out his piece of the week, slowly, almost painfully. He was better than last week, and learning was a slow process. That's what Graham would say. Graham said a lot of things.

He had been a mess after Mirinda's death, and together we had talked through a lot of his issues, which were surprisingly similar to my own. I was insecure about my looks, and Graham was insecure about his abilities. I was haunted by my decision to date and marry Brett, and Graham was haunted, always, by his past drug use. I had been hurt by my husband and—now I could admit it—by my mother too, and Graham had been damaged by his father's expectations. We found we could empathize with each other.

Gage finished his piece, and I clapped my hands and had him start his last song. Through the window I could see Dad and Olivia, who had finally started spending time together outside of work. They were pulling a half-finished table out of the garage and into the yard. Before Gage got to the end of the page, the shrill of the sander could be heard through the thin walls, and his eyebrows lifted.

"It's just a power tool," I said. "And perfect timing too because I see your daddy driving up."

"Thanks, Miss Ross." Gage bounded across the room, leaving the door open as he left.

I settled back in my chair, listening to the sander and the voices in the yard. Olivia talked to Al over the racket, and Dad hummed the tune he had just heard Gage playing. And I was happy. Content. Pleased with myself and my life and my situation. Things could still improve, but I had determined not to dwell on the negative. Instead, I focused on the best thing that had come out of all the heartache: we were keeping our property.

Michael Divins had begged Dad to allow him to pay off Mom's medical debts. Michael couldn't bear the thought of buying the property without Mirinda, and he said if he wasn't going to start his family there, he wanted to be sure it stayed in ours. Dad refused at first, but in the end, Graham talked him into it, saying it would help Michael if he was given the opportunity to help someone else.

I could see the wisdom in that.

Gage and Al drove away as Graham pulled up, and I smiled at the happy flurry in our yard.

Graham had finally convinced me to take him rappelling, and Dad had prepared the gear for us that morning. Probably my dad would've enjoyed teaching him more than I would because the two of them were spending more and more time together lately, working on projects around the house while they discussed everything from politics to sports.

The front door was still open, and as I sat on the couch and tied my tennis shoes, a soft knock prompted me to look up.

Graham stood on the porch, watching me. "Mind if I come in?"

"Sure, but I'm almost ready."

He took a step over the threshold, then hesitated. "Actually, can we talk for a few minutes before we go down to the canyon?"

"You're not getting cold feet, are you?"

He smiled widely. "No, I just have a question for you."

"Have a seat."

"I'd rather stand."

He took my hand and pulled me up from the couch.

"What's this about?" I asked.

Silently, he drew me to the side of the room where Mom's antique mirror hung on the wall, then he turned me so that I was looking at my reflection with him standing behind me and peering over my shoulder.

I lifted my eyebrows.

"What do you see?" he asked softly.

"Me." I shrugged. "And you."

"What else?"

"My new and improved sleeve?"

He lifted my left arm and inspected the ivy that now covered it. A high-priced tattoo parlor in Amarillo had transformed my barbed wire into curling green ivy with tiny white and yellow flowers. It was still pink around the edges, healing. *"Nice,"* said Graham, "but what else?" He directed my attention back to the mirror.

He was smiling at my reflection with an open-mouthed grin, so I stated the obvious. "You're happy."

"Yes, but what else?"

He wasn't looking at my reflection now. He had leaned forward to look at my profile, and his gaze traveled up and down my face. When his eyes found mine again in the mirror, I knew what he was getting at.

"I'm . . . not ugly?"

He sighed, an exaggerated demonstration of patience. "Rephrase."

Rephrase. Rephrase. Rephrase. It had become his latest keyword in our happy-thoughts regime. But positive self-talk was still difficult for me. "I'm . . . all-right looking."

"Little stronger."

"I'm pretty enough, I guess." I swallowed. "*Okay*, I'm beautiful."

He grinned. "Did you hear that, Cecily? You just looked in a mirror and said you were beautiful. You know what that means?"

"Does it mean you've gone crazy?"

"It means you're so, so much healthier than you were." He stepped between me and the mirror, and when he looked down at me, his grin softened. "It means you're happy and well adjusted."

"So?"

He chuckled. "We should start dating again. It's time."

I couldn't speak at first, but then I sputtered. "But I thought . . . I thought you didn't want a relationship."

His eyes widened. "Why would you think that?"

"After everything happened, you pulled away."

"No." His head slowly moved back and forth. "When we broke up I just wanted to take a break. You needed to heal, and I was pushing you. It wasn't healthy."

"But I thought—" It seemed like so long ago, and so much had happened right after, that I couldn't seem to remember any of it clearly.

"You—" Graham squinted. "You still want me, right?"

I stared at him, not believing what I was hearing, but desperately wanting what he had offered. "Yes." I smiled. "I still want you."

And this time I wanted him for the right reasons. So I could help and support him too, not just so I could be supported. I wanted us to be a partnership, not a hero saving a damsel. I wanted him for life.

When he took my face in his hands and gently kissed my lips, desire welled inside me, but when he pulled me into a hug, I felt the peace I'd been longing for my entire life. We were right together, and I didn't need to see our reflection in the mirror to know it.

THE END

SHANTY'S BE YOU CHALLENGE

1. Make a list of things you like about yourself. Name at least five.
2. Write and tell yourself you are beautiful and amazing. Then tell yourself why.
3. Write about a mistake you made and how it impacted your life in a positive way.
4. Make a list of people who have committed offenses against you. Then forgive them.
5. Write about a time in your childhood when you didn't feel good about yourself.
6. Close your eyes and think about self-esteem for a while. Write whatever comes to mind.
7. List things for which you are thankful. Keep going until you can't think of any more.
8. Jot down the names of three people who could use a hug today.
9. Draw a picture of YOU, being as kind to yourself as you would to your best friend.
10. Write about something that made you happy in the past year.

NOTE TO THE READER

To my knowledge, there has never been a suicide at Palo Duro Canyon, though there have been a handful of deaths due to falls while hiking. To the friends and families of these victims, I offer my heartfelt condolences.

Even though I only lived in the Panhandle for a few months during my freshman year at college, the region has become a favorite setting, mainly due to the fabulous views at the canyon and the open expanse of the surrounding farmland. Because it's been a while since my college years, I'm sure many details are skewed (some accidentally and some intentionally). So to the residents of Canyon, I apologize for the inaccuracies, which I'm sure irritate you beyond distraction. Midnight Oil is actually the Palace Coffee Company, and several other shops were invented from my imagination, but what a nostalgic square you guys have! Any author would be inspired to set a story there.

Writing about the canyon brought me great joy, and I hope I managed to take you on a mental sightseeing trip where you could envision the jagged cliffs, feel the breeze in your hair, and hear the eagle cawing overhead. My goal was to contrast the glory of nature with our culture's warped definition of physical beauty.

This book was difficult for me to write because I'm fighting my own battle with self-esteem, and as you can probably tell, I don't have all the answers. However, I have a jumble of tools, and Cecily and I will continue to work the plan. If you share our struggle, I pray this story has helped you in your journey and that you are soon able to look away from the mirror and see the rest of the world out there. A world that needs you.

Clearly I am not a counselor. The knowledge that Graham Harper and Shanty Espinosa bestowed on my characters came from several excellent books: *Boundaries*, by Dr. Henry Cloud and Dr. John Townsend; *Forgive and Love Again*, by John W. Nieder and Thomas M. Thompson; *Every Heart Restored*, by Fred and Brenda Stoeker; *Who Switched Off My Brain? Controlling Toxic Thoughts and Emotions*, by Dr. Caroline Leaf; *Healing for Damaged Emotions*, by David A. Seamands; *Untangled*, by Carey Scott; *Taming Your Gremlin*, by Richard Carson; and *The Healing Choice*, by Susan Allen and Brenda Stoeker.

Find me online at www.VarinaDenman.com or on social media. I'd love to hear from you.

Thanks for reading!

Varina

ACKNOWLEDGMENTS

It turns out I don't know as much about the Texas Panhandle as I thought I did, and I've picked the brains of many family, friends, and strangers who are now avoiding my calls and emails. Someday I will learn to write stories about things I'm more familiar with . . . maybe.

I owe a huge thanks to the McNeill family of Happy, Texas, for figuratively loaning me your property on the rim of Palo Duro Canyon and for giving me a glimpse of the love you have for the region, your passion for family, and your affinity for stories of life in the Panhandle. This book would not be the same without your influence.

Thank you to Jeff Davis, park interpreter at Palo Duro Canyon State Park, for answering a bajillion questions about the day-to-day responsibilities of a park ranger, for giving me a written tour of the gatehouse, and for pointing me toward that sheer cliff on the CCC trail. I suppose this means you're partly responsible for Mirinda's death.

Thank you to Kelsea and Drew for tutoring me on the code of ethics for professional counselors, for telling me all the crazy things Cecily could be experiencing, and for driving up and down the streets of Canyon, snapping pictures and recording videos, so I could create a more factual story for my readers.

Thank you to Dustin Hahn for giving me a crash course (pun intended) on the various bike trails at the state park, for sending pictures that helped me feel as though I were back at the canyon again, and for mentioning that our favorite dentist once flipped over his handlebars. But most of all, thank you for sharing your love of the sport, which helped me to write not only a better setting but also a better character.

Thank you to Amy Elkins and my other friends for holding me steady on my journey and for inadvertently helping me figure out what to do for Cecily in the process.

My most heartfelt thanks goes to my husband, Don, for your tireless, unquestioning, and much-needed support; and to my kiddos Jessica, Colton, Drew, Kelsea, Dene, Micah, Jillian, and Janae for putting up with my distracted conversations, my absence at family functions, and my ever-diminishing cooking and cleaning skills.

Thank you to my agent, Jessica Kirkland, for encouraging me through the writing process once again, and to all the folks at Waterfall Press, for bringing Cecily's story to life.

BOOK CLUB GUIDE

1. In the beginning of the story, Cecily feels unattractive and depressed. What events lead up to this status? Could she have avoided falling into despair? How? Can you empathize with her?

2. Soon after her return home, Cecily goes out with Michael Divins. What motivates her to make this decision? What happens during the date to cause her depressive episode later that night?

3. Cecily is so disgusted with her appearance, her life situation, and her past that she deliberately cuts herself. Can you explain her actions? How does she feel afterward? Fortunately, her self-abuse prompts her to seek help, but what might have happened if she hadn't?

4. When Cecily is alone in front of mirrors, she thinks negative thoughts. Some people might call this "the voice inside her head" or "bad memories" or "Satan's influence." How do you look at it? What causes Cecily's mind to wander in that direction? What steps does she take to silence the voice?

5. When Cecily goes to the support group, it isn't what she was expecting. How do Shanty and Nina compare to Cecily's expectations? Is she surprised when they eventually help her? What else surprises Cecily about her new friends?

6. Cecily's dad has his own set of problems, which affect Cecily

indirectly. What kinds of emotional problems is he facing, and how do they work for or against Cecily's struggle? How do the two characters grow closer as they walk along their journeys?

7. Shanty assigns Cecily several homework projects, one of which is to journal about herself. Do the assignments help? Why or why not? What is most difficult for Cecily? What helps her most?

8. During the demonstration at the mall, Cecily grows more confident as she watches Shanty and the way the crowd reacts to her. Why do you think the event affects Cecily in that way? Do you think Cecily would ever want to do a demonstration? Why does Shanty do it? How does it affect Shanty's self-esteem?

9. When Cecily finally acknowledges her feelings for Graham, why is she hesitant? How does their backstory affect the plot? What do you think brought them together? In what ways are they good or bad for each other?

10. Cecily is intimidated by Mirinda's beauty. What factors cause her to be so judgmental? Is she justified in her bias? How do Mirinda's actions add to Cecily's stereotype of her?

11. Shanty and Al seem to have the perfect marriage, but things are not always as they seem. What events lead to their problems? How might they have avoided their issues? What steps should they take to reconcile their marriage?

12. At the class reunion, Cecily realizes she wants Graham to come to her rescue like a knight in shining armor. How long has she had this warped sense of what a man's role should be in a relationship? What causes her to perceive men in this way? How has this expectation hurt or helped her over the years? How does she overcome it?

13. How does Nina's demonstration differ from Shanty's? How does it affect Nina? How does it affect Cecily as she watches it? What does Cecily learn from the demonstration? If you could rewrite the scene, what would you change?

14. Throughout the book, an unknown man is shown as he falls into an addiction to pornography, then gradually works his way out. His identity is left a secret until the end, but let's pretend you don't know it was Michael. How might each of the female characters (Cecily, Shanty, and Nina) have reacted if it had been a man close to them? Would their reactions mirror Mirinda's? Why or why not?

15. Cecily and Graham decide to take a break from their romantic relationship. What are each of their reasons for this decision? Do you think it was a healthy decision? How does it help Cecily? Could things have worked out well had they not broken up? Explain.

16. At Shanty's encouragement, the girls are able to vent their frustrations by beating up an old car. Why does this help them? Have you ever just wanted to hit something? What are some therapeutic (and nondestructive) ways to vent anger?

17. When Mirinda kills herself, all three women in the support group make huge leaps in their recovery. Why do you think this is? How does Mirinda's death change the way Cecily and the other women view themselves? What else changes?

18. After Mirinda's death, Cecily realizes how badly Graham must be hurting, and she rushes to comfort him. Why is this a pivotal scene in the storyline? What does it tell you about Cecily's emotional growth?

19. All through the story, there are references to lies, both real and metaphorical. Why do you think the author inserted so many "little white lies" between Cecily and the supporting characters? How might these lies have affected Cecily's emotional growth and slowed her healing process?

20. At the end of the book, Cecily is able to look into a mirror and tell herself she's beautiful. Do you think she is sincere? Why or why not? Her appearance has not actually changed, so what has made the difference? Explain.

AUTHOR BIOGRAPHY

Photo © 2017 Monica Faram

Varina Denman is the award-winning author of the Mended Hearts series, a compelling blend of women's fiction and romance. A native Texan, Varina lives near Fort Worth with her husband and children, and she has taught creative writing and literature at her local home-school cooperative. To connect with Varina, find her on the web at www.VarinaDenman.com.